ALSO BY HILARY MANTEL

Every Day Is Mother's Day

Vacant Possession

A Place of Greater Safety

Eight Months on Ghazzah Street

A Change of Climate

An Experiment in Love

The Giant O'Brien

Fludd

Giving Up the Ghost

Mandy Coughlan came in. Her eyes were red-rimmed and her lips compressed. "Another one who's had a bad night," Gemma said. "Princess?"

"Morris," Mandy said. She rummaged bad-temperedly at the breakfast buffet and slammed a banana down on the table. "I've passed the whole night under psychic attack."

"Tea or coffee?" the waitress said.

"Got any rat poison?" Mandy said. "I wish I'd had some last night for that little bastard. You know, I pity Alison, I really do, I wouldn't be in her shoes for any money. But can't she get him under control? I'd hardly got into bed before he was there trying to pull the duvet off me."

"He always did fancy you," Cara said, flapping the newspaper. "Ooh, look at poor little Prince Harry. Look at his liddle face, bless him."

"Pulling and tugging till nearly three o'clock. I thought he'd gone, I got out of bed to go to the loo, and he just jumped out from behind the curtains and put his filthy paw right up my nightie."

"Yeah, he does that," Colette said. "Hides behind the curtains. Alison says she finds it very annoying."

Alison winced in a moment later, looking green.

"Oh, poor love," Mandy breathed. "Look at her."

"I see you didn't manage to do anything with your hair after all," Cara said sympathetically.

"At least she doesn't look like a bloody pixie," Colette snapped.

"Tea, coffee?" the waitress said.

Al pulled her chair well out from the table and sat down heavily. "I'll get changed later," she said, by way of explaining herself. "I was sick in the night."

"Too much of that red," Gemma said. "You were sozzled when you went up."

"Too much of everything," Al said. Her eyes, dull and downcast, rested on the dish of cornflakes Colette had placed before her. Mechanically, she picked up a spoon.

"That's nice," Gemma said. "She gets your cereal for you. Even though she's not your maid, she says."

"Could you just shut up?" Colette enquired. "Could you just give her a minute's peace and let her get something inside her?"

"Mandy—" Alison began.

Mandy waved a hand. "Nugh about it," she said, her mouth full of muesli. "Id nig. Nobbel self."

"But I do blame myself," Al insisted.

Mandy swallowed. She flapped a hand, as if she were drying her nail varnish. "We can talk about it another time. We can stay in separate hotels, if we have to."

"I hope it won't come to that."

"You look done up," Mandy said. "I feel for you, Al, I really do."

"We were up talking till late, me and Colette. And other people came through, that I used to know when I was a kid. And you know I said, paramilitaries were tormenting me? The thing is, they broke through and smashed up my feet. I had to take two Distalgesic. By dawn I was just dropping off to sleep. Then Morris came in. He yanked out the pillow from under my head and started boasting in my ear."

"Boasting?" Gemma said.

"What he'd done with Mandy. Sorry, Mandy. It's not that—I mean, I didn't believe him or anything."

"If he were mine," Gemma said, "I'd get him exorcised."

Cara shook her head. "You could control, Morris, you know, if you were to approach him with unconditional love."

Colette said, "Could you manage a tomato juice, Alison?"

Alison shook her head, and put down her spoon. "I suppose we're in for another day of the princess."

"Another day, another dollar," Merlin said.

"Snivel, bloody snivel," Al said. "Do they ever think what it's like for us? Down I go, *whoosh*. Plunged head first into their shit. Like a lavatory brush."

"Well, it's a living, Al," Mandy Coughlan said, but Cara, startled, dropped her knife on the *Mail*'s Full-Colour Tribute and smeared butter on the Prince of Wales.

Last night, Saturday, the first card Al had laid down was the Page of Hearts: significator of her pale companion, the emblem of the woman who appeared in the cards at the Harte and Garter, Windsor, on the morning when Colette first came into her line of vision: white hair, pale eyes, red-rimmed like the eyes of some small scurrying pet you ought to be kind to.

She looked up, at the woman, the client, who was sitting there sniffling. The reading Al was getting was close to home, it was for herself, not for the client before her. You can't control the cards; they will only give the messages they want to give. Here's the King of Spades, reversed: probably, what was his name . . . Gavin. Colette is aching for a man to come into her life. Nighttimes, she can feel it, in the flat at Wexham, the slow drag of desire beyond the plasterboard wall. Colette's busy little fingers, seeking solitary pleasure. . . . What turn of fate brought Colette my way? Did I take up with her for my own advantage, for an advantage not yet revealed even to me: for some purpose that is working itself out? She pushed the thought away, along with any guilt that attended it. I can't help what I do. I have to live. I have to protect myself. And if it's at her expense . . . so what if it is? What's Colette to me? If Mandy Coughlan offered her a better prospect I wouldn't see her for dust, she'd have her stuff rolled up in that holdall of hers and she'd be on the next train to Brighton and Hove. At least, I hope she would. I hope she wouldn't steal my car.

Diana is the Queen of Hearts; every time the card turns up in a spread, this week and next, she will signify the princess, and the clients' grief will draw the card time and time again from the depth of the pack. Already the first sightings of her have been reported, peeping over the shoulder of her ancestor Charles I in a portrait at St. James's Palace. Some people who have seen the apparition say that she is wearing a dress the colour of blood. All agree that she is wearing her tiara. If you look hard you will see her face in fountains, in raindrops, in the puddles on service station forecourts. Diana is a water sign, which means she's the psychic type. She's just the type who lingers and drips, who waxes and wanes, breathes in and out her tides; who, by the slow accretion of tears, brings ceilings down and wears a path into stone.

When Alison had seen Colette's horoscope (cast by Merlyn as a favour), she had quailed. "Really?" she'd said. "Don't tell me, Merlyn. I don't want to know." Farking air signs, Merlyn had said, what can you bloody do? He had felt for Alison's hand with his damp Pisces palm.

•   •   •

Sunday morning: she gave readings in a side room, tense, waiting to go on the platform at 2 P.M. From her clients, through the morning, it was more of the same. Diana, she had her problems; I have my problems too. I reckon she had her choice of men, but she was a bad picker. After an hour of it, a feeling of mutiny rose inside her. Mutiny on the Bounty was the phrase that came into her head. She put her elbows on the table, leaned towards the punter and said, "Prince Charles, you think he was a bad pick? So you'd have known better, eh? You'd have turned him down, would you?"

The client shrank back in her chair. A moment, and the little poor woman sat there again, in the client's lap: "Excuse me, miss, have you seen Maureen Harrison? I've been seeking Maureen for thirty year."

About lunchtime she sneaked out for a sandwich. She and Gemma split a pack of tuna and cucumber. "If I had your problems with the Irish," Gemma said, "I'd be straight on the phone to Ian Paisley. We all have our crosses to bear, and mine personally tend to be derived from my ninth life, when I went on crusade. So any upheaval east of Cyprus, and frankly, Al, I'm tossed." A sliver of cucumber fell out of her sandwich, a sliding green shadow on her white paper plate. She speared it artfully and popped it into her mouth.

"It's not just the Irish," Al said. "With me, it's everybody, really."

"I used to know Silvana, in that life. 'Course, she was on the other side. A Saracen warrior. Impaled her prisoners."

"I thought that was Romanians," Al said. "It just goes to show."

"You were never a vampire, were you? No, you're too nice."

"I've seen a few today."

"Yes, Di's brought them out. You can't miss them, can you?" But Gemma did not say what signs she looked for in a vampire. She balled up her paper napkin and dropped it on her plate.

Two-twenty P.M. She was on the platform. It was question time.

"Could I get in touch with Diana if I used a Ouija board?"

"I wouldn't advise it, darling."

"My gran used to do it."

And where's your gran now? She didn't say it: not aloud. She thought: that's the last thing we need, Amateur Night, Diana pulled about and puzzled by a thousand rolling wineglasses. The young girls in the audience bounced up and down in their seats, not knowing what a Ouija board was. Being the current generation, they didn't wait to be told, they yipped at her and whistled and shouted out.

"It's just an old parlour game," she explained. "It's not a thing any serious practitioner would do. You put out the letters and a glass rolls around and spells out words. Spells out names, you know, or phrases that you think mean something."

"I've heard it can be quite dangerous," a woman said. "Dabbling in that sort of thing."

"Oh, yes, dabbling," Al said. It made her smile, the way the punters used it as a technical term. "Yes, you don't want to go dabbling. Because you have to consider who would come through. There are some spirits that are—I'm not being rude now, but they are on a very low level. They're only drifting about earthside because they've got nothing better to do. They're like those kids you see on sink estates hanging about parked cars—you don't know if they're going to break in and drive them away or just slash the tyres and scratch the paintwork. But why find out? Just don't go there! Now those sort of kids, you wouldn't ask them in your house, would you? Well, that's what you're doing if you mess about with a Ouija board."

She looked down at her hands. The lucky opals were occluded, steamy, as if their surfaces were secreting. There are things you need to know about the dead, she wanted to say. Things you really ought to know. For instance, it's no good trying to enlist them for any good cause you have in mind, world peace or whatever. Because they'll only bugger you about. They're not reliable. They'll pull the rug from under you. They don't become decent people just because they're dead. People are right to be afraid of ghosts. If you get people who are bad in life—I mean, cruel people, dangerous people—why do you think they're going to be any better after they're dead?

But she would never speak it. Never. Never utter the word *death* if she could help it. And even though they needed frightening, even though they deserved frightening, she would never, when she was with her clients, slip a hint or tip a wink about the true nature of the place beyond black.

At teatime, when the event was over and they went down in the lift with their bags, Colette said, "Well now!"

"Well now what?"

"Your little outburst at breakfast! The less said about that, the better."

Al looked sideways at her. Now that they were alone together, and with the drive home before them, Colette was obviously about to say a great deal.

As they stood at the desk, checking out, Mandy came up behind them. "All right, Al? Feeling better?"

"I'll be okay, Mandy. And look, I really want to apologize about Morris last night—"

"Forget it. Could happen to any of us."

"You know what Cara said, about unconditional love. I suppose she's right. But it's hard to love Morris."

"I don't think that trying to love him would get you anywhere. You've just got to get clever about him. I don't suppose there's anyone new on the horizon, is there?"

"Not that I can see."

"It's just that round about our age, you do sometimes get a second chance—well, you know yourself how it is with men, they leave you for a younger model. Now I've known some psychics who, frankly, they find it devastating when their guide walks out, but for others, let me say, it's a blessed relief—you get a fresh start with a new guide, and before you know where you are your trade's taken an upturn and you feel twenty years younger." She took Al's hand. Her pink-frosted nails caressed the opals. "Alison, can I speak frankly to you? As one of your oldest friends? You've got to get off the Wheel of Fear. Onto the Wheel of Freedom."

Al pushed her hair back, smiling bravely. "It sounds a bit too athletic for me."

"Enlightenment proceeds level by level. You know that. If I had to take a guess, I'd say that thinking was at the source of your problems. Too much thinking. Take the pressure off, Al. Open your heart."

"Thanks. I know you mean well, Mandy."

Colette turned from the desk, credit card slip between her fingers, fumbling with the strap of her bag. The nail of Mandy's forefinger dug her in the ribs. Startled, Colette looked up into her face. Her mouth was set in a grim pink line. She's quite old, Colette thought; her neck's going.

"Look after Al," Mandy said. "Al is very gifted and very special, and you'll have to answer to me for it if you let her talent bring her to grief."

In the car park, Colette strode briskly ahead with her holdall. Alison was dragging her case—one of the wheels had come off—and she was still limping, in pain from her smashed-up feet. She knew she should call Colette back to help her. But it seemed more suitable to suffer. I ought to suffer, she thought, though I am not sure why.

"The amount you take away!" Colette said. "For one night."

"It's not that I pack too much," Al said meekly. "It's that my clothes are bigger." She didn't want a row, not just at this minute. There was a quivering in her abdomen which she knew meant that someone was trying to break through from Spirit. Her pulse was leaping. Once again she felt nauseated, and as if she wanted to belch.

Sorry, Diana, she said, I just had to get that wind up, and Colette said— well, she said nothing, really, but Al could see she was annoyed about being told off by Mandy. "She was only advising you," she said. "She didn't mean any harm. Me and Mand, we go back a long way."

"Put your seat beat on," Colette said. "I'm hoping to get home before dark. You'll need to stop somewhere to eat, I suppose."

"Fucking will," Morris said, settling himself into the rear seat. "Here, don't drive off yet, wait till we get settled."

"We?" Al said. She swivelled in her seat; was there a thickening of the air, a ripple and disturbance, a perturbation below the level of her senses? A smell of rot and blight?

Morris was in wonderful spirits, chortling and bouncing. "Here's Donald Aitkenside hitching a ride. Donnie, what I've been trying to meet up wiv. You know Donnie, don't you? 'Course you do! Donnie and me, we go back a long way. Donnie knew MacArthur. You remember MacArthur, from the old days? And here's young Dean. Don't know Dean, do you? Dean's new at this game, he don't know nobody—well, he knows Donnie but he don't know the army crowd nor any of that lot from the old fight game. Dean, meet the missus. That? That's the missus's pal. Like a length o' string, ain't she? Would you? No, not me, no chance, I like a bit of meat on their bones."

He laughed raucously.

"Tell you what, gel, tell you what, stop off south of Leicester somewhere, and we might meet up with Pikey Pete. For Pikey Pete," he told Dean, "he is such a man, if he's down on his luck you'll see him picking fag ends off the road, but let him have a win on the dogs and he will see you and slot a cigar in your top pocket, he's that generous."

"Should we pull in south of Leicester?" Al asked.

Colette was irritated. "That's no distance."

"Look, it's not worth antagonizing him."

"Morris?"

"Of course, Morris. Colette, you know the tape, you know those men that were coming through?"

"Paramilitaries?"

"No. Forget them. I mean the fiends, the fiends I used to know."

"Can we please not talk about it? Not while I'm driving."

The service stations were quiet, winding down after the weekend trade, though it had been an odd sort of weekend, of course, because of Di. The fiends swarmed out of the back of the car, yipping and squeaking. Inside the building, Al wandered around the food court, an anxious expression on her face. She lifted the lid of a mock-rustic tureen and gazed into the soup, and picked up filled rolls and tugged at their wrappings, turning them up to look at them end on. "What's in this one, do you think?" she said. The film was misty, as if the lettuce had been breathing out.

"For God's sake sit down," Colette said. "I'll bring you some pizza."

When she came back, edging among the tables with her tray, she saw that Al had taken out her tarot cards.

She was amazed. "Not here!" she said.

"I just have to—"

The card's scarlet wrappings flowed over the table, and puddled in Colette's lap as she sat down. Alison drew out one card. She held it for a moment, flipped it over. She didn't speak, but laid it down on top of the pack.

"What is it?"

It was the Tower. Lightning strikes. The masonry of the tower is blasted away. Flames shoot out of the brickwork. Debris is thrown into space. The occupants hurtle towards earth, their legs scissoring and their arms outflung. The ground rushes up at them.

"Eat your pizza," Colette said, "before it goes all flabby."

"I don't want it." The Tower, she thought; it's my least favourite. The death card I can handle. I don't like the Tower. The Tower means—

Colette saw with alarm that Al's eyes had slipped out of focus; as if Al were a baby whom she were desperate to placate, whose mouth she was desperate to fill, she grabbed the plastic fork and plunged it into the pizza. "Look, Al. Try a bit of this."

The fork buckled against the crust; Al snapped back, smiled, took the fork from her hand. "It may not be so bad," she said. Her voice was small and tight. "Here, Col, let me. When you get the Tower it means your world blows up. Generally. But it can have a—you know, quite a *small* meaning. Oh, blast this thing."

"Pick it up in your fingers," Colette advised.

"Wrap my cards up, then."

Colette shrank; she was afraid to touch them.

"It's all right. They won't bite. They know you. They know you're my partner."

Hastily, Colette bundled them into their red wrappings.

"That's right. Just drop them in my bag."

"What came over you?"

"I don't know. I just had to see. It gets you that way sometimes." Al bit into a piece of raw-looking green pepper, and chewed it for a while. "Colette, there's something you ought to know. About last night."

"Your baby voice," Colette said. "Talking to nobody. That made me laugh. But then I thought at one point you were having a heart attack."

"I don't think there's anything wrong with my heart."

Colette looked meaningfully at her pizza slice.

"Well, yes," Alison said. "But that's not going to finish me off. Nobody perishes of a pizza slice. Think of all those millions of Italians, running round quite healthy."

"It was a horrible weekend."

"What did you expect?"

"I don't know," Colette said. "I didn't have any expectations. That card— what do you mean by a *small* meaning?"

"It can be a warning that the structure you're in won't contain you anymore. Whether it's your job or your love life or whatever it is, you've outgrown it. It's not safe to stay put. The Tower is a house you know. So it can mean just that. Move on."

"What, leave Wexham?"

"Why not? It's a nice little flat but I've got no roots there."

"Where would you like to move?"

"Somewhere clean. Somewhere new. A house that nobody's lived in before. Could we do that?"

"New-build is a good investment." Colette put down her coffee cup. "I'll look into it."

"I thought—well, listen, Colette, I'm sure you're as tired of Morris as I am. I don't know if he'd ever agree to—you know—take his pension—I think Mandy was being a bit optimistic there. But our lives would be easier, wouldn't they, if his friends didn't come round?"

"His friends?" Colette said blankly.

Oh, Jesus, Al said to herself, it's all uphill work. "He's beginning to meet up with his friends," she explained. "I don't know why he feels the need, but it seems he does. There's one called Don Aitkenside. I remember him. He had a mermaid on his thigh. And this Dean, now, he's new to me, but I don't like the sound of him. He was in the back of the car just now. Spotty kid. Got a police record."

"Really?" Colette's flesh crawled. "In the back?"

"With Morris and Don." Al pushed her plate away. "And now Morris is off looking for this gypsy."

"Gypsy? But there won't be room!"

Alison just looked at her sadly. "They don't take up room, in the usual way," she said.

"No. Of course not. It's the way you talk about them."

"I can't think how else to talk. I only have the usual words."

"Of course you do, but it makes me think—I mean it makes me think they're ordinary blokes, except I can't see them."

"I hope they're not. Not ordinary. I mean, I hope the standard is better than that."

"You never knew Gavin."

"Did he smell?"

Colette hesitated. She wanted to be fair. "Not more than he could help."

"He'd take a bath, would he?"

"Oh yes, a shower."

"And he wouldn't, sort of, undo his clothes and take out private bits of himself in public?"

"No!"

"And if he saw a little girl on the street, he wouldn't turn around and make comments about her? Like, look at it waggle its little arse?"

"You frighten me, Al," Colette said coldly.

I know, Al thought. Why mention it now?

"You have a very peculiar imagination. How can you think I would marry a man like that?"

"You might not know. Till you'd tied the knot. You might have had a nasty surprise."

"I wouldn't have been married to that kind of a man. Not for an instant."

"But he had magazines, did he?"

"I never looked at them."

"It's on the Internet, these days."

Colette thought, I should have searched his systems. But those were early days, as far as technology went. People weren't sophisticated, like they are now.

"He used to call hotlines," she admitted. "Once I myself, just out of curiosity—"

"Did you? What happened?"

"They kept you hanging on for ages. Just messing you about, basically, while you were running up a bill. I put the phone down. I thought, what will it be? Just some woman pretending to come. Moaning, I suppose."

"You could do that for yourself," Al said.

"Precisely."

"If we moved, we might be able to lose them. I suppose Morris will stick, but I'd like to shake off his friends."

"Wouldn't they come after us?"

"We'd go somewhere they don't know."

"Don't they have maps?"

"I don't think they do. I think it's more like . . . they're more like dogs. They have to pick up the scent."

In the LADIES, she watched her own face in the mirror, as she washed her hands. Colette must be coaxed towards a house move, she must be made to see the sense. Yet she must not be terrified too much. Last night the tape had frightened her, but how could that have been prevented? It was a shock to me too, she said to herself. If Morris has caught up with Aitkenside, can Capstick be far behind? Will he be bringing home MacArthur, and lodging him in the bread bin or her dressing table drawer? Will she sit down to breakfast one day and find Pikey Pete lurking under the lid of the butter dish? Will she get a sudden fright, as Bob Fox taps at the window?

Move on, she thought: it might baffle them for a bit. Even a temporary bewilderment could keep them off your back. It might cause them to disperse, lose each other again in those vast tracts the dead inhabit.

"Oi, oi, oi oi!" Morris called, yelling right in her ear. "Bob's your uncle!"

"Is he?" she'd said, surprised. "Bob Fox? I always wanted a relative."

"Blimey, Emmie," Morris said, "is she simple, or what?"

That night, when they got home, Morris crept in with them; the others, his friends, seemed to have melted away, somewhere in Bedfordshire between Junctions 9 and 10. To check for them, she lifted the carpet in the boot of the car, peered into the cold metal well; no one was there, and when she dragged out her case she found it was no heavier than it had been when she packed it. So far so good. To keep them out permanently—that would be another matter. Once inside she was solicitous to Colette, recommending a hot bath and the *Coronation Street* omnibus edition.

"If it's on," Colette said. All she could summon up was funeral coverage. "For God's sake. I wish they'd give it a rest. They've buried her now. She's not going to get up again." She slumped on the sofa with a bowl of breakfast cereal. "We ought to get a satellite dish."

"We can when we move."

"Or cable. Whatever."

She's resilient, Al thought, as she climbed the stairs—or maybe she's just forgetful? At the stop back in Leicestershire, Colette had turned the shade of porridge, when it was broken to her about the menagerie riding in the back seat of the car. But now she was her usual self, carping away, always with some petty grievance. You couldn't say her colour had come back, because she never had any colour; but when she was frightened, Al had noticed, she sucked her lips inwards so that they seemed almost to disappear; at the same time, her eyes seemed to shrink back in her skull, so you noticed their pink rims even more.

In her own room, Al sank down onto the bed. Hers was the master bedroom; Colette, when she moved in, had squeezed into what even the estate agent, when he'd sold the flat to Al, had the grace to describe as a *small* double. It was a good thing she had few clothes and no possessions; or, to put it as Colette did, a capsule wardrobe and a minimalist philosophy.

Al sighed; she stretched her cramped limbs, checking out her body for spirit aches and pains. Some entity was tweaking her left knee, some desolate soul was trying to hold her hand; not now, kids, she said, give me a break. I need, she thought, to give Colette more of a stake in life. Get her name on the house deeds. Give her more reason to stick around, so she's less inclined to take off in a sulk or on a whim, or under the pressure of unnatural events. For we all have our limits; though she's brave—brave with the true-blue staunchness of those who lack imagination.

I could, she thought, go downstairs and tell her face-to-face how much I appreciate her; I could, as it were, pin a medal on her: Order of Diana (deceased). She levered herself upright. But her resolution failed. No, she thought; as soon as I see her she'll irritate me, sitting sideways with her legs flung over the arm of the chair, swinging her feet in her little beige ankle socks. Why doesn't she get slippers? You can get quite acceptable kinds of slippers these days. Moccasins, something like that. Then there will be a bowl half full of milk on the floor by her chair, with a few malted flakes bobbing in it. Why does she drop her spoon into the bowl when she decides she's finished, so that driblets of milk shoot out onto the carpet? And why should such small things work one up to an extreme level of agitation? Before I lived with Colette, she thought, I supposed I was easy to live with, I thought I would be happy if people didn't actually vomit on the carpet, or bring home friends who did. I thought it was quite good to have a carpet, even. I thought of myself as quite a placid person. Probably I was mistaken.

She took the tape recorder out of its bag and set it up on her bedside table. She kept the volume low, whizzing the tape backward to find last night.

MORRIS: Run out for five Woodbine, would you? Thanks Bob, you're a scholar and a gentleman. (*eructation*) Blimey. I should never 'ave 'ad that cheese an' onion pie.

AITKENSIDE: Cheese an' onion? Christ, I 'ad that once, it was at the races, remember that time we went up to Redcar?

MORRIS: Ooh, yer, do I? And Pikey had his motorbike with the sidecar? Redcar, sidecar, we was laughing about that?

AITKENSIDE: Bloody crucified me, that pie. Repeating on me for three bloody weeks.

MORRIS: 'Ere, Dean, they don't make pies like that these days. I remember Pikey Pete, he kept saying, fanks, Donnie, fanks for the memory. Oh, he were a right laugh! 'Ere, Bob, are you going for them fags?

AITKENSIDE: They don't make Woodbine no more.

MORRIS: What, they don't make Woodies? Why not? Why don't they?

AITKENSIDE: And you can't buy five. You've got to buy ten these days.

MORRIS: What, buy ten, and not even Woodies?

BOY'S VOICE: Where've you been, Uncle Morris?

MORRIS: Dead. That's where I bloody been.

BOY'S VOICE: Have we got to stay dead, Uncle Morris?

MORRIS: Well, it's up to you, Dean lad, if you can find some way to bloody recycle yourself you get on and do it, san-fairy-ann, no skin off my blooming nose. If you've got the contacts, you bloody use 'em. I give a hundred pounds, one hundred nicker in notes to a bloke I met that said he could get me restarted. I said to him, I don't want borning in bloody wogland, you hear what I'm saying, I don't want to come back as some nig, and he swore he could get me born in Brighton—or Hove which is near as dammit—born in Brighton and free, white, and twenty-one. Well, not twenty-one, but nar what I mean. And I thought, not bad, Brighton's near the course, and when I'm a tiddler I'll be getting the sea air and all, grow up strong and healthy, besides I always had mates in Brighton, show me the bloke wiv no mates in Brighton and I'll show you a tosser. Anyway, he took my readies and he scarpered. Left me high and dry, dead.

Alison switched off the tape. It's so humiliating, she thought, so crushing and shameful to have Morris in your life and to have lived with him all these years. She put her arms across her body, rocked herself gently. Brighton—well, naturally. Brighton and Hove. The sea air, the horse racing. If only she'd thought about it earlier. That was why he was trying to get inside Mandy, back at the hotel. That was why he kept her up all night, pawing and pulling at her—not because he wanted sex, but because he was plotting to be born, to be carried inside some unknowing hostess . . . the filthy, dirty little sneak. She could imagine him, in Mandy's hotel room, whining, slobbering, abasing himself by crawling across the carpet, slithering towards her on his chin with his pitiful haunches in the air: born me, born me! Dear God, it didn't bear thinking about.

And clearly—at least it was clear to her now—it wouldn't be the first time Morris had tried it on. She well remembered Mandy's pregnancy test, was it last year? She'd been on the phone that very night, I was feeling strange, Al, really queasy, well I don't know what made me but I went out to the chemist, I tested my wee and the line's gone blue. Al, I blame myself, I must have been extremely careless.

In Mandy's mind the solution was straightforward; she had it done away
with. So that was the end of Morris and his hundred pounds. For months afterwards she would say, whenever they met, do you know I'm baffled about
that episode, I can't think who or where—I think it must have been when we
went to that café bar in Northampton, somebody must have spiked my drink.
They'd blamed Raven—though not to his face; as Mandy said, you didn't
want to push it, because if Raven denied it categorically, that would more or
less mean it must have been Merlin or Merlyn.

Those speculations were hard enough and distasteful; she admired the way
Mandy faced them, the putative fathers, at every Psychic Fayre, her chin tilted
up, her eyes cold and knowing. But she'd be sick to her stomach if she knew
what Al was thinking now. I won't tell her, she decided. She's been a good
friend to me over the years and she doesn't deserve that. I'll keep Morris under
control, somehow, when I'm in her vicinity; God knows how, though. A million pounds wouldn't be enough—it wouldn't be enough of a bribe to make
you carry Morris or any of his friends. Imagine your trips to the antenatal
clinic. Imagine what they'd say at your play group.

She clicked the tape back on. I have to make myself do it, she thought, I
have to listen right through: see if I get any insight, any grip on other furtive
schemes that Morris might come up with.

> MORRIS: So what ciggies *can* I 'ave?
> DEAN: You can have a roll-up, Uncle Morris.
> UNKNOWN VOICE: Can we have a bit of respect, please? We're
> here on a funeral.
> DEAN: (*timid*) It is all right if I call you Uncle Morris?
> SECOND UNKNOWN VOICE: This sceptered isle, this precious
> stone set in the silver sea. . . .
> MORRIS, AITKENSIDE: Oi oi oi oi! It's Wagstaffe!
> MORRIS: Mended the bloody hole in your bloody pantaloons yet,
> Wagstaffe?
> WAGSTAFFE: There's rosemary, that's for remembrance.

She recognized voices from her childhood; she heard the clink of beer bottles, and the military rattle, as bone clicked into joint. They were reassem-

bling themselves, the old crew: root and branch, arm and leg. Only Wagstaffe seemed baffled to be there; and the unknown person who had called for respect.

She remembered the night, long ago in Aldershot, when the streetlight shone on her bed. She remembered the afternoon when she had come into the house and seen a man's face looking through the mirror, where her own face ought to be.

She thought, I should phone my mum. If they're breaking through like this, she ought to be tipped off. At her age, a shock could kill her.

She had to scrabble through an old address book, to find Emmie's number in Bracknell. A man answered. "Who is that?" she asked, and he said, "Who's asking?"

"Don't come that with me, matey," she said, in Aitkenside's voice.

The man dropped the receiver. She waited. A static crackle filled her ear. A moment later her mother spoke.

"Who's that?"

"It's me. Alison." She added, she couldn't think why, "It's me, your little girl."

"What do you want?" her mother said. "Bothering me, after all this time."

"Who's that you've got there, in your house?"

"Nobody," her mother said.

"I thought I knew his voice. Is it Keith Capstick? Is it Bob Fox?"

"What are you talking about? I don't know what somebody's been telling you. There's some filthy tongues about, you should know better. You'd think they'd mind their own bloody business."

"I only want to know who answered the phone."

"I answered it. God Almighty, Alison, you always were a bit soft."

"A man answered."

"What man?"

"Mum, don't encourage them. If they come round, you don't let them in."

"Who?"

"MacArthur. Aitkenside. That old crowd."

"Must be dead, I should think," her mother said. "I haven't heard them names in years. Bloody Bill Wagstaffe, weren't he a friend of theirs? That Morris, and all. And there was that gypsy fella, dealt in horses, what did they call him? Yes, I reckon they must all be dead by now. I wouldn't mind it if they did come round. They was a laugh."

"Mum, don't let them in. If they come knocking, don't answer."

"I remember Aitkenside, drove a heavy lorry, always got a wodge in his wallet. Used to do favours, you know. Drop off loads, this and that, he'd say one stiff more or less it don't hardly make no difference to the weight. This gypsy fella—Pete, they called him—now he had a trailer."

"Mum, if they turn up, any of them, you let me know. You've got my number."

"I might have it written down somewhere."

"I'll give it you again."

She did so. Emmie waited till she finished and said, "I haven't got a pencil."

Al sighed. "You go and get one."

She heard the receiver drop. A buzzing filled the line, like flies around a dustbin. When Emmie returned she said, "Found up my eyebrow pencil. That was a good idea, wasn't it?"

She repeated the number.

Emmie said, "Wagstaffe always had a pen. You could rely on him for that."

"Have you got it now?"

"No."

"Why not, Mum?"

"I haven't got a paper."

"Haven't you got anything you can write on? You must have a writing pad."

"Oh, la-di-dah."

"Go and get a bit of toilet paper."

"All right. Don't get shirty."

She could hear Emmie singing, as she moved away; "I wish I was in Dixie, hurrah, hurrah . . ."; then, again, the buzzing occupied the line. She thought, the men came into the bedroom and looked down at me as I lay in my little bed. They took me out of the house by night, into the thick belt of birch trees and dead bracken beyond the pony field. There on the ground they operated on me, took out my will and put in their own.

"Hello?" Emmie said. "That you, Al? I got the toilet paper, you can tell me again now. Oops, hang on, me pencil's rolled off." There was a grunt of effort.

Alison was almost sure she could hear a man, complaining in the background.

"Okay, I got it now. Fire away."

Once again, she gave her number. She felt exhausted.

"Now tell me again," her mother said. "What have I got to ring you, when and if what?"

"If any of them come around. Any of that old crowd."

"Oh yes. Aitkenside. Well, I should hear 'is lorry, I should think."

"That's right. But he might not be driving a lorry anymore."

"What's happened to it?"

"I don't know. I'm just saying, he might not. He might just turn up. If anybody comes knocking at your window—"

"Bob Fox, he always used to knock on the window. Come around the back and knock on the window and give me a fright." Emmie laughed. " 'Caught you that time,' he'd say."

"Yes, so . . . you ring me."

"Keith Capstick," her mother said. "He were another. Keef, you used to call him, couldn't say your tee-haitches; you was a stupid little bugger. Keef Catsick. 'Course, you didn't know any better. Oh, it used to make him mad, though. Keef Catsick. He caught you many a slap."

"Did he?"

"He used to say, I'll skin the hide off her, I'll knock her to Kingdom Come. 'Course, if it weren't for Keith, that dog would have had your throat out. What did you want to let it in for?"

"I don't know. I don't remember now. I expect I wanted a pet."

"Pet? They weren't pets. Fighting dogs, them. Not as if you hadn't been told. Not as if you hadn't been told a dozen times and Keith give you the back of his hand to drive it through your skull. Not that he did succeeded, did he? What did you want to open the back door for? You was all over Keith after that, after he pulled the dog off you. Couldn't make enough of him. Used to call him Daddy."

"Yes, I remember."

"He said, that's worse than Catsick, her calling me Daddy, I don't want to be her daddy, I'll throttle the little fucker if she don't leave off." Emmie chuckled. "He would too. He'd throttled a few, in his time, Keith."

There was a pause.

Al put her hand to her throat. She spoke. "I see. And you'd like to meet up with Keith again, would you? A laugh, was he? Always got a wodge in his wallet?"

"No, that was Aitkenside," her mother said. "God help you, girl, you never could keep anything straight in your head. I don't know if I'd recognize Keith if he come round here today. Not after that fight he had, he was that mangled I don't know if I'd know him. I remember that fight, I see it as if it were yesterday—old Mac with the patch over his eye socket, and me embarrassed, not knowing where to look. We didn't know where to put our loyalties, you see? Not in this house we didn't. Morris said he was putting a fiver on Keith; he said I'll back a man with no balls over a man with one eye. He had a fiver on Keith, oh, he was mad with him, the way he went down. I remember they said, after, that MacArthur must have had a blade in his fist. Still, you'd know, wouldn't you? You'd know about blades, you little madam. By Christ, did I wallop you, when I found you with those whatsits in your pocket."

Al said, "I want to stop you, Mum."

"What?"

"I want to stop you and rewind you."

She thought, they took out my will and they paid my mother in notes for the privilege. She took the money and she put it in that old cracked vase that she used to keep on the top shelf of the cupboard to the left of the chimney breast.

Her mum said, "Al, you still there? I was thinking, you never do know, Keith might have got his face fixed up. They can do wonders these days, can't they? He might have got his appearance changed. Funny, that. He could be living round the corner. And we'd never know."

Another pause.

"Alison?"

"Yes. . . . Are you still taking pills, Mum?"

"On and off."

"You see your doctor?"

"Every week."

"You been in the hospital at all?"

"They closed it."

"You all right for money?"

"I get by."

What else to say? Nothing, really.

Emmie said, "I miss Aldershot. I wish I'd never moved here. There's nobody here worth talking to. They're a miserable lot. Never had a laugh since I moved."

"Maybe you should get out more."

"Maybe I should. Nobody to go with, that's the trouble. Still, they say there's no going back in life." After a longer pause, just as Al was about to say goodbye, her mother asked, "How are you then? Busy?"

"Yes. Busy week."

"Would be. With the princess. Shame, innit? I always think we had a lot in common, me and her. All these blokes, and then you get the rough end of it. Do you reckon she'd have been all right with Dido?"

"I don't know. I haven't an idea."

"Never one for the boys, were you? I reckon you got put off it."

"Do you? How?"

"Oh, you know."

"No, I don't," she was starting to say, I don't know, but I very much want to know, I find this enlightening, you've told me quite a few things—

But Emmie said, "Got to go. The gas is running out," and put the phone down.

Al dropped the handset on the duvet cover. She lowered her head to her knees. Pulses beat; in her neck, in her temples, at the ends of her fingers. She felt a pricking in the palms of her hands. Galloping high blood pressure, she thought. Too much pizza. She felt a low, seeping fury, as if something inside her had broken and was leaking black blood into her mouth.

I need to be with Colette, she thought. I need her for protection. I need to sit with her and watch the TV, whatever she's watching, whatever she's watching will be all right. I want to be normal. I want to be normal for half an hour, just enjoying the funeral highlights; before Morris starts up again.

She opened the bedroom door and stepped out into the small square hall. The sitting room door was closed but raucous laughter was rocking the room where Colette, she knew, kicked up her heels in her little socks. To avoid hearing the tape, Colette had turned the TV volume up. That was natural, very natural. She thought of tapping on the door. But no, no, let her enjoy. She turned away. At once Diana manifested: a blink in the hall mirror, a twinkle. Within a moment she had become a definite pinkish glow.

She was wearing her wedding dress, and it hung on her now; she was gaunt, and it looked crumpled and worn, as if dragged through the halls of the hereafter, where the housekeeping, understandably, is never of the best. She had pinned some of her press cuttings to her skirts; they lifted, in some otherworldly breeze, and flapped. She consulted them, lifting her skirts and peering; but, in Alison's opinion, her eyes seemed to cross.

"Give my love to my boys," Diana said. "My boys, I'm sure you know who I mean."

Al wouldn't prompt her: you must never, in that fashion, give way to the dead. They will tease you and urge you, they will suggest and flatter; you mustn't take their bait. If they want to speak, let them speak for themselves.

Diana stamped her foot. "You do know their names," she accused. "You oiky little grease spot, you're just being hideous. Oh, fuckerama! Whatever are they called?"

It takes them that way, sometimes, the people who have passed: memory lapses, an early detachment. It's a mercy, really. It's wrong to call them back, after they want to go. They're not like Morris and company, fighting to get back, playing tricks and scheming to get reborn, leaning on the doorbell, knocking at the window, crawling inside your lungs and billowing out on your breath.

Diana dropped her eyes. They rolled, under her blue lids. Her painted lips fumbled for names. "It's on the tip of my tongue," she said. "Anyway, whatever. You tell them, because you know. Give my love to . . . Kingy. And the other kid. Kingy and Thingy." There was a sickly glow behind her now, like the glow from a fire in a chemical factory. She's going, Al thought, she's melting away to nothing, to poisoned ash in the wind. "So," the princess said, "my love to them, my love to you, my good woman. And my love to him, to— wait a minute." She picked up her skirts and puzzled over a fan of the press cuttings, whipping them aside in her search for the name she wanted. "So many words," she moaned, then giggled. The hem of her wedding gown slipped from her fingers. "No use, lost it. Love to all of you! Why don't you just bog off now and let me get some privacy."

The princess faded. Al implored her silently, Di, don't go. The room was cold. With a *click*, the tape switched itself on.

> WAGSTAFFE: This sceptered isle. . . .
> MORRIS: My sceptered—

Colette yelled, "Al, are you playing that tape again?"

"Not on purpose, it just switched itself—"

"Because I don't think I can face it."

"You don't want it for the book?"

"God, no. We can't put that stuff in the book!"

"So what shall I do with it?"

> WAGSTAFFE: This other Eden—
> MORRIS: My sceptered arse.

Colette called, "Wipe it."

seven

At Admiral Drive there were these house types: the Collingwood, the Frobisher, the Beatty, the Mountbatten, the Rodney, and the Hawkyns. Colette, initially, was unimpressed. The site was ragged grassland, half of it turned over already by the diggers.

"Why is it called Admiral Drive?"

The woman in the sales caravan said, "We theme all our developments nautically, you know?" She wore a name badge and a bright orange skirt and jersey, like a supermarket cashier.

"Awful uniform," Colette said. "Wouldn't navy be more appropriate?"

"We'll be glad of it," the woman said, "once the building starts. Orange stands out against the landscape. We'll have to wear hard hats when we go out there. It'll be mud up to your knees. Like a battlefield." One of nature's saleswomen, Colette thought. "What I'm saying is," the woman added, "it's really much better to buy off-plan?"

Colette picked up a fistful of brochures from the desk, banged them end-on to tidy them, and dropped them into her bag.

"Can I help you there at all?" the woman said. She looked aggrieved at the loss of her leaflets. "How many beds were you looking at?"

"I don't know. Three?"

"Here you are then. The Beatty?"

Colette was puzzled by the woman, who turned most of her statements into questions. It must be what they do in Surrey, she decided; they must have had it twinned with Australia.

She opened the brochure for the Beatty and took it to the light. "Are these the actual room sizes, Suzi?"

"Oh no. It's for information purposes only?"

"So it's information, but it's wrong?"

"It's guidelines?"

"So the rooms could be bigger than this?"

"Probably not."

"But they could be smaller?"

"Some contraction could occur."

"We aren't midgets, you know? What are the four-beds like? We could merge the rooms, or something."

"At this stage, subject to building regulations, some redesign is possible?" Suzi said. "Extra costs may be incurred?"

"You'd charge for walls you didn't put up?"

"Any alteration to the basic plan may be subject to extra costs," Suzi said, "but I don't say it will. Might you be interested in the Frobisher at all? It comes with a spacious utility area?"

"Wait a minute," Colette said. "Wait a minute, I'll get my friend." She skipped out of the sales caravan and across the hardstanding to where the car was parked. The builders had put up a flagpole to dignify their sales area, and Alison was watching their emblem sailing in the wind. Colette swung open the car door. "Al, you'd better come in. The Frobisher comes with a spacious utility area. So I'm told."

Al released her seat belt and stepped out. Her knees were stiff after the short drive down into Surrey. Colette had said, new-build appeals, but I need time to do my research. You have to go back beyond paint finishes and colour schemes, back beyond bricks and mortar, look at the ground we'll be standing on. It isn't just a place to live. It's an investment. We need to maximize the profit. We need to think long-term. After all, she said, you appear to have no pension plans in place. Don't be silly, Al had said. How could I retire?

Now she stood looking about her. She sensed the underscape, shuddering as it waited to be ripped. Builders' machines stood ready, their maws crusted with soil, waiting for Monday morning. Violence hung in the air, like the smell of explosive. Birds had flown. Foxes had abandoned their lairs. The bones of mice and voles were mulched into mud, and she sensed the minute snapping of frail necks and the grinding into paste of muscle and fur. Through the soles of her shoes she felt gashed worms turning, twisting and repairing themselves. She looked up, to the grassland that remained. The site was framed by a belt of conifers, like a baffle wall; you could not guess what lay beyond it. In the middle distance was a stand of young birch trees. She could see a ditch running with water. Towards the main road to Guildford, she could see a hedge, a miscarried foetus dug in beneath it. She could see ghost horses, huddled in the shadow of a wall. It was an indifferent place; no better nor worse than most others.

Colette said briskly, "Is something upsetting you?"

"No."

"Was there something here before?"

"Nothing. Just country."

"Come in the caravan. Talk to Suzi."

Al caught the scent of standing water; the ditch, a pond, a sludgy canal, widening into a basin that reflected faces looking down at her from the sky, sneering. The dead don't ascend, or descend, so properly speaking they can neither leer down at you from the treetops nor grumble and toss beneath your feet; but they can give the appearance of it, if it takes them that way.

She followed Colette and heaved herself into the caravan. The metal steps were flimsy; each tread, under her weight, bowed a little and came snapping back.

"This is my friend," Colette said.

"Oh, hello?" Suzi said. She looked as if she meant to say, we discourage friends. For a few minutes she left them alone. She took out a duster and passed it over her model drawer fronts and cupboard doors, clicking them backwards and forwards on their swivel-jointed display stand with a sound like the gnashing of giant dentures. She blew some dust off her carpet samples, and found a spot of something disagreeable on her stack of vinyl tiles, which she worked at by spitting on it and then scrubbing at it with her fingernail.

"You could offer us a coffee?" Colette said. "We're not time wasters."

"Some people make a hobby of it. Driving around the new developments on a Sunday afternoon, comparing prices? With their friends?"

I never got this far with Gavin, Colette thought. She tried to imagine the life they might have had, if they'd been planning to have a family. She would have said to him, what kitchen do you want, and he'd have said, wot's the choice? And when she pointed to the model drawer fronts and cupboards, he'd have said, are they kitchens? And when she had said yes, he'd have said, wotever.

But here was Alison, studying the details of the Frobisher, behaving just like a normal purchaser. Suzi had put her duster away and, her back still turned, was edging towards the counter by degrees. Al looked up. "It's tiny, Col. You can't do anything with these rooms, they're just dog kennels." She handed the leaflet back to the woman. "No thank you," she said. "Have you got anything bigger?" She rolled her eyes and said to Colette, "Story of my life, eh?"

Suzi enquired, "Which lady is the purchaser?"

"We are both the purchaser."

Suzi turned away and snatched up the coffeepot from its hotplate. "Coffee? Milk and sugar?" She turned, the pot held defensively before her, and gave them a wide smile. "Certainly," she said. "Oh, yes, of course. We don't discriminate. Far from it. Far on the other side. We've been away for a training day. We are enthused to play our part to enhance the diversity of the community. The very special kind of community that's created wherever you find a Galleon Home?"

Colette said, "What do you mean, far on the other side?"

"I mean, no discrimination at all?"

Al said, "No sugar, thanks."

"But you don't get a bonus? I mean, if we were lesbians? Which by the way we aren't? Would you get extra commission?"

Just then a normal couple came up the steps. "Hello?" Suzi called to them, with a warmth that almost scared them down again. "Coffee?" she sang. A few drips from the poised pot leaked onto the plans of the Frobisher, and widened like a fresh fecal stain.

Alison turned away. Her cheeks were plum-coloured.

Colette followed her. "Ignore her. This is Surrey. They don't get many gays and they're easily upset." She thought, if I *were* a lesbian, I hope I'd get a woman who wasn't so bulky.

"Could we come back later?" Alison asked. "When there are houses here?"

Suzi said coldly, "Half of these plots are under offer."

Colette took Al back to the car and laid the facts before her. This is prime building land, she said. She consulted the literature and read it out. Convenient transport links and first-class health and leisure facilities.

"But there aren't," Al said. "It's a field. There's nothing here. No facilities of any sort."

"You have to imagine them."

"It's not even on a map, is it?"

"They'll redraw the map, in time."

She touched Colette's arm, conciliatory. "No, what I mean is, I like it. I'd like to live nowhere. How long would it be before we could move in?"

"About nine months, I should think."

Alison was silent. She had given Colette a free hand in the choice of site. Just nowhere near my old house, she had said. Nowhere near Aldershot. Nowhere near a race course, a dog track, an army camp, a dockyard, a lorry park, or a clinic for special diseases. Nowhere near a sidings or a depot, a customs shed or a warehouse; not near an outdoor market or an indoor market or a sweatshop or a body shop or a bookie's. Colette had said, I thought you might have a psychic way of choosing—for instance, you'd get the map and swing a pendulum over it. God, no, Al had said, if I did that, we'd probably end up in the sea.

"Nine months," she said now. "I was hoping to do it quicker."

She had thought of Dean and Aitkenside and whoever, wondered what would happen if Morris brought them home and they got dug in at Wexham. She imagined them hanging around the communal grounds and making their presence felt: tipping over the bins and scratching the residents' cars. Her neighbours didn't know the nature of her trade; she had been able to keep it from them. But she imagined them talking behind her back. She imagined the residents' meeting, which they held every six months. It was at best a rancorous affair: who moves furniture late at night, how did the stair carpet get frayed? She imagined them muttering, talking about her, levelling spiteful but unspecific accusations. Then she would be tempted to apologize; worse, tempted to try to explain.

"Well, there it is," Colette sighed. "If you want new-build, I don't think we can do it any quicker. Not unless we buy something nobody else wants."

Alison swivelled in her seat. "We could do that, couldn't we? We don't have to want what everybody else wants?"

"Fine. If you're prepared to settle for some peculiar little house next to a rubbish dump. Or a plot next to a main road, with all the traffic noise day and night."

"No, we wouldn't want that."

"Alison, should we give it up for today? You're just not in the mood, are you? It's like dealing with a five-year-old."

"Sorry. It's Morris."

"Tell him to go to the pub."

"I have. But he says there isn't a pub. He keeps going on about his mates. I think he's met up with another one, I can't get the name. Oh, wait. Hush, Col, he's coming through now."

Morris came through, loud, clear, indignant: "What, are we going to come and live in the middle of a field? I'm not living here."

Al said, "Wait. He just said something interesting." She paused, her hand held above her abdomen, as if she were tuning him in. "All right," she said, "if you're going to be like that, you know what you can do. See if you can find a better home to go to. (Not you, Col, I'm talking to Morris.) What makes you think I want you moving in anyway? I don't need you. I've had it up to here! Bugger off!" She shouted the last phrase, staring through the windscreen.

Colette said, "Shh! Keep it down!" She checked over her shoulder that no one was watching them.

Al smiled. "I'll tell you what, Colette, I'll tell you what we should do. Go back in there, and tell that woman to put us down for the biggest house she's got."

Colette placed a small holding deposit and they returned two days later. Suzi was on duty, but it was a weekday morning and the caravan was empty.

"Hello, again. So you're not working ladies?" Suzi enquired. Her eyes skittered over them, sharp as scissors.

"Self-employed," Colette said.

"Oh, I see. Both of you?"

"Yes, is that a problem?"

Suzi took a deep breath. Once again a smile spread over her face. "No problem at all? But you will be wanting our package of personally tailored mortgage advice and assistance?"

"No, thank you."

Suzi spread out the site map. "The Collingwood," she said, "is very unique, on this site we shall only be erecting three. Being exclusive, it is in a preferential situation, here on top of the hill? We don't have a computer-generated image as of this moment, because we're waiting for the computer to generate it. But if you can imagine the Rodney? With an extra bedroom en suite?"

"But what will it look like on the outside?"

"If you'll excuse me?" Suzi got on the phone. "Those two ladies?" she said. "That I mentioned? Yes, those ones. Wanting to know about the Collingwood, the exterior elevations? Like the Rodney with different gob-ons? Yes. Mmm. Just ordinary, really. . . . No, not to look at them. By-eee." She turned back to Colette. "Now, if you can imagine?" She passed her forefinger over the sales leaflet. "For the Rodney you have this band of decorative plasterwork with the nautical knots motif, but with the Collingwood you will get extra portholes?"

"Instead of windows?"

"Oh no, they will just be decorative."

"They won't open?"

"I'll check that for you, shall I?" She picked up the phone again. "Hi, there! Yes, fine. My ladies—yes, those ones—want to know, do the portholes open? That's on the Collingwood?"

The answer took some time to find. A voice in Al's ear said, did you know Capstick was at sea? He was in the merchant navy before he got taken on as a bouncer.

"Colette," she said. She put her hand on Colette's hand. "I think Morris has met Keef Catsick."

"No?" Suzi said. "No! Really? You too? In Dorking? . . . Well, there must

be a plague of them. What can you do? Live and let live, that's what I say. . . .
Yes, will do. By-eee."

She clicked the phone down and turned away politely, believing she was
witnessing a moment of lesbian intimacy.

Colette said, "Keith who?"

Alison took her hand away. "No. It's all right. It's nothing." Her knuckles
looked skinned and darkly bruised. The lucky opals had congealed in their
settings, dull and matt like healing scabs.

Al thought you couldn't bargain with a house builder, but Colette showed her
that you can. Even when they had agreed on a basic price, three thousand below Suzi's target, she kept on pushing, pushing, pushing, until Suzi felt sick
and hot and she began to capitulate to Colette's demands; for Colette made it
clear that until she was dealt with, and dealt with in a way satisfactory to herself, she would keep away any other potential customers—which she did, by
darting her head at them as they climbed the steps and fixing them with her
pale glare; by snapping, "Do you mind, Suzi is busy with me?" When Suzi's
phone rang, Colette picked it up and said, "Yes? No she can't. Call back."
When Suzi yearned after lost prospects as they stumbled down the steps, following them with her eyes, Colette zipped her bag, stood up and said, "I could
come back when you're more fully staffed—say, next Saturday afternoon?"

Suzi grew frantic then, as she saw her commission seeping away. She became accommodating and flexible. When Suzi agreed to upgrade to a power
shower en-suite to Bed Two, Colette signed up for fitted wardrobes. When
Colette hesitated over a double oven, Suzi offered to make it a multifunction
model including microwave. When Colette—after prolonged deliberation—
gave the nod to brass switchplates throughout, Suzi was so relieved she threw
in a carriage lamp free. And when Colette—after stabbing at her calculator
buttons and gnawing her lip—opted for wood-style flooring to kitchen and
utility, Suzi, sweating inside her orange skin, agreed to turf the back garden
at Galleon's expense.

Meanwhile, Alison had plummeted down on the click 'n' fix korner group
seating. I can afford it, she thought, I can probably afford it. Business was

booming, thanks in part to Colette's efficiency and bright ideas. There was no shortage of clients; and it was just as Colette said, one must invest, one must invest against leaner times. Morris sat in the corner, picking at the carpet tiles, trying to lift one. He looked like a toddler, absorbed, his short legs and potbelly thrust out, his tongue between his teeth.

She watched Colette negotiating, small rigid hand chopping the air. At last she got the nod and limped out to the car after her. Colette jumped into the driving seat, whipped out her calculator again, and held it up so that Al could see the display.

Al turned away. "Tell me in words," she said. Morris leaned forward and poked her in the shoulder. Here's the lads coming, he shouted. Here's the cheeky chappies. Knew you'd find me, knew you would, that's the spirit.

"You could take more of an interest," Colette snapped. "I've probably saved us ten K."

"I know. I just can't read the panel. The light's in my eyes."

"Plain ceilings or Artex?" Colette said. Her voice rose to a squeak, imitating Suzi. "They think you'll give them money to stop them making plaster swirls."

"I expect it's harder to make plaster smooth."

"That's what *she* said! I said, smooth should be standard! Silly bitch. I wouldn't pay her in washers."

Aitkenside said, we can't live here. There's no bleeding accommodation.

Dean said, Morris, are we going camping? I went camping once.

Morris said, how was it, mate?

Dean said, it were crap.

Aitkenside said, call it a porthole and it don't bleeding open? Won't do for Keef, you know, it won't do for Keef.

"Brilliant," Al said. "Couldn't be better. What won't do for Keith will do just fine for me." She put out her hand and squeezed Colette's cold bony fingers.

That summer, the birch trees were cut down and the last birds flew away. Their song was replaced by the roaring of road drills, the beeping of the earth movers backing up, the cursing of hod carriers and the cries of the wounded, and scrubland gave way to a gashed landscape of trenches and moats, of mud chutes and standing pools of yellow water; which within a year, in its turn, gave way to the violent emerald of new turf, the Sunday morning roar of mowers and strimmers, the tinkling of the ice-cream vans, the trundling of gas barbecues over paving and the stench of searing meat.

The flat in Wexham had sold to the first people who saw it. Alison wondered, will they sense something: Morris glugging inside the hot-water tank, or murmuring in the drains? But they seemed delighted, and offered the full asking price.

"It seems so unfair," Colette said, "when our flat in Whitton wouldn't sell. Not even when we dropped the price."

She and Gavin had sacked Sidgewicks, tried another agent; still no takers. Eventually, they had agreed Gavin should stay there, and buy her out by installments. "We have hopes the arrangement will be persuasive to Mrs. Waynflete," his solicitor had written, "as we understand she is now living with a partner." Colette had scrawled over the letter, *Not that sort of partner!!!* It was just for her own satisfaction that she wrote it; it was no business of Gavin's, she thought, what kind of partnership she was in now.

On the day they moved from Wexham, Morris was fuming and snarling in a corner. "How can I move," he said, "when I have given out this as my address? How will Nick find me, how will my old mates know where to come?" When the men came to take the pine dresser away, he lay on top of it to make it heavy. He infiltrated Al's mattress and infused his spirit sulks among the fibres, so that it bucked and rippled in the men's hands, and they almost dropped it in alarm. When the men slammed the tailgate and vaulted into the driver's cab, they found their whole windscreen had been spattered with something green, viscid, and dripping. "What kind of pigeons do you have around here?" they said. "Vultures?"

As the Collingwood was Galleon's top-of-the-range model, it had more gobons than any other house type in the development, more twiddles and teases, more gables and spindles; but most of them, Colette predicted, would fall off within the first six months. Down the hill they were still building, and yellow machines picked and pecked at the soil, their stiff bending necks strangely articulated, like the necks of prototype dinosaurs. Trucks jolted up with glue-on timbers of plastic oak, bound together in bundles like kindling. Swearing men in woolly hats unloaded paper-thin panels of false brickwork, which they pinned to the raw building blocks; they disembarked stick-on anchor motifs, and panels of faux pargetting with dolphin and mermaid designs. The beeping, roaring, and drilling began promptly at seven, each morning. Inside the house there were a few mistakes, like a couple of the internal doors being hung the wrong way around, and the Adam-style fireplace being off-centre. Nothing, Al said, that really affected your quality of life. Colette wanted to keep arguing with the builders till she got compensation, but Al said, let it go, what does it matter, just close the door on it. Colette said, I would but the frame's warped.

The day their kitchen ceiling fell in, she strode off to the sales caravan, where Suzi was still selling off the last remaining units. She made a scene; punters fled back to their cars, thinking they'd had a lucky escape. But when she left Suzi and began splashing uphill, picking her way between stacked paving slabs and lengths of piping, she found that she was shaking.

The Collingwood stood at the top of a rise; its portholes stared out over the neighbours like blind eyes. Is this my life now? she thought. How will I ever meet a man? At Wexham there were one or two young bachelors she used to glimpse down by the bins. One had never met her eye and only grunted when she greeted him. The other was Gavin to the life and went about swinging his car keys around his forefinger; the sight of him had almost made her nostalgic. But the men who had moved into Admiral Drive were married with two kids. They were computer programmers, systems analysts. They drove minivans like square little houses on wheels. They wore jackets with flaps and zips that their wives chose for them from mail order catalogues. Already the postman could be seen, ploughing across the furrows carrying flat boxes containing these jackets, and splattered white vans bounced over the ruts, delivering gob-ons for their home computers. At weekend they were outside, wearing their jackets, constructing playhouses and climbing frames of primary-coloured plastic. They were hardly men at all, not men as Colette knew them; they were dutiful emasculates, squat and waddling under their burden of mortgage debt, and she despised them with an impartial, all-embracing spite. Sometimes she stood at her bedroom window, as the men drove away in the mornings, each edging his square-nosed vehicle cautiously into the muddy track; she watched them and hoped they got into a pileup on the M3, each folding neatly, fatally, into the back of the vehicle in front. She wanted to see their widows sitting in the road, daubing themselves with mud, wailing.

The Collingwood still smelled of paint. As she let herself in at the front door, kicking off her shoes, it caught in her throat and mingled with the taste of salt and phlegm. She went upstairs to her own room—Bed Two, 15 by 14 feet with en-suite shower—and slammed the door, and sat down on the bed. Her little shoulders shook, she pressed her knees together; she clenched her fists and pressed them into her skull. She cried quite loudly, thinking Al might hear. If Al opened the bedroom door she would throw something at her, she decided—not anything like a bottle, something like a cushion—but there wasn't a cushion. I could throw a pillow, she thought, but you can't throw a pillow hard. I could throw a book, but there isn't a book. She looked around her, dazed, frustrated, eyes filmed and brimming, looking for something to throw.

But it was a useless effort. Al wasn't coming, not to comfort her: nor for any other purpose. She was, Colette knew, selectively deaf. She listened into spirits and to the voice of her own self-pity, carrying messages to her from her childhood. She listened to her clients, as much as was needful to get money out of them. But she didn't listen to her closest associate and personal assistant, the one who got up with her when she had nightmares, the friend who boiled the kettle in the wan dawn: oh no. She had no time for the person who had taken her at her word and given up her career in event management, no time for the one who drove her up and down the country without a word of complaint and carried her heavy suitcase when the bloody wheels fell off. Oh no. Who carried her case full of her huge fat clothes—even though she had a bad back.

Colette cried until two red tracks were scored into her cheeks, and she got hiccoughs. She began to feel ashamed. Every lurch of her diaphragm added to her indignity. She was afraid that Alison, after her deafness, might now choose to hear.

Downstairs, Al had her tarot pack fanned out before her. The cards were face down, and when Colette appeared in the doorway she was idly sliding them in a rightward direction, over the pristine surface of their new dining table.

"What are you doing? You're cheating."

"Mm? It's not a game."

"But you're fixing it, you're shoving them back into the pack! With your finger! You are!"

"It's called Washing the Cards," Al said. "Have you been crying?"

Colette sat down in front of her. "Do me a reading."

"Oh, you have been crying. You have *so*."

Colette said nothing.

"What can I do to help?"

"I'd rather not talk about it."

"So I should make general conversation?"

"If you like."

"I can't. You start."

"Did you have any more thoughts about the garden?"

"Yes. I like it as it is."

"What, just turf?"

"For the moment."

"I thought we could have a pond."

"No, the children. The neighbours' children."

"What about them?"

"Cut the pack."

Colette did it.

"Children can drown in two inches of water."

"Aren't they ingenious?"

"Cut again. Left hand."

"I could get some quotes for landscaping."

"Don't you like grass?"

"It needs cutting."

"Can't you do it?"

"Not with my back."

"Your back? You never mentioned it."

"You never gave me the chance."

"Cut again. Left hand, Colette, left hand. Well, I can't do it. I've got a bad back too."

"Really? Where did that originate?"

"When I was a child." I was dragged, Alison thought, over the rough ground.

"I'd have thought it would have been better."

"Why?"

"I thought time was a great healer."

"Not of backs."

Colette's hand hovered.

"Choose one," Al said. "One hand of seven. Seven cards. Hand them to me." She laid down the cards. "And your back, Colette?"

"What?"

"The problem. Where it began?"

"Brussels."

"Really?"

"I was carrying fold-up tables."

"That's a pity."

"Why?"

"You've spoiled my mental picture. I thought that perhaps Gavin had put you in some unorthodox sexual position."

"How could you have a picture? You don't know Gavin."

"I wasn't picturing his face." Alison began to turn the cards. The lucky opals were flashing their green glints. Alison said, "The Chariot, reversed."

"So what do you want me to do? About the garden?"

"Nine of swords. Oh dear."

"We could take it in turns to mow it."

"I've never worked a mower."

"Anyway, with your weight. You might have a stroke."

"Wheel of Fortune, reversed."

"When you first met me, in Windsor, you said I was going to meet a man. Through work, you said."

"I don't think I committed to a time scheme, did I?"

"But how can I meet a man through work? I don't have any work except yours. I'm not going out with Raven, or one of those freaks."

Al fluttered her hand over the cards. "This is heavy on the major Arcana, as you see. The Chariot, reversed. I'm not sure I like to think of wheels turning backward. . . . Did you send Gavin a change-of-address card?"

"Yes."

"Why?"

"As a precaution."

"Sorry?"

"Something might come for me. For forwarding. A letter. A package."

"A package? What would be in it?"

Al heard tapping, tapping, at the sliding glass doors of the patio. Fear jolted through her; she thought, Bob Fox. But it was only Morris, trapped in the garden; beyond the glass, she could see his mouth moving.

She lowered her eyes, turned a card. "The Hermit reversed."

"Bugger," Colette said. "I think you were reversing them on purpose, when you were messing about. *Washing* them."

"What a strange hand! All those swords, blades." Al looked up. "Unless it's just about the lawn mower. That would make some sense, wouldn't it?"

"No use asking me. You're the expert."

"Colette . . . Col . . . don't cry now."

Colette put her elbows on the table, her head on her hands, and howled away. "I ask you to do a reading for me and it's about bloody garden machinery. I don't think you have any consideration for me at all. Day in, day out I am doing your VAT. We never go anywhere. We never do anything nice. I don't think you have any respect for my professional skills whatever, and all I have to listen to is you rabbitting on to dead people I can't see."

Alison said gently, "I'm sorry if it seems as if I don't appreciate you. I do remember, I know what my life was like when I was alone. I do remember, and I value everything you do."

"Oh, stop it. *Burbling* like that. Being professional."

"I'm trying to be nice. I'm just trying—"

"That's what I mean. Being nice. Being professional. It's all the same to you. You're the most insincere person I know. It's no use pretending to me. I'm too close. I know what goes on. You're rotten. You're a horrible person. You're not even normal."

There was a silence. Alison picked up the cards, dabbing each one with a damp fingertip. After a time she said, "I don't expect you to mow the lawn."

Silence.

"Honest, Col, I don't."

Silence.

"Can I be professional for a moment?"

Silence.

"The Hermit, reversed, suggests that your energy could be put to better use."

Colette sniffed. "So what shall we do?"

"You could ring up a gardening service. Get a quote. For, let's say, a fortnightly cut through the summer." She added, smiling, "I expect they'd send a man."

A thought about the garden had gone through her head: it will be nice for the dogs. Her smile faded. She pushed the thought violently away, seeing in her mind the waste ground behind her mother's house at Aldershot.

Colette had taken on the task of contacting Al's regular clients, to let them know about the move. She made a pretty lilac-coloured card, with the new details, which they handed out to contacts at their next big Psychic Fayre. In return they got cards back. "You'll want a bit of Goddess Power, I expect," said a nice woman in a ragged pullover, as she unloaded her kit from her beat-up old van. "You'll want to come into alignment with the Path." When they saw her next she was wearing a hairpiece and a push-up bra, charging forty pounds and calling herself Siobhan, palms and clairvoyance.

"Shall I come up and do your feng shui?" Mandy Coughlan asked. "It's nice that you're nearer to Hove."

Cara rolled her eyes. "You're not still offering feng shui? Are you getting any uptake? I'm training as a vastu consultant. It's five thousand years old. This demon falls to earth, right? And you have to see which way his head comes down and where his feet are pointing. Then you can draw a mandala. Then you know which way the house should go."

"It's a bit late," Al said. "It's finished and we've moved in."

"No, but it can still apply. You can fit your existing property into the grid. That's advanced, though. I've not got up to that yet."

"Well, come round when you do," Al said.

• • •

Al said, I don't want the neighbours to know what we do. Wherever I've lived I've kept away from the neighbours, I don't want this lot around asking me to read their herbal teabags. I don't want them turning up on our doorstep saying, you know what you told me, it hasn't come true yet, can I have my money back? I don't want them watching me and commenting on me. I want to be private.

The development progressed piecemeal, the houses at the fringes going up before the middle was filled in. They would look over to the opposite ridge, against the screen of pines, and see the householders running out into the streets, or where the streets would be, fleeing from gas leaks, floods, and falling masonry. Colette made tea for their next-door neighbours in the Beatty when their kitchen ceiling came down in its turn; Al was busy with a client.

"Are you sisters?" Michelle asked, standing in the kitchen and jiggling an infant up and down on her hip.

Colette's eyes grew wide. "Sisters? No."

"There, Evan," she said to her husband. "Told you they couldn't be. We thought perhaps one of you wasn't staying. We thought perhaps she was helping the other one settle in."

Colette said, "Are those boys or girls?"

"One of each."

"Oh. But which is which?"

"You work at home?" Evan asked. "A contractor?"

"Yes." He was waiting. She said, flustered. "I'm in communications."

"British Telecom?"

"No."

"It's so confusing now," Michelle said. "All these different tariffs you can go on. What's the cheapest for phoning my nan in Australia?"

"That's not my side of it," Colette said.

"And what does your—your friend—do?"

"Forecasting," Colette said. For a moment, she began to enjoy herself.

"Met Office, eh?" Evan said. "Bracknell, aren't they? Bloody murder, getting onto the M3. Bet you didn't know that till you moved in, eh? Three-mile tailback every morning. Should have done your research, eh?"

Both infants began to squall. The grown-ups watched as a workman came out of the Beatty, damp to his knees, carrying a bucket. "I'll sue those fuckers," Evan said.

Later, Colette said to Al, "How could he ever have thought we were sisters? I would have thought half sisters, at the most. And even that would be stretching a point."

"People aren't very observant," Alison said kindly, "so you mustn't be insulted, Colette."

Colette didn't tell Alison that the neighbours thought she worked for the meteorological office. Word spread, around the estate, and the neighbours would call out to her, "No joke you know, this rain! Can't you do better than this?" Or simply, with a wave and a grin, "Oi! I see you got it wrong again."

"I seem to be a personality around here." Al said. "I don't know why."

Colette said, "I should think it's because you're fat."

As Easter approached, Michelle popped her head over the fence and asked Al what she should pack for their holiday in Spain. "I'm sorry," Al said, aghast, "I simply wouldn't be able to forecast anything like that."

"Yes, but unofficially," Michelle coaxed. "You must know."

"Off the record," Evan said, wheedling.

Colette ran her eyes over Michelle. Was she pregnant again, or just letting herself go? "Cover up, would be my advice," she said.

The weather affects the motorway as it affects the sea. The traffic has its rising tides. The road surface glistens with a pearly sheen, or heaves its black wet deeps. They find themselves at distant service stations as dawn breaks, where yellow light spills out into an oily dimness and a line of huddled birds watches them from above. On the M40 near High Wycombe, a kestrel glides on the updraught, swoops to pluck small squealing creatures from the rough grass of the margins. Magpies toddle amid the roadkill.

They travel: Orpington, Sevenoaks, Chertsey, Runnymede, Reigate, and Sutton. They strike out east of the Thames barrier, where travellers' encampments huddle beneath tower blocks and seagulls cry over the floodplains, where the smell of sewage is carried on the cutting wind. There are flood-lights and bunkers, gravel pits and pallet yards, junctions where traffic cones cluster. There are featureless hangars with TO LET signs pinned to them, tyres spun away into shabby fields. Colette puts her foot down; they pass vehicles mounted on the backs of vehicles, locked in oily copulation. They pass hous-ing developments just like theirs—"Look, portholes," Al says—their dormers and their Juliet balconies staring out over low hills made of compacted Lon-don waste. They pass Xmas tree farms and puppy farms, barnyards piled with scrap. Pictures of salivating dogs are hung on wire fences, so that those who don't read English get the point. Crosswinds rock them; cables lash across a fast sky. Colette's radio is tuned to traffic reports—trouble at Trellick Tower, an insurmountable blockage afflicting the Kingston bypass. Al's mind drifts, across the central reservation. She sees the walls of warehouses shining silver like the tinny armour of the tarot knights. She sees incinerators, oil storage tankers, gas holders, electricity substations. Haulage yards. Portakabins, un-derpasses, subways, and walkways. Industrial parks and science parks and re-tail parks.

The world beyond the glass is the world of masculine action. Everything she sees is what a man has built. But at each turnoff, each junction, women are waiting to know their fate. They are looking deep inside themselves, into their private hearts, where the foetus forms and buds, where the shape forms inside the crystal, where fingernails click softly on the backs of the cards, and pictures flutter upwards, towards the air: Justice, Temperance, The Sun, The Moon, The World.

At the motorway services, there are cameras pointing, watching the queues for fish and chips and tepid jellified cheesecake. Outside there are notices af-fixed to poles, warning of hawkers, peddlers, itinerant sellers, and illegal traders. There are none that warn against the loose, travelling dead. There are cameras guarding the exits, but none that register the entrances of Pikey Pete.

"You don't know what will trigger them," Al says. "There's a whole pack of them, you see. Accumulating. It worries me. I'm not saying it doesn't worry me. The only thing is, the only good thing—Morris doesn't bring them home. They fade away somewhere, before we turn into Admiral Drive. He doesn't like it, you see. Says it's not a proper home. He doesn't like the garden."

They were coming back from Suffolk—or somewhere, at any rate, where people still had an appetite—because they were behind a van that said WRIGHT'S FAMOUS PIES, SAVORIES, CONFECTIONERY.

"Look at that," Al said, and read it out, laughing. At once she thought, why did I do that? I could kick myself. They'll claim they're hungry now.

Morris gripped the passenger seat and rocked it, saying, "I could murder a Famous Pie." Said Pikey Pete, "You can't beat a Savoury." Said young Dean, with his customary politeness, "I'll have a Confectionery, please."

Colette said, "Is that headrest rocking again, or is it you fidgetting? God, I'm starving, I'm going to pull in at Clacket Lane."

When Colette was at home she lived on vitamin pills and ginseng. She was a vegetarian except for bacon and skinless chicken breasts. On the road they ate what they could get, when they could get it. They dined in the theme pubs of Billaricay and Egham. In Virginia Water they ate nachos and in Broxborne they ate fat pillows of dough that the baker called Belgian Buns. In lay-bys they ate leaking seafood sandwiches and when spring came, in the pedestrianized zones of small Thameside towns they sat on benches with warm Cornish pasties, nibbling daintily around the frills. They ate broccoli and three-cheese bake straight from the cash-and-carry, and wholesaler's quiche Lorraine with sinewy nuggets of ham as pink as a scalded baby, and KrispyKrum Chickettes, and lemon mousse that reminded them of the kind of foam you clean carpets with.

"I have to have something sweet," Alison said. "I have to keep my energy levels up. Some people think it's glamorous having psychic powers. They're dead wrong."

Colette thought, it's hard enough keeping her tidy, never mind glamorous. She served her time with Al, in the shopping precincts of small towns, standing outside fitting rooms the size of sentry boxes, with curtains that never pulled straight across. There were creaks and sighs from the other sentry boxes; the thin smell of desperation and self-hatred hung in the air. Colette had made a vow to take her upmarket, but Al was uncomfortable in posh shops. She did have some pride, though. Whatever she bought, she decanted into a carrier bag from a shop that catered to normal-sized women.

"I have to keep body and mind receptive and quiet," she said. "If carrying a bit of flesh is the price I have to pay, so be it. I can't tune in to Spirit if I'm bouncing around in an aerobics class."

Morris said, have you seen MacArthur, he is a mate of mine and Keef Capstick, he is a mate of Keef's too. Have you seen MacArthur, he is a mate of mine and he wears a knitted weskit. Have you seen MacArthur, he has only one eye, have you seen him, he has one earlobe ripped off, a sailor ripped it off in a fracas, that's what he tells people. How did he lose his eye? Well, that's another story. He blames that on a sailor too, but round here, we know he's lying. And Morris gave a dirty laugh.

When spring came, the gardening service sent a man. A truck dropped him, and his mower, then rattled off. Colette went to the door to administer him. No use waiting for Al to do it.

"It's only I don't know how to start it?" he said. He stood pushing a finger under his woolly hat, as if, Colette thought, he were making some sort of secret sign to her.

She stared at him. "You don't know how to start the mower?"

He said, "What do I look like, in this hat?"

"I can't imagine," she said.

"Do you think I look like a brickie?"

"I couldn't say."

"You can see 'em all over the place, they're building walls." He pointed. "Down there."

"You're soaked through," Colette said, noticing this.

The man said, "No, it's not up to much, is it, this cardigan, parka, jacket? I could do with a fleece."

"A fleece wouldn't keep the rain out."

"I could get a plastic, a plastic to put over it."

"Whatever you think best," Colette said coldly.

The man trudged away. Colette shut the door.

Ten minutes later the doorbell rang. The man had pulled his hat over his eyes. He was standing on the doormat, dripping under the porch. "So, starting it? Could you?"

Colette's eyes swept him, up and down. She saw with disgust that his toes were poking out of his shoes, waggling the cracked leather up and down. "Are you sure you're qualified for this job?"

The man shook his head. "I've not been trained on a mower," he said.

"Why did they send you?"

"I suppose they thought you could train me on it."

"And why would they think that?"

"Well, you look a lovely girl."

"Don't try it on," Colette said. "I'm ringing your manager." She slammed the door.

Al came to the head of the stairs. She had been having a lie-down, after seeing a bereaved client. "Col?"

"Yes?"

"Was that a man?" Her voice was vague, sleepy.

"It was the gardening service. He was crap. He couldn't start the mower."

"So what happened?"

"So I told him to bugger off and I'm ringing them to complain."

"What sort of man was he?"

"An idiot."

"Young, old?"

"I don't know. I didn't look. He was wet. He had a hat on."

In summer, they drove through countryside perfumed by the noxious vapours of pesticides and herbicides, and by the sweet cloud that lay over the golden fields of oil-seed rape. Their eyes streamed, their throats dried and tightened; Al groped in her bag for antiseptic lozenges. Autumn: she saw the full moon snared in the netting of a football field, caught there bulging, its face bruised. When a traffic snarl-up brought them to a halt, she noticed the trudging shopper with her grocery bags, leaning into the wind. She noticed the rotted wood of a balcony, London brick weeping soot, winter mould on a stack of garden chairs. A curve in the road, a pause at traffic lights, brings you close to another life, to an office window where a man leans on a filing cabinet in a crumpled shirt, as close as some man you know; while a van backs into the road, you halt, you are detained, and the pause makes you intimate with a man stroking his bald head, framed in the lighted cavity of his garage beneath the up-and-over door.

At journey's end comes the struggle with randomly arriving trivia, zinging through the ether. You are going to get a new sofa. You are a very tenacious person. Morris was supposed to act as a sort of doorman, ushering the spirits and making them queue up, threatening them so they don't all talk at once. But he seemed to have fallen into a prolonged sulk, since they moved to Admiral Drive. Nothing suited him, and he left her to be teased and tormented by Diana imitators, Elvis imitators, the petty dead purveying misinformation, working tricks and setting riddles. From her audiences, the same old questions: for example, is there sex in Spirit World?

She would answer, giggling, "There's an elderly lady I know who's very psychic, and I'll tell you what she says: she says, there's a tremendous amount of love in Spirit World, but there's none of that funny stuff."

It would get a laugh. The audience would relax. They didn't really suppose there could be an answer to this question. But once when they got home, Colette had said, "Well, is there sex in Spirit World? I don't want to know what Mrs. Etchells says, I want to know what you say."

"Mostly, they don't have body parts," Al said. "Not as such. There are exceptions. There are some really low spirits that are—well, just genitals, really. The others, they just . . . they like to watch us doing it."

"Then we can't provide them with much entertainment," Colette said.

Winter: from the passenger seat Al turns her face towards the lighted windows of a school. Children's drawings are pinned up, facing away from her: she sees the backs of triangular angels, with pointing frosted wings. Weeks after Christmas, into the new year, the cardboard stars still hang against the glass, and polyester snowflakes fall dryly, harmlessly down the inside of the panes. Winter and another spring: on the A12 towards Ipswich the lamps overhead burst into flower, their capsules splitting; they snap open like seedpods, and from their metal cups the rays of light burst out against the sky.

One day in early spring Alison looked out over the garden, and saw Morris squatting in the far corner, crying—or pretending to. Morris's complaint about the garden was that, when you looked out the window, all you could see was turf, and fence, and him.

They had paid extra for a plot backing south. But that first summer the light beat in through the French windows, and they were forced to hang voile panels to protect themselves. Morris spent his time sequestered in these drapes, swathed in them; he did not care for the light of the sun or the unshaded moon. After the idiot from the gardening service, they had bought their own mower, and Colette, complaining, had trimmed the lawn; but I'm not grubbing about in flower beds, she said, I'm not planting things. Al was embarrassed at first, when the neighbours stopped her and offered her magazine articles about garden planning, and recommended certain television programmes with celebrity horticulturalists, that they felt sure she would enjoy. They think we're letting the side down, she thought; as well as being sexual deviants, we don't have a pond or even decking. Morris complained there was no cover for his nefarious activities. His mates, he said, were jeering at him, crying "Hup! Hup! Hup! Morris on parade! By the left, quick march; by the right, quick march. . . . Fall out! Morrr-iisss, report for special fucking kitchen duties and licking ladies' shoes."

Al sneered at him. "I don't want you in my kitchen." No chance, she thought; not amongst our hygienic granite-look worktops. There is no crack or corner and there is no place to hide in our stainless-steel double oven, not without the risk of being cooked. At her mum's house in Aldershot the sink had an old-style wooden draining board, reeking, mouldy, sodden to the touch. For Morris, after he passed, it had been his natural home. He insinu-ated himself through the spongy fibres and lay there breathing wetly, puffing through his mouth and snorting through his nose. When this first happened she couldn't bear to do the washing up. After she had left it for three days in a row her mother had said, "I'll have you, young lady," and came after her with a plastic clothesline. Emmie couldn't decide whether to lash her, or tie her up, or hang her: and while she was deciding, she wobbled and fell over. Alison sighed and stepped over her. She took one end of the clothesline and drew it through her mother's half-closed hand until Emmie yielded the last foot, the last inch. Then she took it outside and hung it back, between the hook driven into the brickwork and the sloping post that was sunk into the grass.

It was twilight, a moon rising over Aldershot. The line was not taut, and her amateurish, womanly knots slipped away from their anchors. Some spirits fluttered down onto the line, and fluttered away again, squawking, when it dipped and swayed under their feet. She threw a stone after them, jeering. She was only a girl then.

At first, Morris had mocked the new house. "This is posh, innit? You're doing very well out of me, ducks." Then he threatened her. "I can take you over, you cheeky bitch. I can have you away airside. I can chew you up and spit you out. I'll come for you one night and the next day all they'll find is your torn knickers. Don't think I've not done it before."

"Who?" she said, "Who have you taken over?"

"Gloria, for one. Remember her? Tart with red hair."

"But you were earthside then, Morris. Anybody can do it with knives and hatchets but what can you do with your spirit hands? Your memory's going. You're forgetting what's what. You've been kicking around too long." She spoke to him roughly, man to man, as Aitkenside might: "You're fading, mate. Fading fast."

Then he began to coax her. "We want to go back to Wexham. It was a nice area in Wexham. We liked going down Slough, we liked it there because we could go down the dog track, where the dog track used to be. We liked it because you could go out fighting, but here there ain't the possibility of fighting. There ain't a bit of land where you can set up a cockfight. Young Dean enjoys nicking cars, but here you can't nick 'em, these buggers have all got alarms and Dean don't do alarms, he's only a kid and he ain't got trained on alarms yet. Donnie Aitkenside, he says we'll never meet up with MacArthur if we stay around these parts. He says, we'll never get Keef Capstick to stick around, Keef he likes a bit of a roughhouse and the chance of a ruckus." Morris's voice rose, he began to wheedle and whine. "Suppose I got a parcel? Where'm I going to keep me parcel?"

"What kind of parcel?" Al asked him.

"Suppose I got a consignment? Supposing I got a package? Supposing I had to keep guard on a few packing cases or a few crates. To help out me mates. You never know when your mate is going to come to you and say, Morris, Morris old son, can you keep an eye on these for me, ask me no questions and I'll tell you no lies?"

"You? You don't know anything but lies."

"And if that happens, where am I going to keep 'em? Answer me that, girl."

Alison told him, "You'll just have to say no, won't you?," and Morris said, "Say no, say no? Is that a way to treat a mate of yours? If old stringbean asked you, keep this package for me, would you refuse her, would you say, Colette, me old mate, no can do?"

"I might."

"But what if Nick asked you? What if old Nick himself was to come to you with a proposition, what if he was to say, cut you in on this my friend, trust me and I'll see you right, what if he was to say, least said soonest mended; what if he was to say, I'd regard it as a special favour?"

"What's Nick to me? I wouldn't cross the road for him."

"Because Nick, he don't ask you, he tells you. Because Nick, he hangs you from a tree and shoots off your kneecaps, I've seen it done. Because you don't say no to Nick or if you do you're bloody crippled. I seen him personally poke out a man's eye with a pencil. Where 'is eye would be."

"Is that what happened to MacArthur? You said he only had one eye."

A jeering, incredulous look spread over Morris's face. "Don't play the innocent wiv me," he said. "You evil baggage. You know bloody fine how his eye got took out." He headed, grumbling, for the French windows and wrapped his head in the curtain. "Tries it on wiv me, plays the innocent, fucking 'ell it won't wash. Tell it to Dean, try it on some kid and see if it will wash wiv him, it won't wash wiv me. I was there, girl. You claim my memory's gone. Nothing wrong with mine, I'm telling you. Could be something wrong with yours. I don't bloody forget his eye springing out. You don't forget a thing like that."

He looked frightened, she thought. Going up to bed, she hesitated outside Colette's room, Bed Two with en-suite shower. She would have liked to say, I am lonely sometimes, and—the brute fact is—I want human company. Was Colette human? Just about. She felt a yawning inside her, an unfilled space of loss, as if a door in her solar plexus were opening on an empty room, or a stage waiting for a play to begin.

• • •

The day Morris said he was going, she could hardly wait to tell people the news. "He's been called away," she said. "Isn't that great?" Smiles kept breaking out. She felt as if she were fizzing inside.

"Oh, that's wonderful," Mandy said on the phone. "I mean, it's good news for all of us, Al. Merlin said he was at the limit of his tolerance, and so did Merlyn. Your Morris had a really nasty way with him, he upset me dreadfully that night of Di's funeral. I never felt clean afterwards. Well, you don't, do you?"

"You don't think it's a trick?" Al said, but Mandy reassured her.

"It's his time, Al. He's pulled towards the light. He can't resist, I bet you. It's time he broke out of that cycle of criminality and self-destructive behaviour. He'll be moving upwards. You'll see."

Colette was in the kitchen making decaffeinated coffee. Al told her, "Morris is leaving. He's been called away."

Colette raised her eyebrows and said, "Called away by who?"

"I don't know, but he says he's going on a course. I talked to Mandy, she says it means he's moving to a higher level."

Colette stood waiting for the kettle to boil, her fingers tapping. "Does that mean he won't be bothering us in the future?"

"He swears he's leaving today."

"And it's like, a residential course, is it?"

"I suppose."

"And how long is it? Will he be coming back?"

"I think it takes as long as it takes. I can't believe he'll come back to the Woking area. Spirits don't generally go backwards. I've never heard of that happening. When he's moved towards the light he'll be free to—" She stopped, perplexed. "Whatever they do," she said finally. "Melt. Disperse."

The kettle clicked itself off. "And all those other people he talks about— Dean, those others we get in the back of the car—will they be melting too?"

"I don't know about Dean. He doesn't seemed very evolved. But yes, I think, it's Morris who attracts them, not me, so if he goes they'll all go. You see, it might be the end of Morris as we know him. It had to happen one day."

"Then what? What will it be like?"

"Well, it'll be—silent. We'll have some peace. I can get a night's sleep."

Colette said, "Could you move, please, so I can get to the fridge? . . . You won't be giving up the business, will you?"

"If I gave up, how would I make a living?"

"I just want the milk. Thanks. But what will you do for a spirit guide?"

"Another one could turn up any day. Or I could borrow yours."

Colette almost dropped the milk carton. "Mine?"

"Didn't I tell you?"

Colette looked horrified. "But who is he?"

"It's a she. Maureen Harrison, her name is."

Colette poured her milk all over the granite-style work surface, and stood watching it stupidly as it dripped. "Who's that? I don't know her. I don't know anyone of that name."

"No, you wouldn't. She passed before you were born. In fact, it took me a while to locate her, but her poor old friend kept calling around, asking for her. So I thought I'd do a good action, link them up together. Okay, I should have told you! I should have mentioned it. But what's your problem? She won't make any difference to you. Look, relax, she's not doing you any harm, she's just one of those grannies who lose the buttons off their cardigans."

"But can she see me? Is she looking at me now?"

"Maureen," Al said softly. "You around, love?"

From a cupboard came the chink of a teacup.

"There," Al said.

"Can she see me in my room at night?"

Alison crossed the kitchen and began to mop up the spilled milk. "Go and sit down, Colette, you've had a shock. I'll make you another cup."

She boiled the kettle again. Decaf's not much use for a shock. She stood looking out over the empty garden. When Morris actually goes, she thought, we'll have champagne. Colette called out to know where Maureen Harrison came from, and when Al called back, "Somewhere up north," she sounded shocked, as if it would have been more natural to have a spirit guide from Uxbridge.

Al couldn't help smiling to herself. "Look on the bright side," she said, bringing the coffee through; she'd put out some chocolate biscuits as the beginning of her celebration. "Look on the bright side, you might have been lumbered with a Tibetan." She imagined the Collingwood, ringing with temple bells.

There was an unusual calm in their sitting room. She stared hard at the voile panels, but Morris's form was not bulking them out, nor was he lying, stretched, along the hem. No Aitkenside, no Dean, no Pikey. She sat down. "Here we are," she said, beaming. "Just the two of us." She heard a moaning, a scraping, a metallic rattle; then the flap of the letter box, as Morris made his exit.

eight

As the millennium approached, their trade declined. It was nothing personal, no misstep in Colette's business plan. All the psychics called up to grouch about it. It was as if their clients had put their personal curiosity on pause, as if they had been caught up in some general intake of breath. The new age was celebrated at Admiral Drive with fireworks, released by careful fathers from the raw back plots. The children's play area, the natural site for the fiesta, had been fenced off and KEEP OUT notices erected.

The local free sheet said Japanese knotweed had been found. "Is that a good thing?" Michelle asked, over the back fence. "I mean, are they conserving it?"

"No, I think it's noxious," Al said. She went inside, worried. I hope it's not my fault, she thought. Had Morris pissed on the plot, on his way out of her life?

Some people didn't buy into the knotweed theory. They said the problem was an unexploded bomb, left over from the last war—whenever that was. Evan leaned over the fence and said, "Have you heard about that bloke over Reading way, Lower Earley? On a new estate like this? He kept noticing his paint was blistering. His drains filled up with black sludge. One day he was digging in his vegetable plot, and he saw something wriggling on his spade. He thought, hell, what's this?"

"And what was it?" Colette asked. Sometimes she found Evan entrancing.

"It was a heap of white worms," he said. "Where you've got white worms you've got radioactivity. That's the only thing you need to know about white worms."

"So what did he do?"

"Called in the council," Evan said.

"If it were me I'd call in the army."

"Of course it's a cover-up. They denied everything. Poor beggar's boarded the place up and cut his losses."

"So what caused it?"

"Secret underground nuclear explosion," Evan said. "Stands to reason."

At Admiral Drive a few people phoned the local environmental health department, putting questions about the play area, but officials would only admit to some sort of blockage, some sort of seepage, some sort of contamination the nature of which they were unable as yet to confirm. They insisted that the white worm problem was confined to the Reading area and that none of them had made their way to Woking. Meanwhile the infants remained shut out of paradise. They roared with temper when they saw the swings and the slide, and rattled the railings. Their mothers dragged them uphill, towards their Frobishers and Mountbattens, out of harm's way. Nobody wanted news of the problem to leak, in case it affected their house prices. The populace was restless and transient, and already the first FOR SALE signs were going up, as footloose young couples tried their luck in a rising market.

New Year's Eve was cold at Admiral Drive, and the skies were bright. The planes didn't fall out of them, and there was no flood or epidemic—none, anyway, affecting the southeast of England. The clients gave a listless, apathetic sigh and—just for a month or two—accepted their lives as they were. By spring, trade was creeping back.

"They're coming to take samples from the drains," Michelle told Alison.

"Who are?"

"Drain officials," Michelle said fearfully.

• • •

After Morris left, their life was like a holiday. For the first time in years, Alison went to bed knowing she wouldn't be tossed out of it in the small hours. She could have a leisurely late-night bath without a hairy hand pulling out the plug, or Morris's snake tattoo rising beneath the rose-scented bubbles. She slept through the night and woke refreshed, ready for what the day might bring. She blossomed, her plumped-out skin refining itself, the violet shadows vanishing from beneath her eyes. "I don't know when I've felt so well," she said.

Colette slept through the nights too, but she looked just the same.

They began to talk about booking a last-minute holiday, a break in the sun. Morris on an aircraft had been impossible, Al said. When she was checking in, he would jump on her luggage, so that it weighed heavy and she was surcharged. He would flash his knuckle-dusters as they walked through the metal detector, causing the security staff to stop and search her. If they made it as far as the plane, he would lock himself in the lavatory or hide in some vulnerable person's sick bag and come up—*boom!*—into their face when they opened it. On the way to Madeira once, he had caused a cardiac arrest.

"You don't have to worry about that anymore," Colette said. "Where would you like to go?"

"Dunno," Al said. Then: "Somewhere with ruins. Or where they sing opera. It's night, and you hold candles, and they sing in an arena, an amphitheatre. Or they perform plays wearing masks. If I were an opera singer I'd be quite alluring. Nobody would think I was overweight."

Colette had been thinking in terms of sex with a Greek waiter. There was no reason, on the face of it, why Alison's cultural yearnings and her sexual ones shouldn't be fulfilled within five hundred yards of each other. But she pictured her hot-eyed beau circling their table on the terrace, his sighs, his raised pulse, his fiery breath, his thoughts running ahead: is it worth it, because I'll have to pay a mate of mine to sleep with the fat girl?

"Besides," Al said, "it would be nice to have somebody with me. I went to Cyprus with Mandy but I never saw her, she was in and out of bed with somebody new every night. I found it quite squalid. Oh, I love Mandy, don't get me wrong. People should enjoy themselves, if they can."

"It just happens you can't," Colette said.

It didn't matter what she said to Al, she reasoned. Even if she didn't speak out loud, Al would pull the thoughts out of her head; so she would know anyway.

Alison withdrew into a hurt silence; so they never got the holiday. A month on, she mentioned it again, timidly, but Colette snapped at her, "I don't want to go anywhere with ruins. I want to drink too much and dance on the table. Why do you think this is all I want to do, live with you and drive you to sodding Oxted to a Celtic Mystery Convention? I spend my sodding life on the M25, with you throwing up in the passenger seat."

Alison said timidly, "I'm not sick much, since Morris went." She tried to imagine Colette dancing on a table. She could only conjure a harsh tango on the blond wood of the coffee table, Colette's spine arched, her chicken-skin armpits exposed as if for a bite. She heard a buzz in her ear; the meek little woman came through, saying, 'scuse me, 'scuse me, have you seen Maureen Harrison?

"Look in the kitchen," Al said. "I think she's behind the fridge."

When 9/11 came, Colette was watching daytime TV. She called Alison through. Al rested her hands on the back of the sofa. She looked without surprise as the Twin Towers crumbled, as the burning bodies plunged through the air. Alison watched till the news looped itself around again and the same pictures were played. Then she left the room without comment. You feel as if you should say something, but you don't know what it is. You can't say you foresaw it; yet you can't say no one foresaw it. The whole world has drawn this card.

Merlyn rang up later that day. "Hello," she said. "How's you? Seen the news?"

"Awful," Merlyn said, and she said, "Yes, awful, And how's Merlin?"

"No idea," he said.

"Not seen him on the circuit?"

"I'm quitting that."

"Really? You're going to build up the psychic detective work?"

Or psychic security services, she thought. You could certainly offer them. You could stand at airports and X-ray people's intentions.

"No, nothing like that," Merlyn said. He sounded remarkably buoyant. "I'm thinking of becoming a life coach. I'm writing a book, a new one. *Self-Heal Through Success*. It's using the ancient wisdom traditions for health, wealth, and happiness. Believe the world owes you: that's what I say."

Alison excused herself, put the receiver down, and went into the kitchen to get an orange. When she came back, she wedged the receiver under her chin while she peeled it. You don't want to waste your time, Merlyn was saying, with these young girls and grandmas. Here we are in the heartland of the hi-tech boom. Affluence is as natural as breathing. Each morning when you rise you stretch out your arms and say, I possess the universe.

"Merlyn, why are you telling me this?"

"I was hoping you'd buy a franchise. You're very inspirational, Alison."

"You'd have to talk to Colette. She makes the business decisions."

"Oh, does she?" said Merlyn. "Let me tell you now, and I'll tell you for free, you alone are responsible for your health and your wealth. You cannot delegate what is at the core of your being. Remember the universal law: you get what you think you deserve."

Peel fell on the carpet, fragrant and curly. "Really?" she said. "Not much, then, in my case."

"Alison, I'm disappointed by your negativity. I may have to put the phone down, before it contaminates my day."

"Okay," she said, and Merlyn said, "No, don't go. I'd hoped—oh, well, I was thinking along the lines of a partnership. Well, there you are. I've said it. What do you think?"

"A business partnership?"

"Any kind you like."

She thought, he thinks I'm stupid, just because I'm fat; because I'm fat, he thinks I'm stupid.

"No."

"Would you be more specific?"

"More specific than no?"

"I value feedback. I can take it on the chin."

The trouble is, she thought, you don't have a chin. Merlyn was running to fat, and his damp grey skin seemed to sweat out, in public, the private moisture contained within the shell of his trailer home. She looked, in imagination, into his chocolate-coloured eyes, and saw how his pastel shirt stretched over his belly.

"I couldn't," she said. "You're overweight."

"Well, *pardonnez-moi*," Merlyn said. "Look who's talking."

"Yes, I know, me too. But I don't like the way your shirt buttons are bursting off. I hate sewing, I'm no good with a needle."

"You can get staplers," Merlyn said nastily. "You can get dedicated staplers nowadays. Anyway, who told you that I would require you to sew on my shirt buttons?"

"I thought you might."

"And you are seriously giving me this as a reason why you are turning down my offer of a business arrangement?"

"But I thought you were offering something else."

"*Who knows?*" Merlyn said. "That's the technical term, I believe, that people use when advertising. "For friendship and *who knows?*"

"But in your case, what you want is my money in your bank, and who knows? Come on, Merlyn! You just think I'm an easy touch. And by the way it's no good ringing up Mandy—Natasha, I mean—or any of the girls. They all don't like you, for the reason I don't like you." She paused. No, that's unfair, she thought. There is a particular reason I don't like Merlyn. "It's your tie pin," she said. "I don't like the sight of a tie pin. I always think it's dangerous."

"I see," Merlyn said. "Or rather, I don't, I don't at all."

She sighed. "I'm not sure I can account for it myself. Goes back to a past life, I suppose."

"Oh, come on!" Merlyn sneered. "Martyred with a tie pin? In antiquity they didn't have tie pins. Brooches, I grant you."

"Maybe it was me who did the martyring," she said. "I don't know, Merlyn. Look, good luck with your book. I hope you do get all that wealth. I do really. If you deserve it, of course. And I'm sure you do. Whatever. Whatever you think. When you leave your mobile home for Beverly Hills, let us have your new address."

Colette came in five minutes later, with the shopping. "Do you want a fudge double-choc brownie?" she asked.

Al said, "Merlyn phoned. He's doing a new book."

"Oh yes?" Colette said. "You do like these yogurts, don't you?"

"Are they high-fat?" Al said happily. Colette turned the pot about in her fingers, frowning. "They must be," Al said, "if I like them. By the way, Merlyn asked me to go and live with him."

Colette continued stacking the fridge. "Your chops are past their sell-by," she said. She hurled them in the bin and said, *"What?* In his trailer?"

"I said no."

"Who the fuck does he think he is?"

"He propositioned me," Al said.

She wiped her hand down her skirt. "What about our book, Colette? Will it ever be finished?"

Colette had accumulated a little pile of printout upstairs; she guarded it, locking it in her wardrobe—a precaution Al found touching. The tapes still gave them trouble. Sometimes they would find their last session had been replaced entirely by gibberish. Sometimes their conversation was overlaid by squeaks, scrapes, and coughs, as if a winter audience were tuning up for a symphony concert.

COLETTE: So, do you regard it as a gift or more as a—what's the opposite of a gift?

ALISON: Unsolicited goods. A burden. An infliction.

COLETTE: Is that your answer?

ALISON: No. I was just telling you some expressions.

COLETTE: So . . . ?

ALISON: Look, I just am this way. I can't imagine anything else. If I'd had somebody around me with more sense when I was training, instead of Mrs. Etchells, I might have had a better life.

COLETTE: So it could be different?

ALISON: Yes. Given a more evolved guide.

COLETTE: You seem to be doing okay without Morris.

ALISON: I told you I would.

COLETTE: After all, you've said yourself, a lot of it is psychology.

ALISON: When you say *psychology*, you're calling it cheating.

COLETTE: What would you call it?

ALISON: You don't call Sherlock Holmes cheating! Look, if you get knowledge, you have to use it however it comes.

COLETTE: But I'd rather think, in a way—let me finish—I'd rather think you were cheating, if I had your welfare at heart. Because a lot of people who hear voices, they get diagnosed and put in hospital.

ALISON: Not so much now. Because of cutbacks, you know? There are people who walk around believing all sorts of things. You see them on the streets.

COLETTE: Yes, but that's just a policy. That doesn't make them sane.

ALISON: I make a living, you see. That's the difference between me and the people who are mad. They don't call you mad, if you're making a living.

Sometimes Colette would leave the tape running without telling Al. There was some obscure idea in her mind that she might need a witness. That if she had a record she could make Al stick to any bargains she made; or that, in an unwary moment while she was out of the house, Al might record something incriminating. Though she didn't know what her crime might be.

COLETTE: My project for the new millennium is to manage you more efficiently. I'm going to set you monthly targets. It's time for blue-skies thinking. There's no reason why you shouldn't be at least ten percent more productive. You're sleeping through the night now, aren't you? And possibly I could handle a more proactive role. I could pick up the overflow clients. Just the ones who require fortune-telling. After all, you can't really tell the future, can you? The cards don't know it.

ALISON: Most people don't want to know about the future. They just want to know about the present. They want to be told they're doing all right.

COLETTE: Nobody ever told me I was doing all right. When I used to go to Brondesbury and places.

ALISON: You didn't feel helped, you didn't feel you'd had any emotional guidance?

COLETTE: No.

ALISON: When I think back to those days, I think you were trying to believe too much. People can't believe everything at once. They have to work up to it.

COLETTE: Gavin thought it was all a fraud. But then Gavin was stupid.

ALISON: You know, you still talk about him a lot.

COLETTE: I don't. I never talk about him.

ALISON: Mm.

COLETTE: Never.

"So okay, okay," Al said. "If you want to learn. What do you want to try first, cards or palms? Palms? Okay."

But after five minutes, Colette said, "I can't see the lines, Al. I think my eyes are going." Al said nothing. "I might get contacts. I'm not having glasses."

"You can use a magnifying glass, the punters don't mind. In fact, they think they're getting more for their money."

They tried again. "Don't try to tell my future," Al said. "Leave that aside for now. Take my left hand. That's where my character is written, the capacities I was born with. You can see all my potential, waiting to come out. Your job is to alert me to it."

Colette held her hand tentatively, as if she found it disagreeable. She glanced down at it, and up at Alison again. "Come on," Al said. "You know my character. Or you say you do. You're always talking about my character. And you know about my potential. You've just made me a business plan."

"I don't know," Colette said. "Even when I look through a magnifier I can't make sense of it."

"We'll have a go with the cards then," Al said. "As you know, there are seventy-eight to learn, plus all the meaningful combinations, so you'll have a lot of homework. You know the basics, you must have picked that up by now. Clubs rule the fire signs—you know the signs, don't you? Hearts rule water, diamonds earth."

"Diamonds, earth," Colette said, "that's easy to remember. But why do spades rule air?"

"In the tarot, spades are swords," Al said. "Think of them cutting through the air. Clubs are wands. Diamonds are pentacles. Hearts are cups."

Colette's hands were clumsy when she shuffled; pictures cascaded from the pack and she gave herself paper cuts, as if the cards were nipping her. Al taught her to lay out a consequences spread and a Celtic Cross. She turned the major arcana face up so she could learn them one by one. But Colette couldn't get the idea. She was diligent and conscientious, but when she saw the cards she couldn't see beyond the pictures on them. A crayfish is crawling out of a pond: why? A man in a silly hat stands on the brink of a precipice. He carries his possessions in a bundle and a dog is nipping at his thigh. Where is he going? Why doesn't he feel the teeth? A woman is forcing open the jaws of a lion. She seems happy with life. There is a collusive buzz in the air.

Al said, "What does it convey to you? No, don't look at me for an answer. Close your eyes. How do you feel?"

"I don't feel anything," Colette said. "How should I feel?"

"When I work with the tarot, I generally feel as if the top of my head has been taken off with a tin opener."

Colette threw down the cards. I'll stick to my side of the business, she said.

Al said, that would be very wise. She couldn't explain to Colette how it felt to read for a client, even if it was just psychology. You start out, you start talking, you don't even know what you're going to say. You don't even know your way to the end of the sentence. You don't know anything. Then suddenly you do know. You have to walk blind. And you walk slap into the truth.

In the new millennium Colette intended to lever her away from low-rent venues, where there are recycling bins in the car parks, crisps ground into the carpet, strip lighting. She wanted to see her in big well-furbished auditoriums with proper sound-and-lighting crews. She detested the public nature of public halls, where tipsy comics played on Saturday night and gusts of dirty laughter hung in the air. She loathed the worn grubby chairs, stained with beer and worse; hated the thought of Al attuning to Spirit in some broom cupboard, very often with a tin bucket and a string mop for company. She said, I don't like it down there by the Gymnastics Club, by the Snooker Centre. I don't like the types you get. I want to get down to the south coast where they have some lovely restored theatres, gilt and red plush, where you can fill the stalls and the royal circle, fill the balcony right to the back.

At Admiral Drive the early bulbs pushed through, points of light in the lush grass. The brick of the Mountbatten and the Frobisher was still raw, the tiled roofs slicked by April rain. Al was right when she said that the people down the hill would have a problem with damp. Their turf squelched beneath their feet, and a swampish swelling and bubbling lifted their patios. At night the security lights flittered, as if all the neighbours were creeping from house to house, stealing each other's game consoles and DVD players.

Gavin never called, though his monthly payment for his share of the flat in Whitton continued to arrive in her bank account. Then one day, when she and Al were shopping in Farnham, they ran straight into him; they were coming out of Elphicks department store, and he was going in.

"What are you doing in Farnham?" she said, shocked.

Gavin said, "It's a free country."

It was just the sort of inane reply he always used to make when you asked him why he was doing anything, or why he was wherever he was. It was the kind of reply that reminded her why she had been right to leave him. He couldn't have done much better if he'd pre-meditated it for a week.

Al's glance took him in. When Colette turned to introduce her, she was already backing away. "I'll just be . . ." she said, and melted in the direction of cosmetics and perfume. Tactfully, she averted her eyes, and stood spraying herself with one scent and then another, to distract herself from tuning in to what they were saying.

"That her? Your friend? Gavin said. "Christ, she's a size, isn't she? That the best you could do?"

"She's a remarkably sound businesswoman," Colette said, "and a very kind and thoughtful employer."

"And you live with her?"

"We have a lovely new house."

"But why do you have to live in?"

"Because she needs me. She works twenty-four/seven."

"Nobody does that."

"She does. But you wouldn't understand."

"I always thought you were a bit of a lezzie, Col. I'd have thought so when I first saw you, only you came down the bar—that hotel, where was it, France—you walked straight up to me with your tongue hanging out. So I thought, could be wrong on this one."

She turned her back and walked away from him. He called, "Colette . . ." She turned. He said, "We could meet up for a drink, sometime. Not her, though. She can't come."

Her mouth opened—she stared at him—a lifetime of insults swallowed, insults swallowed and digested, gushed up from deep inside her and jammed in her throat. She hauled in her breath, her hands formed claws; but the only words that came out were "Get stuffed." As she dived into the store, she caught sight of herself in a mirror, her skin mottled with wrath and her eyes popping, and for the first time she understood why when she was at school they had called her Monster.

The following week, in Walton-on-Thames, they got into a parking dispute with a man in a multistorey car park. Two cars nosing for the same space; it was just one of those crude suburban flare-ups, which men easily forget but which make women cry and shake for hours.

Nine times out of ten, in these spats, Al would put her restraining hand on Colette's hand, as it tightened on the wheel, and say, forget it, let him have what he wants, it doesn't matter. But this time, she whizzed down her window and asked the man, "What's your name?"

He swore at her. She was inured to bad language, from the fiends; but why should you expect it from such a man, an Admiral Drive sort of man, a mail-order-jacket sort of man, a let's-get-out-the-barbecue sort of man?

She said to him, "Stop, stop, stop! You should have more on your mind than cursing women in car parks. Go straight home and boost your life insurance. Clean up your computer and wipe off those kiddie pictures, that's not the sort of thing you want to leave behind you. Ring up your GP. Ask for an early appointment and don't take no for an answer. Tell them, left lung. They can do a lot these days, you know. If they catch these things before they spread." She whizzed up the window again. The man mouthed something; his car squealed away.

Colette slotted them neatly into the disputed space. She glanced sideways at Al. She didn't dare question her. They were running late, of course; they did need the space. She said to Al, testing her, "I wish I had done that." Al didn't answer.

When they got home that night and had poured a drink, she said, "Al, the man in the car park. . . ."

"Oh, yes," Al said. "Of course, I was just guessing." She added, "About the pornography."

These days when they travelled there was blissful silence from the back of the car. Didcot and Abingdon, Blewberry and Goring: Shinfield, Wonersh, Long Ditton, and Lightwater. They knew the lives they glimpsed on the road were lives more ordinary than theirs. They saw an ironing board in a lean-to, waiting for its garment. A grandma at a bus stop, stooping forward to pop a biscuit into a child's open mouth. Dirty pigeons hanging in the trees. A lamp shining behind a black hedge. Underpasses dropping away, lit by dim bulbs: Otford, Limpsfield, New Eltham, and Blackfen. They tried to avoid the high streets and shopping malls of the denatured towns, because of the bewildered dead clustered among the dumpsters outside the burger bars, clutching door keys in their hands or queuing with their lunch boxes where the gates of small factories once stood, where machines once whirred and chugged behind sooty panes of old glass. There are thousands of them out there, so pathetic and lame-brained that they can't cross the road to get where they're going, dithering on the kerbs of new arterial roads and bypasses, as the vehicles swish by: congregating under railway arches and under the stairwells of multistorey car parks, thickening the air at the entrance to underground stations. If they brush up against Alison they follow her home, and start pestering her the first chance they get. They elbow her in the ribs with questions, always questions; but never the right ones. Always, where's my pension book, has the Number 64 gone, are we having a fry-up this morning? Never, am I dead? When she puts them right on that, they want to go over how it happened, trying to glean some sense out of it, trying to throw a slippery bridge over the gap between time and eternity.

"I had just plugged in the iron," a woman would say, "and I was just starting on the left sleeve of Jim's blue striped shirt . . . of his . . . our Jim . . . his stripes. . . ." And her voice will grow faint with bafflement until Alison explains to her, puts her in the picture, and "Oh, I see now," she will say, quite equable, and then, "I get it. These things happen, don't they? So I'll not take up your time any further. I'm very much obliged. No thanks, I've my own tea waiting for me when I get home. I wouldn't want to cut into your evening. . . ."

And so she passes, her voice fading until she melts into the wall.

Even the ones who went over with plenty of warning liked to recall their last hours on the ward, dwelling in a leisurely fashion on which of their family showed up for the deathbed and which of them left it too late and got stuck in traffic. They wanted Alison to put tributes in the newspaper for them—*Thanks, sincerely meant, to the staff at St. Bernard's*—and she promised she would, for I'll do anything, she would say, that will make them lie down, wait quietly and waft to their next abode instead of making themselves at home in mine. They will finish their ramblings with, "Well, that's all from me for now," and "Hoping this finds you well," and "Let me have your family news soon": sometimes with a quiet, stoical, "I ought to go now." Sometimes, when they bob back, with a cheery, "Hello, it's me," they are claiming to be Queen Victoria, or their own older sister, or a woman who lived next door to them before they were born. It's not intentional fraud; it's more that a mingling and mincing and mixing of personality goes on, the fusing of personal memory with the collective. You see, she explains to Colette, you and me, when we come back, we could manifest as one person. Because these last years, we've shared a lot. You could come back as my mum. I could come over, thirty years from now, to some psychic standing on a stage somewhere, and claim I was my own dad. Not that I know who my dad is, but I will one day, perhaps after I've passed.

But Colette would say, panicked for a moment, stampeded into belief, what if I die? Al, what shall I do, what shall I do if I die?

Al would say to her, keep your wits about you. Don't start crying. Don't speak to anybody. Don't eat anything. Keep saying your name over and over. Close your eyes and look for the light. If somebody says, follow me, ask to see their ID. When you see the light, move towards it. Keep your bag clamped to your body—where your body would be. Don't open your bag, and remember the last thing you should do is pull out a map, however lost you feel. If anybody asks you for money ignore them, push past. Just keep moving towards the light. Don't make eye contact. Don't let anyone stop you. If somebody points out there's paint on your coat or bird droppings in your hair, just keep motoring, don't pause, don't look left or right. If a woman approaches you with some snotty-nosed kid, kick her out of the way. It sounds harsh, but it's for your own safety. Keep moving. Move towards the light.

And if I lose it? Colette would say. What if I lose the light and I'm wandering around in a fog, with all these people trying to snatch my purse and my mobile? You can always come home, Alison would tell her. You know your home now, Admiral Drive. I'll be here to explain it all to you and put you on the right path so that you can manage the next bit, and then when I come over in the fullness of time we can get together and have a coffee and maybe share a house again if we think it will work out.

But what if you go before me, Colette would say, what if we go together, what if we're on the M25 and a wind blows up and what if it's a mighty wind and we're blown into the path of a lorry?

Alison would sigh and say, Colette, Colette, we all get there in the end. Look at Morris! We end up in the next world raw, indignant, baffled or furious, and ignorant, all of us: but we get sent on courses. Our spirits move, given time, to a higher level, where everything becomes clear. Or so people tell me, anyway. Hauntings can persist for centuries, for sure, but why wouldn't they? People have no sense of urgency, airside.

Inside the Collingwood the air was serene. Weekly, Colette polished the crystal ball. You had to wash it in vinegar and water and rub it up with a chamois. Al said, the tools of the trade are what keep you on track. They focus the mind and direct the energy. But they have no magic in themselves. Power is contained in domestic objects, in the familiar items you handle every day. You can look into the side of an aluminium pan and see a face that's not your own. You can see a movement on the inside of an empty glass.

The days, months, blurred into one. The venues offered a thousand grannies with buttons missing; a thousand hands raised. Why are we here? Why must we suffer? Why must children suffer? Why does God mistreat us? Can you bend spoons?

Smiling, Al said to her questioner, "I should give it a go, shouldn't I? Give me something to do in the kitchen. Stop me raiding the fridge."

The truth was—though she never admitted it to anyone—that she had once tried it. She was against party tricks, and generally against showing off and being wasteful, and wrecking your cutlery seemed to come under those heads. But one day at Admiral Drive the urge overcame her. Colette was out: all well and good. She tiptoed into the kitchen and slid out a drawer. It snagged, bounced back. The potato masher had rolled forward spitefully and was catching its rim on the front of the unit. Unusually irritated, she slid in her hand, dragged the utensil out and threw it across the kitchen. Now she was in the mood for spoon-bending, she wasn't to be thwarted.

Her hand jumped for the knives. She picked one out, a blunt round-edged table knife. She ran her fingers around the blade. She put it down. Picked up a soupspoon. She knew how to do this. She held it loosely, fingers caressing its neck, her will flowing from her spinal column sweetly into the pads of her fingers. She closed her eyes. She felt a slight humming behind them. Her breathing deepened. She relaxed. Then her eyes snapped open. She looked down. The spoon, unaltered, smiled up at her; and suddenly she understood it, she understood the essence of spoonhood. Bending it wasn't the point, anymore. The point was that she would never feel the same about cutlery. Something stirred deep in her memory, as if she had been cross-wired, as if some old source of feeling had been tapped. She laid the spoon to rest, reverently, snug inside a fellow spoon. As she closed the drawer her eye caught the glint of the paring knife, a more worthwhile blade. She thought, I understand the nature of it. I understand the nature of spoon and knife.

Later, Colette picked up the potato masher from where it had fallen. "It's bent," she said.

"That's all right. I did it."

"Oh. You're sure?"

"Just a little experiment."

"I thought for a minute it must be Morris come back." Colette hesitated. "You would tell me, wouldn't you?"

But truly, there was no sign of him. Al sometimes wondered how he was doing on his course. It must be that he's going to a higher level, she reasoned, you wouldn't get sent on a course to go to a lower level.

"No, not even Morris," Colette said, when she mentioned it. If Morris were on a lower level, he'd be no good, he'd not even scrape up to standard as an ordinary spirit, let alone get employed anywhere as a guide. He'd be just an agglomeration of meaninglessness, a clump of cells rolling around through the netherworld.

"Colette," she said, "when you're sweeping, have a look at the vacuum cleaner bag from time to time. If you find any big lumps you can't account for, check it out with me, okay?"

Colette said, "I don't think that sifting through the vacuum cleaner bag was in my job description."

"Well, write it in, there's a good girl," Al said.

There are some spirits, she knew, who are willing to sink: who are so tenacious of existence that they will assume any form, however debased, ridiculous, and filthy. That was why Al, unlike her mother, made sure to keep a clean house. She thought that she and Colette, between them, could keep down the lower sort, who drift in dust rolls under beds and make streaks and fingerprints on windowpanes. They cloud mirrors and sometimes vanish with a chortle, leaving the mirror clear and unkind. They clump in hairbrushes, and when you comb them out, you think, can this thin grey frizz be mine?

Sometimes, when Alison came into a room, she thought the furniture had shifted slightly; but no doubt that was Colette, pushing it around as she cleaned. Her own boundaries seemed invisible, uncertain. Her core temperature tended to fluctuate, but there was nothing new in that. Her extremities drifted, in time and space. Sometimes she thought an hour, an afternoon, a day had gone missing. Less and less did she want to go out; her clients e-mailed her, the phone rang less often; Colette, who was restless, could always be persuaded to shop for them. It was the house's silence that entranced her, lulled her. Her daydreams and night dreams ran together. She thought she saw two cars—trucks, really—parked outside the Collingwood; it was dark, Colette was in bed, she pulled her coat around her shoulders and went outside.

The carriage lamp flared into life, and the thump of a hi-fi came from a Hawkyns. There was no one around. She looked into the cab of one truck and it was empty. The cab of the other was empty too, but in the back there was a grey blanket tied with twine, covering something irregular and lumpy.

She shivered, and went back inside. When she woke the next morning the trucks had gone.

She wondered about them; whose were they? Had they not looked a bit old-fashioned? She wasn't good on makes of cars, but there was something about their lines that suggested her childhood. "Colette," she said, "when you're at Sainsbury's, you wouldn't pick up a car magazine? One of those with lots and lots of pictures of every car anyone might want?" She thought, at least I could exclude all modern makes.

Colette said, "Are you winding me up?"

"What?" she said.

"Gavin!"

"There you are! I told you that you're always talking about him."

Later, she was sorry for upsetting Colette. I meant no harm, she said to herself, I just didn't think. As for the trucks, they were spirit vehicles, probably, but whose? Sometimes she rose in the night to look down from the landing porthole over Admiral Drive. Around the children's playground, warning lamps shone from deep holes in the ground. Great pipes, like troglodyte dwellings, lay gaping at the landscape; the moon's single eye stared down at them.

Colette would find her, standing by the porthole, tense and cold. She would find her and draw her back to bed; her touch was like a spirit touch, her face hollow, her feet noiseless. By day or night, Colette's aura remained patchy, wispy. When she was out and Alison found traces of her about the house—a discarded shoe, a bangle, one of her elastic hairbands—she thought, who ever is she, and how did she get here? Did I invite her? If so, why did I do that? She thought about Gloria and Mrs. McGibbet. She wondered if Colette might disappear one day, just as suddenly as they did, fading into nothingness and leaving behind only snatches of conversation, a faint heat trace on the air.

They had been given a breathing space. Time to reconsider. To pause. To reevaluate. They could see middle age ahead of them. Forty is the new thirty, Colette said. Fifty is the new forty. Senescence is the new juvenility, Alzheimer's is the new acne. Sometimes they would sit over a bottle of wine and talk about their future. But it was difficult for them to plan in the way other people did. Colette felt that maybe Al was withholding information, information about the future that she could very well part with. Her questions about this life and the next were by no means resolved in a way that satisfied her; and she was always thinking of new ones. But what can you do? You have to make an accommodation. You have to accept certain givens. You can't waste time every day worrying about the theory of your life, you have to get on with the practice. Maybe I'll get into Kaballah, Al said. That seems to be the thing now. Colette said, maybe I'll get into gardening. We could have some shrubs, now Morris isn't here to hide behind them. Michelle and Evan keep hinting we should do something at the back. Get some flags laid, at least.

"They keep talking to me about the weather," Al said. "I don't know why."

"Just being English, I suppose," Colette said innocently. She sat brooding over the Yellow Pages. "I might ring up a gardening service. But not the one that sent that idiot last time, the one who couldn't start the mower."

"Do the next-doors still think we're lesbians?"

"I expect so." Colette added, "I hope it spoils their enjoyment of their property."

She rang up the gardening service. A few flagstones, so less grass to mow, she thought. Her imagination didn't stretch beyond an alleviation of her weekly routine. She made sure it didn't. If she allowed herself to think about her life as a whole she felt an emptiness, an insufficiency: as if her plate had been taken away before she'd finished eating.

Meanwhile Evan leaned on the fence, watching her mow. She wondered if he was wearing an expression of lechery, but when she turned, it was actually an expression of sympathy. "I sometimes think, Astroturf," he said. "Don't you? They're bringing in an auto-mower, one you preprogramme. But I suppose it'll be a while before they hit the shops."

His own plot was scuffed up and worn bald by the skirmishing of his two older brats. Colette was amazed at the speed with which they had grown. She remembered Michelle jiggling them on a hip; now they were out at all hours, scavenging and savaging, leaving scorched earth behind them, like child soldiers in an African war. Inside the house, Michelle was training up another one; when they had the French windows open, you could hear its stifled wails and roars.

"What you need there is a shed," Evan said. "Stop you needing to get your mower out of the garage and walk it round the side."

"I'm going to hire a man," Colette said. "It didn't work out before, but I'm trying somebody different. Going to do some planting."

"There it is," Evan said. "You need a man for some things, you see."

Colette banged into the house. "Evan says we need a man."

"Oh, surely not," Alison said. "Or not any man we know."

"He also says we need a shed."

Alison looked surprised, a little hesitant. She frowned. "A shed? I suppose that'll be all right," she said.

On Sunday they went down the A322 to a shed supplier. Alison wandered around looking at the different kinds. There were some like Regency arbours, and some like miniaturized Tudor houses, and some with cupolas and arabesque cornices. There was one that reminded her of a Shinto shrine; Cara would probably go for that, she thought. Mandy would want the one with the onion dome. She liked the Swiss chalets, with little porches. She imagined hanging gingham curtains. I could go in there, she thought, shrunk (in thought form) to a small size. I could have a doll's tea set and little cakes with pastel fondant icing and candied fruit on top.

Colette said, "We were hoping, my friend and I, to buy a shed."

"Nowadays," the man advised, "we call them garden buildings."

"Okay, a garden building," Al said. "Yes, that would be nice."

"We only need something basic," Colette said. "What sort of price are we looking at?"

"Oh," said the man, "before we discuss price, let's study your needs."

Alison pointed to a sort of cricket pavilion. "What if our need were that one?"

"Yes, the Grace Road," the man said. "An excellent choice where space is no object." He thumbed his lists. "Let me tell you what that comes at."

Colette peered over his shoulder. "Good God!" Colette said. "Don't be silly, Al. We don't want that."

The man ushered them to a revolving summerhouse. "This is nice," he said, "for a lady. You can envisage yourself, as the day closes, sitting with your face turned to the west, a cooling drink in hand."

"Give over!" Colette said. "All we want is a place to keep the mower."

"But what about your other essential equipment? What about your barbecue? And what about your winter storage? Tables, waterproof covers for tables, parasols, waterproof covers for parasols—"

"Garage," said Colette.

"I see," the man said. "So forcing you to park your car in the open, exposing it to the elements and the risk of theft?"

"We've got Neighbourhood Watch."

"Yes," Alison said. "We all watch each other, and report each other's movements." She thought of the spirit trucks, and the mound beneath the blanket: she imagined the nature of it.

"Neighbourhood Watch? I wish you joy of it! In my opinion, householders should be armed. We in the Bisley area are run ragged by opportunistic thieves and every type of intruder. Police Constable Delingbole gave us a lecture on home security."

"Can we get on?" Colette said. "I've set aside this afternoon for buying a shed, and I want to get it sorted. We still have to do our food shopping."

Alison saw her dreams of dolls' teatime fading. Come to think of it, had she ever had a doll? She followed the salesman towards a small log cabin.

"We call this one 'Old Smokey,'" he said. "It takes its inspiration, the designers claim, from railway buildings in the golden days of the Old West."

"I'll say this for you. You don't give up easily." Colette turned her back and stalked away in the direction of the honest working sheds.

Just as Alison was about to follow her, she thought she saw something move inside Old Smokey. For a second she saw a face, looking out at her. Bugger, she thought, a haunted shed. But it was nobody she knew. She trailed after Colette, thinking, we're not going to get anything nice, we're just going to get one of these tidgy sheds that anybody could have. What if I were to lie down on the ground and say, it's my money, I want one of those cream-painted Shaker-style ones with a porch?

She caught up with them. Colette must be in an exceptionally nice mood today, because she hadn't struck the salesman. "Pent or Apex?" he demanded.

Colette said, "It's no good trying to blind me with science. The pent are the ones with a sloping roof, and the apex are the ones with pointy roofs. That's obvious."

"I can do you a Sissinghurst. Wooden garden workshop, twelve-by-ten, double door, and eight fixed-glass windows, delivery date normally one month but we could be flexible on that: 699.99 pounds, on-the-road price."

"You've got a nerve," Colette said.

Alison said, "Did you see somebody, Colette? Inside Old Smokey?"

The salesman said, "That will be a customer, madam."

"He didn't look like a customer."

"Nor do I," Colette said. "That's obvious. Are you going to sell me something, or shall I drive up to Nottcutts on the A30?"

Al pitied the man; like her, he had his job to do, and part of his job was to stimulate the customer's imagination. "Don't worry," she said, "we'll have one from you. Honest. If you can just point us to the kind my friend wants."

"I've lost my bearings here," the man said. "I confess to a certain amount of total bafflement. Which of you ladies is the purchaser?"

"Oh, let's not go through that again." Colette groaned. "Al, you take over." She walked away, giggling, between the ornamental wheelbarrow planters, the cast-iron conservatory frogs and the roughcast Buddhas. Her thin shoulders twitched.

"Will you sell one to me?" Al asked. She smiled her sweetest smile. "What about that one?"

"What, the Balmoral?" The man sneered. "Eight-by-ten pent with single-pitch roof? Well, that seems like a decision made, at last. Thank you, madam, it seems we've found something to suit you. The only problem is, as I could have told you if you'd let me get a word in edgewise, it's the end of the range."

"That's okay," Al said. "I'm not bothered about whether it's in fashion."

"No," the man said, "what I'm saying to you is this, it would be futile, at this stage in the season, for me to ask the manufacturer to supply."

"But what about this one? The one standing here?" Al tapped its walls. "You could send it right away, couldn't you?"

The man turned away. He needed to struggle with his temper. His grand-dad had come through in spirit and was sitting on the Balmoral's roof—its pent—ruminatively working his way through a bag of sweets. When the man spoke, granddad flapped his tongue out, with a melting humbug on the end of it.

"Excuse me madam—"

"Go ahead."

"—are you asking me and my colleagues to dismantle that garden building and supervise its immediate transport, for a price of some four hundred pounds plus VAT plus our normal service charge? While the World Cup's on?"

"Well, what else are you going to do with it?" Colette came up to rejoin them, her hands thrust deep in the pockets of her jeans. "You planning to leave it there till it falls down by itself?" Her foot scuffed the ground, kicked out casually at a concrete otter with its concrete pup. "If you don't sell it now, mate, you never will. So come on, look sharp. Whistle up your crew, and let's get on with the job."

"What about your hardstanding?" the man said. "I don't suppose you've given a thought to your hardstanding. Have you?"

As they walked back to the car, Colette said, "You know, I really think, when men talk, it's worse than when they don't."

Alison looked at her narrowly, sideways. She waited for more.

"Gavin never said much. He'd say nothing for such a long time that you wanted to lean over and poke your finger in him to see if he was dead. I used to say, tell me your thoughts, Gavin. You must have thoughts. You remember when we met him, in Farnham?"

Alison nodded. She had smelled, trailing after Gavin, the reek of a past life: an old tweed collar rancid with hair oil. His aura was oatmeal, grey, it was as tough as old rope.

"Well," Colette said. She flicked her remote to open the car doors. "I wonder what he was doing in Farnham."

"Having a run out?"

"He could shop in Twickenham."

"Change of scene?"

"Or Richmond." Colette chewed her pale lip. "I wonder what he wanted in Elphicks? Because when you think, he gets all he needs at car shops."

"Perhaps he wanted a new shirt."

"He has a wardrobe full of shirts. He has fifty shirts. He must have. I used to pay a woman to iron them. Why did *I* pay? He seemed to think, if I didn't want to do it myself, I ought to pay. When I look back now, I can't for one minute imagine what was going through my head when I agreed to that."

"Still," Al said. She eased herself into her seat. "Some years have passed. Since you were together. They might be—I don't know—frayed? His neck might have grown."

"Oh yes," Colette said. "He looks porky, all right. But he never did up his top button. So. Anyway. Plenty shirts."

"But a new tie? Socks, underpants?" She felt shy; she'd never lived with a man.

"Knickers?" Colette said. "Car shops every time. Halfords. Velour for the proles, but leather for Gavin, top spec. They stock them in six-packs, shouldn't wonder. Or else he buys them mail order from a rescue service."

"A rescue service?"

"You know. Automobile Association. Royal Automobile Club. National Breakdown."

"I know. But I didn't think Gavin would need rescuing."

"Oh, he just likes to have a badge and a personal number."

"Have I got a personal number?"

"You are in all the major motoring organizations, Alison."

"Belts-and-braces approach?"

"If you like." Colette swung them out of the shed sellers' compound, carelessly scattering a party of parents and children who were clustering about the hot-dog stand. "That's done their arteries a favour," Colette said. "Yes, you have several, but you don't need to know them."

"Perhaps I do," Al said. "In case anything happened to you."

"Why?" Colette was alarmed. "Are you seeing something?"

"No, no, nothing like that. Colette, don't drive us off the road!"

Colette corrected their course. Their hearts were beating fast. The lucky opals had paled on Alison's fists. You see, she thought. That's how accidents happen. There was a silence.

"I don't really like secrets," Alison said.

"Bloody hell!" Colette said. "It's only a few digits." She relented. "I'll show you where I keep them. On the computer. Which file." Her heart sank. Why had she said that? She'd just bought an elegant little laptop, silver and pleasingly feminine. She could perch it on her knees and work in bed. But when Al loomed up with a cup of coffee for her, the keyboard started chattering and scrambled itself.

"So what about when you lived with Gavin, did he tell you his personal number?"

Colette tilted up her chin. "He kept it secret. He kept it where I couldn't access it."

"That seems a bit unnecessary," Alison said, thinking, now you know how it feels, my girl.

"He wouldn't put me on joint membership. I think he was ashamed, to phone them up and mention my car. It was all I could afford, at the time. I used to say, what's your problem, Gavin? It gets me from A to B."

Alison thought, if I were a great enthusiast for motoring, and somebody said "It gets me from A to B," I think I would sneak up on them and smash their skull in with a spanner—or whatever's good to smash skulls in, that you keep in the back of a car.

"We'd have rows." Colette said. "He thought I should have a better car. Something flash. He thought I should run up debt."

Debt and dishonour, Al thought. Oh dear. Oh dear and damnation. If somebody said to me, "What's your problem?" in that tone of voice, I would probably wait till they were snoring and drive a hot needle through their tongue.

"And as it worked out, I was putting so much into the household—his ironing and so on—I went through a whole winter without cover. Anything could have happened. I could have broken down in the middle of nowhere—"

"On a lonely road at night."

"Exactly."

"On a lonely motorway."

"Yes! You stop on the hard shoulder, if you get out—Jesus," Colette slapped the wheel, "they just drive into you."

"Or suppose a man stopped to help you. Could you trust him?"

"A stranger?"

"He would be. On a lonely road at night. He wouldn't be anyone you knew."

"You're advised to stay put and lock your doors. Don't even put your window down."

"By the rescue services? Is that what they say?"

"It's what the police say! Alison, you drove yourself around, didn't you? Before me? You must know."

She said, "I try to imagine."

For think of the perils. Men who wait for you to break down just so they can come and kill you. Men hovering, monitoring the junctions. How would you know a sick car, to follow it? Presumably, smoke would come out of it. She herself, in her driving days, had never thought of such disasters; she sang as she drove, and her engine sang in tune. At the least whine, stutter, or hiccough, she sent it her love and prayers, then stuffed it in the garage. She supposed they were fleecing her, at the garage; but that's the way it goes.

She thought, when me and Colette bought the car, soon after we got together, it was quite easy, a good afternoon out, but now we can't even buy a Balmoral without Colette nearly driving us off the road, and me thinking of ways to stove her skull in. It shows how our relationship's come on.

Colette careered them to a halt in the Collingwood's drive, and the handbrake groaned as she hauled at it. "Bugger," she said. "We should have food-shopped."

"Never mind."

"You see, Gavin, he didn't care if I was raped, or anything."

"You could have been drugged with date-rape drugs, and taken away by a man who made you live in a shed. Sorry. Garden building."

"Don't laugh at me, Al."

"Look, the man back there asked us a question. Have we given a thought to our hardstanding?"

"Yes! Yes! Of course! I got a man out of the local paper. But I got three quotes!"

"That's okay then. Let's go in. Come on, Colette. It's okay, sweetheart. We can have a cheese omelette. I'll make it. We can go back. We can shop later. For God's sake, they're open till ten."

Colette walked into the house, and her eyes roamed everywhere. "We'll have to replace that stair carpet," she said, "in under a year."

"You think so?"

"The pile's completely flattened."

"I could avoid wearing it, if I jumped down the last three steps."

"No, you might put your back out. But it seems a shame. Only been here two minutes."

"Three years. Four."

"Still. All those marks rubbed along the walls. Do you know you leave a mark? Wherever your shoulders touch it, and your big hips. You smear everything, Al. Even if you're eating an orange, you slime it all down the wall. It's a disgrace. I'm ashamed to live here."

"At the mercy of shed merchants," Al said. "Ah dear, ah dear, ah dear."

At first she didn't recognize who was speaking, and then she realized it was Mrs. McGibbet. She urged Colette towards the kitchen by slow degrees and consoled her with a microwaved sponge pudding, with hot jam and double cream. "You seriously think I'm going to eat this?" Colette asked; then gulped it down like a hungry dog.

They went to bed all tucked up safe that night. But she dreamed of snapping jaws, and temporary wooden structures. Of Blighto, Harry and Serene.

nine

It was about 2 A.M.; Colette woke in darkness, to the screeching of garden birds. She lay suffering under her duvet, till birdsong was replaced by the long swish of waves against a shingle beach. Then came some twitters, scrapes, and squeaks. What's it called? Oh yes, rain forest. She thought, what is rain forest anyway? We never had it when I was at school.

She sat up, grabbed her pillow, and beat it. Beyond the wall the croaking and chirping continued, the twittering of strange night fowl, the rustling of the undergrowth. She lay back again, stared at the ceiling: where the ceiling would be. The jungle, she thought, that's what we had; but they don't call it the jungle now. A green snake looped down from a branch and smiled into her face. It unravelled itself, falling, falling . . . she slept again. A need to urinate woke her. Al's sodding relaxation tapes had reached the waterfall track.

She stood up, dazed, passing her hand over her hair to flatten it. Now she could see the outlines of the furniture; the light behind the curtains was brilliant. She crept into her en-suite and relieved herself. On her way back to bed she pulled aside the curtain. A full moon silvered the Balmoral, and frosted its pent.

There was a man on the lawn. He was walking around it in circles, as if under an enchantment. She pulled back, dropped the curtain. She had seen him before, perhaps in a dream.

She lay down again. The waterfall track was finished, and had given way to the music of dolphins and whales. In the cradle of the deep she swayed, slept, and slept more deeply still.

It was 5 A.M. when Al came down. Her guts were churning; this happened. She could eat quite an ordinary meal, but her insides would say no-no, not for you. She raised the kitchen blind, and while her bicarb fizzed in a glass at her elbow she looked out over the larch-lap fences swathed in pearly light. Something moved, a shadow against the lawn. In the distance, a milk truck hummed, and nearer at hand an early businessman slammed with a metallic clatter his garage's Georgian door.

Alison unlocked the kitchen door and stepped out. The morning was fresh and damp. From across the estate a car alarm whooped and yodelled. The man on the lawn was young, and had a dark stubble and a blueish pallor. He wore a woolly hat pulled down over his brow. His big sneakers bruised his footprints into the dew. He saw Alison, but hardly checked his stride, simply raising two fingers to his forehead in acknowledgement.

What's your name? she asked him silently.

There was no reply.

It's all right, you can tell Al, don't be shy. The creature smiled shyly and continued to circle.

She thought, you can go under a false name if you like. Just as long as I have something to call you by, to make our life together possible. Look at him, she thought, look at him! Why can't I get a spirit guide with some dress sense?

Yet there was something humble in his manner, that she liked. She stood shivering, waiting for him to communicate. A train rattled away in the distance, up from Hampshire, London bound. She noticed how it gently shook the morning; the light broke up around her, flaking into creamy fragments edged with gold, then settling again. The sun was creeping around the edge of a Rodney. She blinked, and the lawn was empty.

•   •   •

Colette, pouring her orange juice at eight-thirty, said, "Al, you cannot have two pieces of toast." Colette was making her diet; it was her new hobby.

"One?"

"Yes, one. With a scrape—no more than a scrape, mind—of low-fat spread."

"And a scrape of jam?"

"No. Jam will play havoc with your metabolism." She sipped her orange juice. "I dreamed there was a man on the lawn."

"Did you?" Alison frowned, holding the lid of the bread bin before her like a shield. "On the lawn? Last night? What was he like?"

"Dunno," Colette said. "I almost came and woke you."

"In your dream?"

"Yes. No. I think I was dreaming that I was awake."

"That's common," Al said. "Those sorts of dreams, people who are Sensitives have them all the time."

She thought, I dreamed there were trucks outside the house, and a blanket in the back of one, and under that blanket—what? In my dream I came inside and lay down again, and dreamed again, within my dream; I dreamed of an animal, tight and trembling inside its skin, quivering with lust as it wolfed human meat from a bowl.

She said, "I wonder if you're becoming a Sensitive, Colette." She didn't say it aloud.

Colette said, "When I agreed to one slice of bread, I meant one normal-sized one, not one slice two inches thick."

"Ah. Then you should have said."

"Be reasonable." Colette crossed the kitchen and barged into her. "I'll show you what you can have. Give me that bread knife."

Al's fingers yielded it, unwillingly. She and the bread knife were friends.

It was gardening day. The new contractors had brought plans and costed out the decking. They were going to build a water feature; it would be more like a small fountain than a pond. By the time Colette had beaten down their estimate by a few hundred pounds, she had forgotten all about her disturbed night, and her mood, like the day, was sunny.

As the men were leaving, Michelle beckoned her to the fence. "Glad to see you're doing something with it, at last. It was a bit of an eyesore, lying all bare like that. By the way—I don't know if I should mention—when Evan got up this morning he saw a man in your garden. Evan thought he was trying the shed door."

"Oh. Anyone we know?"

"Evan had never seen him before. He rang your doorbell."

"Who, the man?"

"No, Evan. You must have been in the land of dreams, both of you. Evan said, they're not hearing me. He said, all right for some."

"The advantages," Colette said, "of the child-free lifestyle."

"Evan said, they've got no lock on their side gate. And them two women alone."

"I'll get a lock," Colette snapped. "And seeing as the blessed gate is all of five feet high, and anybody but a midget could vault over it, I'll get some barbed wire on top, shall I?"

"Now that would be unsightly," Michelle said. "No, what you should do, come to our next meeting with community policing and get some advice. This is a big time of year for shed crime. Police Constable Delingbole gave us a talk on it."

"I'm sorry I missed that," Colette said. "Anyway, the shed's empty. All the stuff's still locked in the garage, waiting for me to move it. By the way, has Evan found any of those white worms?"

"What?" Michelle said. "White worms? Yuk. Are they in your garden?"

"No, they're in Reading," Colette said. "At the last sighting. A man was digging in his garden and there they were on the end of his spade, huge writhing clusters of them. Did Constable Wossname not mention it?"

Michelle shook her head. She looked as if she might throw up.

"I can't think why he didn't. It's been in all the papers. The poor man's had to board his property up. Now he's asking for an investigation. Thing with worms is, they travel underground, they'll be heading out in search of a food source, and of course being radioactive they won't hang about, they'll be scorching along like buggery. Excuse my language, but being the police he ought to have warned you really."

"Oh God," Michelle said. "Evan didn't mention it either. Didn't want to scare me, I suppose. What can we do? Shall I ring the council?"

"You ask for pest control, I think. And then they come out with very fine mesh nets, and fence all around your garden with them."

"Are you having them?"

"Oh yes. Same time as we get the decking, to save digging up twice near the house."

"Do you have to pay?"

" 'Fraid so. But it's worth it, wouldn't you say?"

She went back into the house and said, "Al, I've told Michelle that gross poisoned worms are going to come and eat her kiddiwinks."

Al looked up, frowning, from her tarot spread. "Why did you do that?"

"Just to see her shit herself." Then she remembered. "By the way, that dream I had, it wasn't a dream. When Evan got up this morning he saw some bloke messing around near the shed."

Alison laid the cards down. Her situation, she saw, needed a rethink. I'll have that rethink, she decided, when Colette goes out.

In the kitchen, out of Colette's earshot, the breakfast dishes were chinking together; a little spirit woman was pushing them around on the worktop, wanting to help, wanting to wash up for them but not knowing how. "Excuse me, excuse me," she was saying, "have you seen Maureen Harrison?"

Honestly, Al thought. A spirit guide is wasted on Colette. I ought to take time out and lay hold of Maureen Harrison and send her zinging to the next stage, out of Colette's way, and then grab her poor little friend and catapult her after. It would be doing them a favour, in the long run. But she imagined their frail flesh shrinking inside the baggy sleeves of their cardigans (where their cardigans would be) as her strong psychic grip fell on their arms; she imagined the old pair weeping and struggling, snapping their feeble bones under her hand. Muscular tactics were seldom any use, she had found, when you needed to send a spirit over. You call it firm action and you think it's for their own good, but they don't think so. Especially not the older generation. She knows psychics who will call in a clergyman at the least excuse. But that's like sending the bailiffs in; it shames them. It's like dosing them with a laxative when they can't get to their commode.

The telephone rang. Al lifted the receiver and said loudly, "Hello, and how's Natasha this fine morning? And the Tsars? Good, good." She dropped her voice confidingly. "Hi, Mandy, how are you, love?"

She smirked to herself. Who needs caller display? Colette, that's who. She saw Colette scowl at her: as if she were taking some mean advantage.

When Colette left the room she said to Mandy, "Guess what? I thought Colette had seen a spirit."

"And had she?"

"It seems not. It looks like it was a burglar."

"Oh dear, anything taken?"

"No, he didn't get in. Just walked about outside."

"Why did she think he was a spirit?"

"It was last night. She thought she was dreaming. It was me who thought it was a spirit. When she said, I saw a man outside by moonlight, I thought I'd got a new guide."

"No sign of Morris coming back?"

"None, thankfully."

"I'll drink to that."

Only I have nightmares, Al wanted to say; but who doesn't, in our trade?

"So did you ring the police?" Mandy said. "Because it's awful down here on the coast. Your teeth aren't safe in your head."

"No, I didn't bother. There's nothing to tell them. I think I saw him myself. He didn't look harmful. If it was the same man. Unless there are different men wandering around our garden. Which is possible, of course."

"Don't take any chances," Mandy said. "Anyway, Al, I won't take up your morning, let's cut to the chase. There's a new psychic supplier opened down in Cornwall, and they've got a very keen price list with some special introductory offers. Also, for a limited period they're doing free postage and packaging. Cara put me on to them. She's got some excellent runes and she says they're going down very well with her regulars. You want a change, don't you, from time to time? A change is as good as a rest."

Alison scribbled down the details. "Okay," she said, "I'll pass it on to Colette. You're a good mate, Mand. I wish I saw more of you."

"Drive down," Mandy said. "We'll have a girl's night out."

"I couldn't. I don't drive anymore."

"How hard can it be? Cut across to Dorking, then straight down the A24."

"I've lost confidence. Behind the wheel."

"Let me know what time you're leaving, and I'll chant for you."

"I couldn't. I couldn't stay out overnight. I couldn't leave Colette."

"Christsake! Get in the car and do it, Al! She doesn't own you."

"She says what toast I can have."

"What?"

"How thick a slice. I can't have butter. Not any. It's awful."

"God, she's such a bossy little madam!"

"But she's very efficient. She's great with the VAT. I couldn't do it, you see. So I have to put up with her."

"Have you heard of accountants?" Mandy said scathingly. "What do you think an accountant is for? Toss your bloody receipts in a brown envelope and stuff them in the post box at the end of the quarter. That's what I do."

"She'd be hurt," Al said. "She's got so little in her life, really. She has this ex with a nasty aura, I only got a glimpse of it but it churns your stomach. She needs me, you see. She needs some love."

"She needs a slap!" Mandy said. "And if I hear any more of this toast business, I'll whiz up there to Woking and give it her myself."

Over the course of the day, it became clear to Al's sharp eye that they had a guest in the shed. Something or someone was lurking; presumably it was the young lad in the hat. Perhaps, she thought, I should take something to defend myself, in case he turns nasty. Hesitating in the kitchen, she had at last picked up the bacon scissors. The blades fitted snugly into her palm, and the bright orange handles looked playfully robust, in a rough-and-tumble sort of way; it was much the sort of weapon you'd choose to break up a fight in a primary school playground. If anybody sees me, she thought, they'll just assume that I'm about some tricky little garden operation; that I'm notching a stem, nipping a bud, cutting a bloom, except there isn't one to cut, we're not up to flowers yet.

When she opened the shed door, she braced herself for the young man to rush at her, try to push past. It could be the best thing, she thought, if he did. I ought to step back and let him go, if it comes to that. Except that if someone's been in my outbuilding I'd like to know why.

The shed was in gloom, its small window spattered, as if it had been raining mud. In the corner was a mournful bundle that barely stirred, let alone made a dash for it. The boy was drawn into a foetal position, arms around his knees; his eyes travelled upwards, and stuck when they reached her right hand.

"I'm not going to hurt you," she said. She peered down at him, perplexed. "Shall I make you a cup of tea?"

He had been living rough at the garden centre, the young man said. "I saw you with your friend, blond-haired lady, innit? You were looking at the Grace Road."

"That's right," Al said.

"Thanks for this tea, by the way, this is good tea. Then after that you looked at Old Smokey, but you gave it the thumbs-down. You gave it the old heave-ho."

As Al leaned back against the wall of the new shed, it shivered slightly, swayed. Not the most solid structure, she thought. "That's where you were," she said, "when I spotted you. You were hanging about inside Old Smokey."

"I thought you saw me." His head drooped. "You didn't say hello."

"I didn't know you, how could I?" She didn't say, I thought you were in spectral form.

"Any more of this tea?"

"Wait a minute."

Alison took the mug from him. She inched open the door of the Balmoral, and peeped out to make sure there was no one in the neighbouring gardens, before she made a dash for the house. She couldn't rule out, of course, being seen by spectators from an upper window. She thought, I've a perfect right to walk across my own lawn, from my own shed, with a china mug in my hand. But she found herself scuttling, head down.

She scurried into the kitchen and slammed the back door after her. She ran to the kettle and slammed down the switch. She rummaged in a cupboard. Better make him a flask, she thought. Can't be running across the lawn, bent double, every time he wants a hot drink.

The flask was at the back of the cupboard, bottom shelf, skidding shyly from her fingertips into the corner. She had to bend deeply to fish it out. The blood rushed to her head and thumped at the back of her nose. As she straightened up, her head swam. She thought, he's my visitor. I can have a visitor, if I want, I suppose?

His mug was on the draining board, marked with grimy fingerprints. He can make do with the top of the flask for his cup, she thought. I'll take him some kitchen roll to wipe it round with. She tore some paper off, waiting impatiently for the kettle. Sugar, she thought, diving into a cupboard. I expect he'll want lots of sugar, tramps always do.

When she got back, Mart—that was his name, he said—was crouching in the corner away from the light. "I thought somebody might look through that window," he said, "while you was away."

"I've been as quick as I could. Here."

He shook as he held the flask top. She put her hand round his to steady it as she poured. "You not having one?" he said.

"I'll have mine inside later." She said gently, "You'd better not come inside. My friend wouldn't like it."

"I used to live in the Far Pavilions," he said. "I lived there nice for two nights. Then they chased me out. They thought I was off the premises but I looped back and broke into Old Smokey. I was just hanging about wondering what I should do next, then I saw you. And later I saw your shed go. So I followed it."

"Where did you live before that?"

"Dunno. One time I slept on me mate's floor. But his floor got took up. They came from the council. The rat officer."

"That was unlucky. People say—Evan, the man next door, he says—that you're never more than three feet from a rat in Britain today. Or is it two feet?" She frowned. "So when the floor was taken up, was that when you went to the garden centre?"

"No, next I went in the park under the bandstand. With Pinto. My mate. Whose floor got took up. We used to go down Sheerwater, they had a drop-in centre. One day we get there and they've put steel shutters up. They said, it's just a policy, don't take it to heart."

Mart wore a khaki jacket with lots of pockets, and beneath it a sweatshirt that was once a colour, and stained cotton pants with some rips in them. I've seen worse things, Alison thought, in the silence of the night.

"Look," she said, "don't misunderstand me, I have no right to ask you questions, but if you're going to be in my garden for much more of today I would like to know if you're violent, or on drugs."

Mart lurched sideways. Though he was young, his joints creaked and snapped. Al saw that he had been sitting on a rucksack. It was a flat one, with very little in it. Perhaps he was trying to hatch something, she thought; some possessions. She felt a rush of pity; her face flushed. It's not an easy life in a shed.

"You feeling all right?" Mart asked her. Out of his rucksack he took a collection of pill bottles and passed them to her one by one.

"Oh, but these drugs are from the chemist," she said. "So that's all right." She peered at the label. "My mum used to have these. And these, too, I think." She unscrewed the cap and put a finger in, swizzling the capsules around. "I recognize the colour. I don't think she liked those ones."

"Those are nice rings you've got," he said.

"They're my lucky opals."

"That's where I went wrong," Mart said. "No luck."

As she passed him the bottles back, she noticed that the surface of the stones had turned a sulky, resistant blue. Stuff you, she thought, I'm not going to be told what to do by a bunch of opals. Mart stowed the bottles carefully in his rucksack.

"So," she said, "have you been in hospital recently?"

"You know, here and there," Mart said. "On and off. As and when. I was going to be in a policy, but then they never."

"What policy was that?"

Mart struggled. "A policy, it's like . . . it's either like, shutting down, or it's like, admissions, or it's . . . removals. You go to another place. But not with a removal van. Because you haven't anything to put in one."

"So when you—when they—when they get a new policy, you get moved to somewhere else?"

"More or less," Mart said. "But they didn't get one, or I wasn't in for it. I don't know if they put me down for it under another name, but I didn't get moved, so I just went, after a bit I just went."

"And this drop-in centre, is it still closed?"

"Dunno," Mart said. "I couldn't go to Sheerwater on the off-chance, with shoes like mine."

•

She looked at his feet and thought, I see what you mean. She said, "I could drive you. That would save you wearing your shoes out any more. But my friend's gone out in our car. So if you could just hide here till she comes back?"

"I dunno," Mart said. "Could I have a sandwich?"

"Yes," she said. She added bitterly, "There's plenty of bread."

Back in the kitchen, she thought, I see it all. Mother scooped into hospital at the last minute, the foetal heart monitor banging away like the bells of hell. Mama unregistered, unweighed, unloved, innocent of antenatal care, and turning up at the hospital because she believes—God love her—that her cramping needs relief: then sweat-streaked, panicked and amazed, she is crying out so hard for a glass of water that by the time they give it her, she prefers a glass of water to her newborn child. She would have sold him, new as he was, in his skin. She would have sold him to the midwives for an early relief from her thirst.

What can I give him? Alison wondered. What would he enjoy? Poor little bugger. You see somebody like that and say, well, his mother must have loved him; but in his case, no. She took out a cold chicken from the fridge and turned it out from its jellied, splintering foil. It was half used, half stripped. She washed her hands, opened a drawer, picked out a sharp little knife and worked away, shearing fragments from the carcass. Close to the bone, the meat was tender. So was the child Mart himself, picked out of the womb; as he was carried away, his legs kicked, the blood on his torso staled and dried.

And then the foster mother. Who stuck for a year or two. Till a policy moved him on to the next. I wish I'd had a foster mother, Al thought. If I'd just been given a break till I was two or three, I might have turned out normal, instead of my brain all cross-wired so I'm forced to know the biographies of strangers. And pity them.

By the time she'd thought all this, she was grilling bacon. As she whipped the rashers over with the tongs, she thought, why am I doing this? God knows. I feel sorry for the bloke. Homeless and down on his luck.

She made towering, toasted sandwiches, oiled with mayonnaise, garnished with cucumber, cherry tomatoes and hardboiled eggs. She made twice as many as one homeless mad person could possibly consume. She made what she anticipated would be the very best plate of sandwiches Mart had ever seen in his life.

He ate them without comment, except for saying, "Not very good bacon, this. You ought to get that kind that is made by the Prince of Wales."

Sometimes he said, "Aren't you having one?" but she knew he hoped she wasn't, and she said, "I'll have mine later." She glanced at her watch. "Is that the time? I've got a telephone client."

"I used to have a watch," Mart said. "But Police Constable Delingbole stamped on it." He looked up at her from the corner and begged, "Don't be long."

Lucky that Colette had gone to Guildford! Al could count on her to be away for some hours. In that time she could give the boy some advice and twenty quid, and set him on his way. Colette had things to do—pop into the occult shop on White Lion Walk with some flyers, etc.—but mainly she would be going shopping, trawling around the House of Fraser for that elusive perfect lip shade, and getting her hair cut into a white pudding-bowl shape. Colette's hair never seemed to grow, not so that you noticed, yet she felt some sort of social obligation to have it trimmed and tweaked every six weeks. When she came home she would stand before the mirror and rage at the stylist, but it never looked any different—not that Alison could see.

Her telephone consultation ran the full hour, and after it Al was so hungry that she had to grab a bowl of cornflakes, standing up in the kitchen. A feeling, something like fellow-feeling, was hauling her back in the direction of Mart; she hated to think of him shrinking from the light, crouching on the hard floor.

"First I was a white-liner," Mart said. "That's where you paint lines on the road, excellent daily rate and no previous experience required. A truck picked us up every morning at the bandstand and took us to where we were lining that day. You see, Pinto was with me. He got bored of it. I didn't get bored of it, I liked it. But Pinto, he started painting little islands in the road, then he said, go on, go on, let's do a box junction. It took us an hour. But when they saw it, they weren't all that keen. They said, you're off the job, mate, and the ganger said, come here while I give you a smack with this shovel." Mart rubbed his head, his eyes distant. "But then they said, we'll give you another chance, you can go on roadworks. We got put on human traffic light. Twirling a sign: STOP–GO. But the motorists wouldn't observe me. Stop-and-go when they fucking well liked. So the boss says, lads, you're not in sync. He says that's your big problem that you've got. You're twirling, but you're not twirling in sync. So I got took off that job."

"And then?"

Al had been to the garage to fetch them two folding garden chairs. She didn't feel she could keep standing, with her back to the shed wall and Mart crouching at her feet. It was natural for Mart to want to tell her his life story, his career history, just to reassure her that he wasn't an axe murderer; not that anything he had told her had actually reassured her of that, but she thought, I would have a feeling, my skin would prickle and I'd know.

"So then . . ." Mart said. He frowned.

"Don't worry," Al said. "You don't have to tell me if you don't want."

All Mart's jobs seemed to have involved hanging about in public places. For a while he was a car park attendant, but they said he didn't attend it enough. He was a park patroller, selling tickets for the attractions. "But some little lads knocked me down and robbed my tickets and threw them in the pond."

"Didn't the hospital give you any help? When you got out?"

"You see, I came through the net," Mart said. "I'm an outloop. I'm on a list, but I'm not computerate yet. I think—the list I was on—I think they lost it."

More than likely, Al thought. I dare say, when I was a kid, people put me on a list. I expect they made a list of bruises, that sort of thing, noticeable marks. But it never came to anything. I guess that list got put in a file; I guess that file got left in a drawer; "I'd like to know," she said, "how you got in trouble with the police."

Mart said, "I was at the zone. I was near the scene. I had to be somewhere. Somebody had to be there. Police Constable Delingbole beat the shit out of me."

"Mart, ought you to be taking your pills? What time do you have them?"

"You see, we got some stickers and we put them on people's cars, that were parked. We waited till we saw them leave and then we came with the stickers and put NO PARKING BY ORDER on their windscreen. Then we hid in the bushes. When they came back we jumped out and fined them a fine."

"Did they pay?"

"No way. One geezer got on his mobile. Delingbole was round like a shot."

"And where were you?"

"Back in the bushes. He didn't catch us that day. It was a good idea, but it caused a description of us to be made and put in the local paper. *Have you seen this distinctively attired man?*"

"But you're not. I wouldn't call you distinctive."

"You didn't see the hat I had in those days."

"No. That's true."

"By the time I came round your place, I'd got a different hat. I was down on the building site, sometimes they give us tea. I said to this Paddy, look mate, can I have your hat? Because it's been in the paper about mine. He says, sure, I says, I'll buy it off you, he says, no, you're all right, I've another one at home, a yellow one. So when I came for mowing your garden, I said to your friend, does this hat make me look like a brickie? Because it belonged to a brickie. And she said, I'd take you for a brickie anywhere."

"So you've met Colette," Alison said. "I see. You're the bloke from the gardening service."

"Yes." Mart gnawed his lip. "And that was another job that didn't last. How about some more tea?"

Alison hurried back across the garden. Michelle's kids were home from their nursery; she could hear their wailing, and the air was loud with their mother's threats and curses. She brought out another flask, with a mug for herself, and a packet of Chocolate Digestives, which Colette allowed her to keep for nervous clients, who liked to crumble and nibble. This time she made sure she got some; she held the packet on her lap, and offered them to Mart one by one. "Missus," he said, "have you ever been described in the paper?"

She said, "I have, actually. In the *Windsor Express*." She'd had three dozen photocopies made: ATTRACTIVE FULL-FIGURED PSYCHIC, ALISON HART. She'd sent one to her mum, but her mum never said anything. She'd sent them out to her friends, but they'd never said anything either. She had plenty of press cuttings now, of course, but none of them mentioned her appearance. They skirt around it, she thought. She had shown the *Windsor Express* cutting to Colette. Colette had sniggered.

"You were lucky," Mart said. "Windsor, you see. That's outside Delingbole's area."

"I've never had any time for the police," she said. I suppose I should have called them, when I was a kid. I suppose I could have laid charges. But I was brought up to be scared of a uniform. She remembered them shouting through the letter box: *Mrs. Emmeline Cheetham?* She thought, why didn't my mum get one of her boyfriends to nail it shut? It isn't as if we had any letters.

Just as Al had finished cleaning the kitchen and tidying away signs of Mart's lunch, Colette came in with a handful of carrier bags and in a state of outrage. "I was putting the car away," she said. "Somebody's swiped our garden chairs! How did that happen? It must have been that man in the night. But how did he get in the garage? There's no sign of forced entry!"

"You sound like Constable Delingbole," Alison said.

"Been talking to Michelle, have you? I can tell you, I wish I'd been a bit more wide awake this morning. I should have rung the police as soon as I spotted him. I blame myself."

"Yes, do," Alison said, in such a commiserating tone that Colette didn't notice.

"Oh well. I'll claim it on the insurance. What have you had to eat while I've been out?"

"Just some cornflakes. And a bit of salad."

"Really?" Colette swung open the fridge door. "Really and truly?" She frowned. "Where's the rest of the chicken?"

"There wasn't much left, I threw it out. And the bread."

Colette looked knowing. "Oh yes?" She lifted the lid of the butter dish. Her eyes swept the worktops, looking for evidence: crumbs, or a slight smearing of the surface. She crossed the kitchen, wrenched open the dishwasher and peered inside; but Al had already washed the grill pan and dishes, and put everything back where it should be. "Fair enough," she said grudgingly. "You know, maybe that bloke down at Bisley was right. If they can get into the garage, they could certainly get into the shed. Maybe it wasn't the best idea. I won't move anything in yet. Till we see. If there's any recurrence, in the neighbourhood. Because I've laid out quite a lot. On forks, and so on."

"Forks?" Alison said.

"Forks, spades. Hoes. Et cetera."

"Oh. Right."

Al thought, she's in such a state of self-reproach that she's forgotten to count the bacon rashers. Or even check the biscuit tin.

"Mart," Al said, "do you hear voices? I mean, inside your head? What's it like when you hear them?"

"My hands sweat," Mart said. "And my eyes go small in my head."

"What do they say?"

Mart looked at her cunningly. "They say, we want tea."

"I don't mean to intrude, but do you find the pills help?"

"Not really. They just make you thirsty."

"You know you can't stay here," Al said.

"Could I just for tonight, missus?"

He calls me missus, she thought, when he wants to be extra-pitiful. "Don't you have a blanket? I mean, I thought if you'd been sleeping rough you'd at least have a blanket, a sleeping bag. Look, I'll sneak something out."

"And a flask refill," said Mart. "And a dinner, please."

"I don't see how I can do that."

She felt ill already—she'd gone all day, on a bowl of cereal and a few biscuits. If she were to bring out her lo-fat turkey strips and vegetable rice to Mart, he would eat it in two swoops, and then she'd probably faint or something—plus, Colette would say, Al, why are you going into the garden with your Ready Meal?

"Suppose I give you some money," she said. "The supermarket's still open."

"I'm barred."

"Really? You could go to the garage shop."

"Barred there too. And the off-licence, or else I could get crisps. They shout, Sod off, you filthy gyppo."

"You're not! A gyppo."

"I tried to get a wash with the hose at the garage, but they chased me out.

They said, you come round here again and we'll run you over. They said I was disgusting the customers and taking their trade away. I blame Deling-bole. I'm barred out of everywhere."

Anger swarmed up from her empty belly. It was unexpected and unfamil-iar, and it created a hot glow behind her ribs. "Here," she said. "Take this, go down the kebab van, I'm sure they'll serve anybody. Don't set off the security lights when you come back."

While Mart was away, and Colette was watching *EastEnders*, she crept out with a spare duvet and two pillows. She tossed them into the Balmoral, and sped back to the house. The microwave was pinging. She ate in the kitchen, standing once again. I am refused bread in my own house, she thought. I am refused a slice of bread.

For a day or two, Mart came and went by night. "If Colette sees you, you're stuffed," she said. "Unfortunately, I can't predict her comings and goings, she's a real fidget these days, always banging in and out. You'll have to take your chances. Evan next door leaves at eight sharp. Don't let him see you. Half-past nine, Michelle takes the kids to nursery. Keep your head down. Post comes at ten; keep out of the postman's way. The middle of the day's not too bad. By three o'clock it gets busy again."

Mart began again, on the story of how PC Delingbole stamped on his watch.

"I'll lend you one of mine," she said.

"I don't want your neighbours to see me," Mart said. "Or they'll think I'm after their kids. Pinto and me, when we lived down Byfleet, some blokes came kicking on the door, shouting, pedos out!"

"Why did they think you were pedophiles?"

"Dunno. Pinto said, it's the way you look, the way you go around, your toes coming out of your shoes, and that hat you have. But that was when I still had my other hat."

"So what happened then? After they kicked the door?"

"Pinto called the police. He had his mobile on him."

"Did they come?"

"Oh, yes. They came in a patrol car. But then they saw it was me."

"And then?"

A slow smile crept over Mart's face. "Drive on, Constable Delingbole!"

She went through her jewellery box for spare watches, and discarded the diamanté ones, which were for onstage. I'd better buy him one, she thought, just a cheap one. And some shoes, I'd have to ask his size. Maybe if he had new shoes he'd move on, before Colette noticed. She had to keep diverting Colette, attracting her attention to spectacles at the front of the house, and chatting to divert her whenever she went into the kitchen. He'll have to be gone, she thought, before she decides to implement any shed security, because as soon as she goes down there she'll see signs of occupation; she imagined the screaming Colette jabbing with her garden fork, and the panic-stricken visitor impaled on its tines.

"Do you think we'd get a bed in here?" Mart asked, when she took him down his flask.

Al said, "Maybe a futon," but then she could have bitten her tongue.

"I should of thought to bring a sun lounger, from the garden centre," Mart said. "I know!" He struck his hat with the flat of his hand. "A hammock! That would do me."

"Mart," she said, "are you sure you haven't got a criminal record? Because I couldn't be responsible, I couldn't take a chance, I'd have to tell somebody, you see. You'd have to go."

"My dad beat my head in with a piece of pipe," Mart said. "Does that count?"

"No," she said. "You're the victim. That doesn't count." Severe blows to the skull, she thought. Colette thinks they're very significant. She asked me about them once, on tape. I didn't know why at the time. I realize now she thought they might have been the beginning of my abnormality.

"Though it was my step-dad, you know? I always thought it was my dad but my mum said not. No, she said, he's your step."

"How many step-dads did you have?"

"A few."

"Me too."

It was a warm day; they were sitting on the garden chairs, the door propped open slightly to give them some air. "Good thing we went for one with a window that opens," Al said. "Or you'd be stifled."

"But then again, not," Mart said. "For reasons of them surveying me, peeking in and tipping off the Big D."

"But then again, not," she agreed. "I thought of getting curtains, at one time."

One of the next-door children darted out of the playhouse, shrieking. Al stood up and watched her scoot across the lawn, skid to a halt, and sink her teeth into her brother's calf. "Ouch!" Al said; she winced as if she had felt the wound herself.

"Mummy, Mummy!" the infant yelled.

Mart banged the shed door and dropped on all fours. Michelle's voice rang out from the kitchen. "I'm coming out there, by God I am, and there'll be slaps all round."

"Get down," Mart pulled her skirt. "Don't let her see you."

"Bite him," Michelle roared, "and I'll bloody bite you."

They knelt on the floor together. Mart was trembling. Al felt she ought to pray.

"Oh Jesus!" Mart said. Tears sprang out of his eyes. He lurched into her. She supported his weight. Sagging against her, he was made of bones and scraps; his flesh breathed the odour of well-rotted manure.

"There, there," she murmured. She patted his hat. Michelle shot across the scabby turf, the baby on her arm and her teeth bared.

Colette answered her cell phone, and a voice said, "Guess who?"

She guessed at once. What other man would be phoning her? "Haven't seen you since we ran into you coming out of Elphicks."

"What?" Gavin said. He sounded dumbstruck, as if she had cursed him.

"The shop," she said. "In Farnham. That Saturday?"

"Out of *what?*"

"Elphicks. Why do you have such trouble, Gavin, with the ordinary names of things?"

A pause. Gavin said uneasily, "You mean that's what it's called? That department store?"

"Yes."

"Why didn't you say so?"

She said, "God give me strength." Then, "Perhaps you should end this call and we could start again?"

"If you like," Gavin said. "Okay." His line went dead. She waited. Her phone buzzed. "Gavin? Hello?"

"Colette? It's me," he said.

"What a nice surprise."

"Is it okay to talk to you now?"

"Yes."

"Were you busy, or something?"

"Let's just forget you called me before. Let's just have another go, and I won't mention where I last saw you."

"If that's what you want," Gavin said airily. His tone showed he thought her capricious in the extreme. "But why couldn't you talk, was it because *she* was around? You know, Fat Girl?"

"If you mean Alison, she's out. She's gone for a walk."

Even as Colette said it, it sounded unlikely to her, but that was what Alison had said she was doing.

"So you can talk?"

"Look, Gavin, what do you want?"

"Just checking up on you. Seeing how you're doing."

"Fine. I'm fine. And how are you doing?" Really, she thought, I'm losing patience with this.

He said, "I'm seeing somebody. I thought you should know."

"It's no concern of mine, Gavin."

But she thought, how odd of him to get it right for once. I may not need to know, but I want to know, of course I want to know. I want her CV, her salary details, and a recent full-length photograph with her body measurements written on the back, so that I can work out what she's got that's so much better than me.

"What's her name?"

"Zoë."

"That won't last. Far too classy for you. Is it serious?" It must be, she thought, or he wouldn't be telling me. "Where did you meet her? Is she in IT?" She must be, of course. Who else did he meet?

"Actually," he said, "she's a model."

"Really?" Colette's voice was cold. She almost said, a model what? She stood up. "Look, I can see Alison coming back. I have to go."

She cut off the call. Alison was lumbering up the hill. Colette stood watching her, the phone still in her hand. Why's she wearing that big coat? Her temperature control must be shot again. She says it's spirits but I bet it's just an early menopause. Look at her! The size of her! Fat Girl!

When Al came in Colette was standing in the hall waiting for her. Her face was savage. "I suppose it's something, that you're taking a bit of exercise!"

Alison nodded. She was out of breath.

"You were practically on your knees, by the time you got halfway up the hill—you should have seen yourself! How far have you waddled, about a mile? You'll have to be sprinting that distance, with weights attached to you, before you see any improvement. Look at you, puffing and sweating!"

Obedient, Al glanced at herself in the hall mirror. There was a flicker of movement; that's Mart, she thought, scooting out of the side gate.

Alison went into the kitchen and out of the back door. She unbuttoned her coat, and—listening out all the time for Colette—disentangled herself from the two supermarket carrier bags that were swinging like saddlebags at her sides. She placed her surreptitious groceries behind the wheelie bin, came in, and shrugged off the coat.

It's like being a reverse shoplifter, she thought. You get to the checkout with your cart and you pay for everything; then, when you get outside, you open your coat and start concealing the bags about your person. People stare at you, but you stare back. If they asked you why you were doing it, what would you say? You can't think of a single good reason, except that you want to do a good action.

It had come to this: either she ate, or Mart did. I'll have to explain to him, she thought. How Colette checks up on me all the time. How she controls the groceries. How she shouted, the day you came, when she finally stock-taked the fridge and realized two eggs were missing. How she accused me of eating them boiled and made me ashamed, even though I never ate them, you did. How she supervises every minute of my day. How I can't just go freelance shopping. How, if I took the car, she'd want to know where. And if I drove off by myself, she'd want to know why.

She thought, on Friday at Sainsbury's they have twenty-four-hour opening. So I could sneak out when she was asleep. Not ordinary asleep, that wouldn't do. I'd have to get her drunk. She imagined herself wedging a plastic funnel into Colette's open throat, and pouring chardonnay through it. I could take the car, she thought, if backing it out of the drive wouldn't wake her. Probably that would only work if I drugged her. Beat her into insensibility. Come here, she thought: would you like a slap with this shovel?

But really, he must be gone by weekend. I'll tell him. Even if she doesn't form the ambition to rehone the forks and the hoes, those water-feature people will be around again early next week.

She locked the back door. She crossed the kitchen, stood at the sink and downed a glass of water. All quiet on the shed front; the door was closed, the ground undisturbed. She refilled her glass. Quick, quick, she thought, before she comes in and says tap-water can kill you, quick, before she says drinking too fast is a notorious cause of death in the obese.

She was aware that the Collingwood was silent.

She went into the hall. "Colette?"

No answer. But from above she heard a bleating, a little trail of bleating that grew louder as she followed it upstairs.

She stood outside Colette's door. She is lying on her bed sobbing, she thought. But why? Can she have regretted what she said to me, about my personal fatness? Has a lifetime of tactlessness flashed before her eyes? This didn't seem likely. Colette didn't think she was tactless. She thought she was right.

Whatever, Al thought. Now is my opportunity. While her emotions are detaining her, I will just sneak down the garden and distribute my haul to Mart. Or, as he's gone out, I will leave it inside his door, for him to find as a happy surprise when he returns.

Yesterday she had taken him three oranges. He had not been impressed when she had explained that she could get away with oranges, by claiming to have juiced them. He had hinted that he preferred a steak, but she couldn't see her way to setting up cooking facilities. So he was getting tinned tuna, that sort of thing. She hoped he would appreciate that tins were extremely heavy.

She creaked down the stairs, away from Colette and her grief: whatever that was. At the foot of the stairs, she saw herself, unavoidably, in the glass. Her face looked as pink as a ham. She thought, I could have got him sliced cold meat, I bet that would have been lighter, though of course it being warm weather he'd have to eat it all the same day. At least, this way, I've built him up a little store that he can put in his rucksack, when he leaves.

She opened the back door, tottered out, reached behind the wheelie bin. The bags had gone. Mart must have darted back, crouching low, and swooped them up on his way in. In which case I hope he's got strong teeth, she thought, as I didn't buy him a can opener.

By close of day, Colette had not come down; but all it would take, Al thought, is a casual glance from her bedroom window, as Mart flits across the lawn by moonlight. Why don't I just give him some money to set him on his way? I can't afford more than, say, a hundred pounds, or Colette will want to know where I drew it out and what I spent it on. She will be quite pleasant about it, knowing I have the right, but she'll be curious all the same.

When it was almost dark, she stepped out of the sliding doors.

"Alison? Is that you?" Michelle was waving.

Who else did she think it was? Reluctantly, she moved towards the fence.

"Lean over," Michelle said. "I want to whisper to you. Have you heard about this plague of rabbit deaths?"

She shook her head.

"It's very strange, you see. Not that I have any time personally for rabbits; I wouldn't have any pets near my kids because they spread all sorts of toxicosis. But these little ones at the nursery, they're crying their eyes out. They go down the garden to feed it and it's keeled over in its hutch with a horrible trickle of black blood coming out of its mouth."

I suppose, Al thought, me keeping Mart in the shed, it's like being a kid again, doing things behind people's backs, stealing food, all that stuff I used to do; running to the corner with any money I got. It's a game really, it's like that dolls' tea party I wanted. We have a lot in common, she thought, me and Mart, it's like having a little brother. She had noticed that Mart was always falling over; that was because of his medication. She thought, my mum, too, she was always falling over.

"So what do the vets say?" she asked Michelle.

"They just say, oh, rabbits, what do you expect? They try to put it on what they've been eating, a bad diet. They blame you, don't they, the owner? That's how they get around it. Evan says personally he has no time for rabbits either, but it's very worrying, in the light of what's going down with the playground. And the vets denying it, you see. He wonders if they know something we don't."

Oh dear, she said. They ought to hold postmortems, maybe. She couldn't think what else to say. Got to go, she said; as she limped away from the fence, Michelle called, will the warm weather last till weekend?

By eight o'clock Al was beginning to feel very hungry. Colette didn't show any sign of coming down and supervising her dinner. She crept upstairs to listen. More and more, this evening reminded her of her youth. The need to tiptoe, listen at doors: sighs and groans from other rooms. "Colette?" she called softly. "I need you to do my calories."

No reply. She eased the door open. "Colette?"

"Go and eat yourself to death," Colette said. "What do I care?"

She was lying face down on the bed. She looked very flat. She looked very out-of-it. Alison drew the door closed, in a manner so quiet that she hoped it showed her complete respect for Colette's state of mind, so quiet that it offered condolences.

She crept down the garden. The moon had not yet turned the corner above the Mountbatten at the curve of the road, and she wasn't clear where she was putting her feet. She felt she ought to knock, but that's ridiculous, she thought, knock at your own shed?

She inched open the door. Mart was sitting in the dark. He had a torch, and batteries, but they were the wrong size; something else for my shopping list, she thought. She could have fixed him up with a candle, but she didn't trust him not to start a fire.

"Get your shopping?"

"What shopping? I'm ravenous in here. Fainting."

"I'm giving you fifty quid," Al said. "Sneak off into Knaphill, will you, and get a takeaway Chinese? Get me a set menu for two, and whatever you want for yourself. Keep the change."

When Mart left, diving low under the light sensors, she tried to make herself comfortable in the canvas garden chair. The earth was cooling, beneath their hardstanding; she lifted her feet and tried to tuck them beneath her, but the chair threatened to overbalance; she had to sit up straight, metal digging into her back, and plant her feet back on the ground. She thought, I wonder what happened to the shopping?

When Mart came back they sat companionably, licking spare ribs and tossing down the bones. "You've got to take the cartons away," she said. "Do you understand that? You mustn't put them in our wheelie bin. Or Colette will see them. You have to be gone soon. The garden design will be coming. They'll probably say, take down that shed, it's an eyesore." She chewed thoughtfully on a sweet-and-sour prawn. "I knew we should get a better one."

"It's late," Mart said, consulting his new watch. "You ought to go in."

"Oh, just so you can finish everything off by yourself!"

"I'm more hungry than you," Mart said, and she thought, that's true. So in she went. Up to bed. All quiet from Colette's room. She didn't dream, for once; or not of being hungry.

It couldn't last, of course. Previously there had been an element of camouflage about Mart, his dirty clothes blending into the earth tones of the gardens, but you noticed his feet now, in the big clean navy and white shoes, seeming to come around the corner before him.

When he saw Colette approaching, he slammed the door of the shed and wedged his rucksack against it; but Colette defeated him with one push. Her yodel of alarm drove him back against the wall.

Al galumphed down the garden, shouting, "Don't hit him! Don't call the police, he's not dangerous."

Mart laughed when Colette said she had seen him on the lawn.

"I bet you thought I was from space, did you? You said, oops, there goes an extraterrestrial! Or did you think I was a brickie from off the building site?"

"I didn't form any opinion," Colette said coldly.

"She thought she was dreaming," Al said.

"Alison, I'll deal with this, please."

"In fact, my troubles started with an alien encounter," Mart said. "Aliens give you a headache, did you know that? Plus they make you fall over. When you've seen an alien, it's like somebody's drilled your middle out." He made a gesture—a gouge and a twist—like someone plunging a corer into an apple. "Pinto," he said, "when we was white-lining up near Saint Albans, he got taken up bodily into an alien craft. Female aliens came and pulled off his overalls and palpitated his body all over."

"He was dreaming," Colette said.

Al thought, she doesn't know how lucky we are, we could have been playing host to Pinto as well.

"He wasn't asleep," Mart said. "He was carried off. The proof of it is, when he got back, he took his shirt off and they'd erased his tattoo."

"You can't stay here any longer," Colette said. "I hope that's perfectly clear to you?"

"A shed wouldn't do for everybody," Mart conceded. "But it'll do nicely for me. Less bugs in a shed."

"I should have thought there'd be more. Though I'm sure you'll find that it's perfectly clean."

"Not crawling bugs. Listening bugs."

"Don't be silly. Who'd want to listen to you? You're a vagrant."

"And there's cameras everywhere these days," Mart said. "Blokes watching you out of control towers. You can't go anywhere without somebody knows about it. You get post from people that don't know you, how do you do that? Even I get post, and I don't have an address. Constable Delingbole says, I've got your number, mate." He added, under his breath, "His is written on him."

"I expect you out of here within ten minutes," Colette said. "I am going back to the house and I shall be counting. Then, whatever you say, Alison, I shall call the police and have you removed."

Al thought, I wonder if Delingbole is real, or in a dream? Then she thought, yes, of course he's real. Michelle knows him, doesn't she? He gave a talk on shed crime. She wouldn't have dreamed that.

• • •

It was some hours before Colette was speaking to her again. There were in-
teractions, chance meetings; at one point Colette had to hand her the telephone to take a call from a client, and later they arrived in the utility room at
the same time, with two baskets of washing, and stood saying coldly, after
you, no, after you.

But the Collingwood wasn't big enough to keep up a feud.

"What do you want me to say?" Al demanded. "That I won't keep a vagrant again? Well, I won't, if you feel that strongly about it. Jesus! It isn't as if
there was any harm done."

"No thanks to you."

"Let's not start again," she said.

"I don't think you realize the kind of people who are out there."

"No, I'm too good," Al muttered. "You don't realize half the evil that is in
the world," she told herself under her breath.

Colette said, "I saw Michelle earlier. She says, guard your shopping."

"What?"

"In the boot of the car. In case it vanishes while you're unlocking the front
door. Don't leave the boot lid open. There's been a spate of grocery theft."

"I don't go shopping by myself, do I?"

Colette said, "Stop muttering like that."

"Truce?" she said. "Peace talks? Cup of tea?"

Colette did not answer but she took it as a yes, standing at the sink filling
the kettle, looking down the garden towards the now-deserted Balmoral. Colette had accused her of harbouring Mart, but not of actually feeding him;
not of actually buying supplies and smuggling them in. She had not actually
slapped her, but she had screamed in her face, asked her if she was insane,
and if it was her intention to bring into the neighbourhood a gang of robbers,
child molesters, terrorists, and would-be murderers.

I don't know, she'd said, I don't think so. I didn't have an intention, I just
wanted to do a good action, I suppose I didn't think; I just felt sorry for him,
because he's got nowhere to go and so he has to go in a shed.

"Sometimes," Colette said, "I think you're retarded as well as fat."

But that's not true, Al thought. Surely not? She knows I'm not stupid. I
might be temporarily muddled by the ingress of memory, some seepage from
my early life. I feel I was kept in a shed. I feel I was chased there, that I ran in the

shed for refuge and hiding place, I feel I was then knocked to the floor, because in the shed someone was waiting for me, a dark shape rising up from the corner, and as I didn't have my scissors on me at the time I couldn't even snip him. I feel that, soon afterwards, I was temporarily inconvenienced by someone putting a lock on the door, and I lay bleeding, alone, on newspapers, in the dark.

She couldn't see the past clearly, only an outline, a black bulk against black air. She couldn't see the present; it was muddled by the force of the scene Colette had made, the scene which was still banging around inside her skull. But she could see the future. She'll be forcing me out for walks, hanging weights— this is what she threatens—on my wrists and ankles. She might drive alongside me, in the car, monitoring me, but probably only at first. She won't want to spare the time from sending out invoices, billing people for predictions I have made and spirits I have raised: To Your Uncle Bob, ten minutes' conversation, £150 plus VAT. So perhaps she won't drive alongside me, she'll just drive me out of the house. And I'll have nowhere to go. Perhaps I, too, can take refuge in someone's outbuilding. First I can go by the supermarket and get a sandwich and a bun, then I can eat them sitting on a bench somewhere, or if it's wet and I can't get into a shed I could go to the park and crawl under the bandstand. It's easy to see how it happens, really, how a person turns destitute.

"So who's stealing the shopping?" she asked: thinking, it could soon be me.

"Illegal immigrants, Evan says."

"In Woking?"

"Oh, they get everywhere," Colette said. "Asylum seekers, you know. The council is taking the benches out of the park, so that no one can sleep on them. Still, we've had our warning, haven't we? With the shed."

She drank the tea Alison had made her, leaning against the work surface as if she were in a station buffet. I moved him on smartly, she thought, he knew better than to mess with me, one look at me and he knew I wasn't a soft touch. She felt hungry. It would have been easy enough to dip into the clients' biscuit tin, when Al wasn't looking, but she denied herself. Michelle had said their wheelie bin had been crammed with takeaway cartons, and she now realized the homeless person must have been responsible for these. Food is over, as far as I'm concerned, she thought. Pictures of Zoë were gnawing at her brain, like rats in a cage with no door.

ten

That summer, black slime came up through the drains of a Frobisher just down the hill. There was a heat wave, with temperatures creeping toward the upper nineties. Animals crawled into the shade. Children turned lobster-red inside their playsuits. Fragile citizens bought charcoal masks to protect against the excess ozone. Sales of ice cream and lager doubled, as did sales of cold and flu remedies. The lawns at Admiral Drive baked until they cracked, and the grass turned to patchy straw. Colette's water feature had to be turned off: as all water features were turned off, by order. Fountains dried, reservoirs dwindled. Hospitals filled. The elderly expired. A plague of psychic shows broke out on TV, crawling all over the schedules.

Colette sat watching them with a sullen expression, denouncing the transparent cheating, the collusion, the simplemindedness of the studio audiences. It's totally irresponsible, she said, to encourage people to think that's the way you go about dealing with the dead. In the days when she and Al first got together, the days when the princess passed, the punters squirmed when they were fingered; they twitched in their seats, desperate to foist the message off on the person next to them or the person in front or just behind. But now, when they came to a dem, the TV shows had tuned up their expectations, they couldn't wait for their messages. When a Sensitive asked, "Who's got a Mike in Spirit World?" fifty hands would shoot into the air. They yelled, cheered, embraced each other, made faces for the camera even though there wasn't one. They shouted, "Oh, my gahhd!" when a message came though, and burst into grating sobs and doggy howls.

I find it exhausting, Al said, just to watch. And I couldn't do television myself, she said. If I were there in the studio something would malfunction. The picture would blank out. The network would go down. Then they'd sue me.

And you're too fat for television, Colette said.

To think I used to blame so much on Morris! Al said. If the lightbulbs started flickering I'd shout, "Oi, Morris!" and if the washing machine overflowed I would just give him a piece of my mind. But even now, your computer goes on the blink whenever I come near it, and we're still not getting anywhere with the recordings, are we? The machine plays back tapes that aren't even in it; we get material coming through from the year before last. All the tapes are speaking on top of each other, it's like a compost heap.

And you're too fat, Colette said.

So I think it's my electromagnetic field. I think it's hostile to modern technology.

They had got all the satellite channels, because Alison liked to home-shop; she often felt shy when she was out, and she complained that people looked at her in a funny way, as if they knew what she did for a living. "It's not shameful," she said. "Not like being a sex worker." Still, it was a comfort to be able to buy some chunky gold chains and glittery earrings, low-taste stuff she could wear onstage.

Once, when they switched on their TV, Cara's pixie face appeared onscreen; another time, Mandy's sharp foxy features bobbed up. Colette said, "Natasha, huh! She doesn't look a bit Russian."

"She's not."

"They could have made her up to look Russian, that's all I'm saying."

When the credits came at the end of the show, the producers put a disclaimer notice on the screen, to say that the programme was "For entertainment purposes only." Colette snorted and stabbed the OFF switch. "You should tell them straight, at your next dem. Tell them what it's really like in Spirit World. Why do you have to be so soft on them? Tell them what Morris used to do to you." She sniggered. "I'd like to see their faces then. I'd like to see Mandy's face, when she's on camera and Morris puts his hand up her skirt. I'd like to see them burbling on about the world beyond, if Morris came back and he was in one of his moods."

"Don't say that," Al begged. "Don't say you'd like to see Morris."

She had never been able to teach Colette the art of self-censorship; never been able to make her understand how simple and literal-minded the organizers of Spirit World could be. You had to guard the words that came out of your mouth and even the words as they formed up in your mind. Wasn't that simple enough? Sometimes she thought Colette couldn't be such a slow learner. Surely she was doing it on purpose, tormenting her?

Gavin rang. He asked for Colette, and Al passed the phone over without speaking to him. She hung about, overhearing; though proximity wasn't really necessary to her. She could tune in to Gavin any time she liked, but the thought tired her. Quite clearly she heard him say, "How's the fat lesbian?"

Colette said, "I've told you, Alison is not a lesbian. In fact, there are several men in her life."

"Who?" Gavin demanded.

"Let me see." Colette paused. "There's Donnie. There's Keith . . . she and Keith go way back."

Al stood in the doorway. "Colette . . . don't."

Colette gestured to her angrily, to go away.

Don't make a joke out of the fiends, Al pleaded; but not out loud. She turned and left the room. You should know better, Colette, but how can you know better? You believe and you half-believe, that's the trouble with you. You want the frisson and you want the money, but you don't want to alter your dumb view of the world. She heard Colette say to Gavin, "There's Dean. Dean really fancies me. But he's quite young."

"What do they do, these blokes?" Gavin said. "Are they fortune-tellers as well?"

"There's Mart," she said "Oh, and our neighbour, Evan. Plenty of men in our lives, you see."

"You're carrying on with a neighbour?" Gavin said. "Married, is he?"

"That's my business."

Colette had that fizzing, crawling feeling you get when you're lying. When she heard what was coming out of her mouth she was frightened. It was quite natural that she should want to put the best face on things, with Gavin, but stop, stop, she said to herself, Donnie and Keith aren't real and Evan is a wanker and Mart lives in the shed. Or used to.

"Fair dos," Gavin said. "I mean, I can't see anybody leaving his wife and kids for you, Colette, but then I've no right to an opinion, have I?"

"Damn right you haven't."

"No, you see who you like," he said—still, she thought, with that lordly air, as if he were giving her permission. "Look, what I called about—they've been having a bit of a shakeout at work. They've let me go."

"I see. When did this happen, this shakeout?"

"Three months back."

"You could have said."

"Yes, but I thought I'd get fixed up. I called a few people."

"And they were out, were they? In a meeting? On holiday this week?"

"There's a downturn, you know?"

"I don't think it's a downturn. I think they've finally rumbled you, Gavin."

"No, it's happening everywhere, all the big consultancies are shedding."

"So how are you managing? Money must be tight."

"It's just a cash-flow problem."

"I'm sure Zoë can help you out."

He seemed to hesitate—so Colette said sharply, "She is still with you, I suppose?"

"Oh, yes, she's very loyal. I mean, she's not the sort of girl to chuck you if you had a temporary setback."

"Not like me, eh? I'd be out of there like a shot."

"So I have to ask you about the payments, for the flat. I have to cut down my outgoings. Just till I get sorted."

"So is there a downturn in the modelling business too? Or is she in hock for her tit lift and her bum suction? Oh, it's all right, Gavin, I can afford to carry you for a while. Alison and I are doing really, really well."

"Yeah, it's all over the TV, psychic shows."

"Yes, but that's fraud. We're not fraud. And we're not dependent on the whims of schedulers, thank you." Something touched her, a small hand on her sleeve: compunction. "So how are you," she said, "apart from poor? How's your car running?"

There was a short silence. "I have to go," Gavin said. "Zoë wants me."

"Probably some bit of her fallen off," Colette said. "By-eee." As she put down the phone she chuckled. Gavin had always lived in anticipation of his next salary cheque, and with his credit cards charged up to their limit. He'll be wanting a loan soon, she said to herself. She sang out to Alison, "Guess what? Gavin's got the boot." But Al was on the other line.

Mandy said, "It's time we started offering something to the punters that they can't get from satellite TV. It's all very well, but who's making money out of it? Not us, for sure. It's three hours hanging about in a back room with a plate of stale biscuits, an hour in makeup with some snooty cow drawing your eyebrows in the wrong place, and then when you see yourself you're edited down to the blink of an eye and you're supposed to be bloody grateful."

"I thought it would be glamorous," Al said wistfully. "Colette says I can't go on because of my size, but I thought it would be nice for you."

"In my view," Mandy said, "we have to reinstate the personal touch. Silvana's been advertising psychic hen parties, and she's getting a very good response. You need to be able to provide one reader to about every six ladies, so I said I'd see if you were willing."

"Be a change, wouldn't it?"

"That's what I think. A change for the guests, too. It's a bit more upmarket than going on the razz and sicking up vodka outside some club. What with date-rape drugs, all that, you wouldn't want to venture out."

"No men," Al suggested. "We don't want Raven droning about ley lines."

"Definitely no men. That's what they've come to get away from."

"And we're not including Mrs. Etchells, are we? We don't want her twittering on about the joys of motherhood."

"Or telling them they need a little op. No, definitely no Mrs. E. I'll sign you up, Al. You know those people in Cornwall, those new suppliers? They offer party packs, sort of goody bags for the clients to take away, minisizes of aromatic oils, three-pack of incense sticks, candle in tin, you know the sort of thing, presented in a velvet-look pouch. We can put a markup on them and sell them to the party organizer and we can bring along our own stocks of angel cards and spiritual CDs. Gemma's got a cash-and-carry card so we could supply the champagne and party snacks. Ideally we'll make it an evening of pampering and relaxation, as well as prediction. We can give nutritional advice—perhaps not you, Al—and we need somebody to do massage and reflexology. Silvana does Reiki, doesn't she? And Cara's got this new therapy she's going in for, I forget what they call it. Anyway, you rub their feet and it brings back memories of life pre-birth."

"Really?" Al said. "Have you tried it, Mandy?"

"Mm. Quite intriguing. Peaceful."

"What was it like?"

"Darkness. Sort of swishing."

She thought, I wouldn't like to have access to my thoughts, before I was born. An image came to her of her mother, patiently fishing for her with a knitting needle.

"Anything else? Besides swishing?"

"Yes. Now you mention it. I think I got reverted to my past life. The closing moments, you know. Bloody great hoof coming down on my head. I could hear my own skull cracking."

At the hen parties, through the summer evenings, Colette sat in other women's kitchens, perched on a stool, frowning as she inputted data into her palm-top organizer. She was cool and neat in her little beige skirts and tiny T-shirts, an inch of flat midriff showing, as fashion decreed. She sat with legs crossed, a sandalled foot swinging, as she squared up Alison's autumn schedule and calculated her expenses. When the Sensitives in their floaty scarves slid away for a break, when they leaned against the fridge and tried to engage her in conversation, she would give them her flat-eyed stare and, with an irritated twitch of her lips, go back to her sums. When they were called back to the party, she would take a long breath, finding herself alone, and look about her. They were working some upmarket locations—Weybridge, Chobham—and there were state-of-the-art kitchen fittings for her to admire: granite worktops like dark mirrors, and brushed steel in which she saw, faintly, her slight and wavering form as she crossed the room to pour herself a glass of

San Pellegrino. When the door opened, New Age music wafted towards her, and dreamy half-clad girls, slippery with aromatic oils, drifted past and sometimes offered her a carrot baton or a bite of sushi.

"Ironic," she said to Al. "You lot, giving advice on love and marriage. There's not an intact relationship between you."

She heard the psychics muttering about her presence, heard herself referred to by Silvana as "that hanger-on." She knew Silvana was jealous, because she herself couldn't afford a manager. She pictured herself hitting back: I'm really the core to the heart of this enterprise. You ask my ex, Gavin. I keep him, these days. I've made this business boom. I have many skills and talents. I could tell the punters what's going to happen in their love lives. You don't need psychic powers.

Alison came into the kitchen looking hot. "I'm just slipping out. Tell the clients I'll be ten minutes. Or shift some of mine over to Cara."

"Certainly." Colette opened the chart on which she kept track of the evening's proceedings.

"Skivving off, eh?" Gemma said, following Alison into the kitchen. "I'm needing some matches, the moon candles keep going out." She cast her eyes around. "There's nothing that needs lighting, is there, in a house like this? And they all don't smoke. Or claim they don't."

Colette opened her bag, and took out a box. She rattled it, looking smug. "Don't," said Al, flinching. They stared at her. "I don't know," she said. "I just don't like people rattling a box of matches. It reminds me of something."

"You were probably burned at the stake," Gemma said. "In a previous existence. You were probably a Cathar."

"When were they?" Colette said.

Gemma frowned. "It's medieval," she said.

"Then I don't think they had matches."

Gemma flounced out. "It's a presence in there," Al said, "blowing out the candles. Cara tried to get it in a corner, but we don't want to be frightening the punters. I'm just popping over the road, because there's a bunch of grannies standing by the hedge."

"Where?" Colette went to the window.

"Spirit grannies. Great-grannies. Great-greats."

"What do they want?"

"Just to say hello. Congratulations. To have a look at the décor. You know how it is."

"You're too soft," Colette said. "Let the grannies stand there, and you get back to your clients."

"I have to explain to them," Al said, "that they're not wanted. I have to put it so as not to cause pain."

As she went out towards the lift, the little woman followed her, saying, "Excuse me, miss, have you seen Maureen Harrison?"

"You again?" Al said. "Haven't you found her yet? Stick around, ducks, follow us home."

Gemma came back into the kitchen with a girl leaning on her shoulder: pin-thin, teetering on high heels, wailing and dripping tears. "Get up, Colette," she said. "This is Charlotte, our hostess. Let Charlotte sit down."

Colette vacated her stool, Charlotte hopped up on it; it wasn't the sort of stool you could sink onto. Her bleating continued, and when Gemma tried to hug her she squealed, "No, no," and beat her away with little flapping motions of her hands. "He just texted her," Gemma said. "The bastard. It's off."

Hens filled the doorway; their mouths were ajar. "Come on back, ladies," Silvana urged, "don't all crowd around, let her get over the shock."

"Christ," Colette said. "She's the bride?"

Cara pushed the hens aside. She looked little and fierce. "Text him back, Charlotte."

"Can you pretext?" Gemma asked. "Is that possible? Would you know, Colette? If she made it look as if she sent a message before he sent his, then she could be the one to call it off."

"Yes, do that," Cara urged. "Your self-esteem's at stake here. Pretend you never got it."

"Now look, darling." Gemma squatted on the ground before Charlotte. Charlotte keened and flapped at her, but Gemma took her hands and squeezed them tight. "Now look, you think the world has stopped turning, but it hasn't. You've had a shock but you'll get over it. This is your lowest ebb and now the only way is up."

"That filthy scumbag," wailed the girl.

"That's the spirit," Gemma said. "You've got to put it behind you, sweetheart."

"Not till she's billed him," Colette said. "Surely. I mean, there'll be deposits. On the venue. And the honeymoon, air tickets paid for. Unless she goes anyway, with a girlfriend."

"At least she's got to text and ask him why," Cara said. "Or she'll never achieve closure."

"That's right," Gemma said. "You've got to move on. I mean, if you've had bad luck in your life, what's the use of brooding?"

"I disagree," Colette said. "It wasn't bad luck. It was bad judgement."

"Will you shut it?" Gemma said.

"There's no point in her moving on until she's sure she's learned something from it."

She glanced up. Alison was wedged in the doorway. "Actually I agree with Colette," she said. "Just on this occasion. You have to think about the past. You ought to. You can work out where it went wrong. There must have been warning signs."

"There, there," Gemma said. She patted the girl's bare bronzed shoulder. Charlotte sniffed, and whispered something; Gemma said, "Witchcraft, oh no!" But Charlotte continued to insist, blowing her nose on a piece of kitchen roll that Al handed to her; until at last Gemma whispered back, "I do know someone in Godalming. If you really want to make him impotent."

"I expect that will cost you," Colette said. She thought, I wonder, if I went in for it, could I get a trade discount? That would be one in the eye for Zoë. She said, "Some girls in your position would go the direct route. What do you need a witch for, when you could go around there with a carving knife? More permanent, isn't it?"

She remembered her own moments of temptation, the night she left Gavin. I can be reckless, she thought, at secondhand.

"You'd go to jail," Gemma said severely. "Don't listen, sweetheart. What do they say? Revenge is a dish best eaten cold?"

Al moaned and clasped a hand to her belly. She made a dash for the kitchen sink, but it was too late. "Oh, that's all I bloody need," said the bride-to-be. She jumped from her stool to fetch a mop and bucket.

Afterwards, Colette said, "I told you prawns were dodgy in weather like this. But you can't curb your appetite, can you? Now you've embarrassed yourself."

"It wasn't the prawns." Hunched in the passenger seat, Al sounded snuffly and depressed. "Prawns are protein, besides."

"Yes," Colette said patiently, "but you can't have the extra protein *and* the carbohydrates *and* the fat, Al, something has to give. It's a simple enough principle to get into your head, I've explained it a dozen times."

"It was when you rattled the matches," Al said. "That's when I started feeling sick."

"That doesn't make any sense at all," Colette said. She sighed. "But I've ceased expecting sense from you. How can you be frightened of a box of matches?"

Between the bride's sudden jilting and Al's sudden vomit, the hen party had broken up early. It was not quite dark when they let themselves into the Collingwood. The air had cooled, and the cats of Admiral Drive tiptoed along the garden fences, their eyes shining. In the hall, Al put her hand on Colette's arm. "Listen."

From the sitting room came two gruff male voices, rising and falling in amicable conversation.

"A tape's playing," she said. "Listen. Is that Aitkenside?"

Colette raised her eyebrows. She flung open the double doors from the hall; though as they were glass, the gesture was superfluous. No one was within; and all she could hear, from the machine on the table, was a faint hiss and twitter that could have been the machine's own workings. "We ought to get some more sophisticated recording equipment," she said. "I'm sure it must be possible to cut out these blips and twitters."

"Shh," Alison said. "Oh dear, Colette."

AITKENSIDE: Here, Morris, you don't get a good gherkin these days. Not like you used to get. Where would you go for a good gherkin?

MORRIS: You don't get a good pickled onion. You don't get a good pickled onion like we used to get after the war.

"It's Morris."

"If you say so."

"Can't you hear him? Maybe his course is finished. But he shouldn't be back." Al turned to Colette, tears in her eyes. "He should have moved on, higher. That's what happens. That's what always happens."

"I don't know." Colette threw her bag down. "You said yourself, you get these cross-recordings from the year before last. Maybe it's old."

"Maybe."

"What's he saying? Is he threatening you?"

"No, he's talking about pickles."

AITKENSIDE: You don't get a mutton pie. Whatever happened to mutton? You never see it.

MORRIS: When you go on the station for a samwidge you can't get ham, you can't get a sheet of pink ham and some hot mustard like you used to get, they want to go stuffing it with all this green stuff—lettuce—and lettuce is for girls.

AITKENSIDE: It's all wog food, pansy food, you can't get a nice pickled egg like you used to get.

MORRIS: Could have some fun with a pickled egg, see a pickled egg and Bob Fox he would start up without fail. Pass it round, lads, he'd say, and when MacArthur comes in you just drop it on the table, say aye-aye, MacArthur, have you lost something, old son? I seen MacArthur turn pale. I seen him nearly drop in his tracks—

AITKENSIDE: I seen him clap his hand to his empty socket—

MORRIS: And Bob Fox, cool as you like take up his fork and stab the little fucker then squeeze it up in his fingers—

AITKENSIDE:—all wobbling—

MORRIS: —and take a bite. Tee-hee. I wonder what happened to Bob Fox?

AITKENSIDE: Used to knock on the window, didn't he? *Tap-tap, tap-tap.* That was Bob.

Towards dawn, Colette came down and found Al standing in the kitchen. The cutlery drawer was open, and Al was staring down into it.

"Al?" she said softly.

She saw with distaste that Al had not bothered to tie up her housecoat; it flapped back at either side to show her round belly and shadowy triangle of pubic hair. She looked up, registered Colette, and slowly, as if half asleep, pulled the thin cotton wrap across her; it fell open again as her fingers fumbled for the ties.

"What are you looking for?" Colette said.

"A spoon."

"There's a drawer full of spoons!"

"No, a particular spoon," Al insisted. "Or perhaps a fork. A fork would do."

"I should have known you'd be down here, eating."

"I feel I've done something, Colette. Something terrible. But I don't know what."

"If you must eat something, you're allowed a slice of cheese." Colette opened the door of the dishwasher and began to take out yesterday's crockery. "Done something terrible? What sort of thing?"

Alison picked out a spoon. "This one."

"Not cornflakes, please! Unless you want to undo all the good work. Why don't you go back to bed?"

"I will," Al said, without conviction. She moved away, the spoon still in her hand, then turned, and handed it to Colette. "I can't think what I did," she said. "I can't quite place it."

A shaft of rosy sunlight lay across the window ledge, and an engine purred as an early Beatty backed out of his garage. "Cover yourself up, Al," Colette said. "Oh, come here, let me." She took hold of the housecoat, wrapped it across Al, and tied a firm double bow. "You don't look well. Do you want me to cancel your morning clients?"

"No. Let them be."

"I'll bring you some green tea at eight-thirty."

Al moved slowly towards the stairs. "I can't wait."

Colette opened the cutlery drawer and slotted the spoon among its fellows. She brooded. She's probably hungry, considering she sicked up all the party snacks. Which she shouldn't have been eating anyway. Maybe I should have let her have some cereal. But who is this diet for? It's not for my sake. It's for her sake. Without me behind her, she goes right off the rails.

She stacked some saucers into the cupboard, *tip-tap, tip-tap*. Did Al have to look so naked? But fat people do. Laid open to the morning shadows, Al's white belly had seemed like an offering, something yielded up; a sacrifice. The sight had embarrassed Colette. Colette disliked her for it.

• • •

The summer heat took its toll on Al. In the week that followed, she lay awake through the nights. In the heat of the day her thighs chafed when she walked, and her feet brimmed over the straps of her sandals.

"Stop moaning!" Colette said, "We're all suffering."

"Sometimes," Al said, "I have a sort of creeping sensation. Do you get that?"

"Where?"

"It runs down my spine. My fingers tingle. And bits of me go cold."

"In this weather?"

"Yes. It's like, my feet won't walk properly. I want to go one way, and they want to go a different way. I'm supposed to come home, but my feet don't want to." She paused. "It's hard to explain it. I feel as if I might fall."

"Probably multiple sclerosis," Colette said. She was flicking though *Slimming* magazine. "You ought to get tested."

Al booked herself in at the health centre. When she rang up, the receptionist demanded to know what was the matter with her, and when Al explained carefully, my feet go different ways, she heard the woman sharing the news with her colleagues.

The woman's voice boomed down the phone. "Do you want me to put you in as an emergency?"

"No, I can wait."

"It's just, you need to be sure you don't wander off," the woman said. There were cackles in the background: screeches.

I could ill-wish them, Al said, but I won't, on this occasion. She thought, are there occasions when I have ill-wished?

"I can fit you in Thursday," the woman said. "You won't get lost on the way here?"

"My manager will drive me," Al said. "By the way, if I were you I should cancel your holiday. I know you'll lose your deposit, but what's a lost deposit compared to being kidnapped by Islamic terrorists and spending several months in leg irons in a tin shack in the desert?"

• • •

When Thursday came, Colette did drive her, of course. "You don't have to wait with me," Al said.

"Of course I do."

"If you leave me your moby, I could call a cab to take me home. You could go to the post office and post off my spells. There's one going airmail that needs to be weighed."

"Do you really think I'd leave you, Alison? To get bad news by yourself? Surely you think more of me than that?" Colette sniffed. "I feel devalued. I feel betrayed."

"Oh, dear," Al said. "Too many of those psychic hens. It's bringing your emotions out."

"You don't realize," Colette said. "You don't understand how Gavin let me down. I know what it's like, you see. I wouldn't do it to someone else."

'There you go again, talking about Gavin."

"I am not. I never mention him."

When they got into reception, Al scrutinized the practice staff behind their glass screens. She couldn't see the one who had laughed at her. Maybe I shouldn't have said anything, but when I saw she was booked on a Nile cruise I just couldn't resist. It's not, it's really not, as if I wished her any ill. I only told her.

"This is interesting," she said, looking around. It was just like the doctors' waiting room that the punters always described: people sneezing and coughing on you, and a long long wait. I'm never ill, she thought, so I don't know, first-hand. I'm ailing, of course. But not in ways doctors can cure. At least, I've assumed not.

They waited, side by side on stacking chairs. Colette talked about her self-esteem, her lack of it, her lonely life. Her voice quavered. Al thought, poor Colette, it's the times we live in. If she can't be in a psychic show, she fancies her chances on a true confession show. She pictured Gavin, stumbling over the cables, drawn from dark into dazzling light, from the dark of his own obtuse nature into the dazzling light of pale accusing eyes. She heard the audience groaning, hissing; saw Gavin tried, convicted, hung by the neck. It came to her that Gavin had been hanged, in his former life as a poacher. That's why, she thought, in this life, he never does up the top button on his shirt. She closed her eyes. She could smell shit, farmyard manure. Gavin was standing with a noose round his neck. He wore sideburns, and his expression was despondent. Someone was bashing a tin drum. The crowd was small but keen. And she? She was enjoying her day off. A woman was selling mutton pies. She had just bought two.

"Wake up, Al," Colette said. "They're calling your number! Shall I come in with you?"

"No." Al gave Colette a shove in the chest, which dropped her back in her chair. "Look after my bag," she said, throwing it into her lap.

When she walked in, her hand—the palm burning and slightly greasy from her second pie—was still outstretched. For a moment the doctor seemed to think he was expected to shake it. He looked outraged at the familiarity, then he remembered his communication skills.

"Miss Hart!" he said, with a smile that showed his teeth. "Sit ye down, sit ye down. And how are you today?"

He's been on a course, she thought. Like Morris. There was a stained coffee mug by his elbow, bearing the logo of a popular pharmaceutical company.

"I take it you're here about your weight?" he said.

"Oh no," she said. "I can't help my weight, I'm afraid."

"Huh. I've heard that a time or two," the doctor said. "Let me tell you, if I had a pound for every woman who's sat in that chair and told me about her slow metabolism, I'd be a rich man now."

Not that riches would help you, Al thought. Not with a liver like yours. Slowly, with a lingering regret, she pulled out her gaze from his viscera and focused on his Adam's apple. "I have tinglings down my arms," she said. "And my feet, when I try to go home, my feet take me somewhere else. My fingers twitch, and the muscles in my hands. Sometimes I can't use my knife and fork."

"And so?" said the doctor.

"So I use a spoon."

"You're not giving me much to go on," the doctor said. "Have you tried eating with your fingers?"

It was his little joke, she saw. I will bear it, she thought. I won't abuse my powers by foreseeing about him. I'll just be calm, and try and be ordinary. "Look, I'll tell you what my friend thinks." She put Colette's theory to him.

"You women!" the doctor exclaimed. "You all think you've got multiple sclerosis! It beats me, why you're all so keen to be in wheelchairs. Shoes off, please, and step on these scales."

Al tried to ease her feet out of her sandals. They were stuck, the straps embedded in her flesh. "Sorry, sorry," she said, bending down to unbuckle them, peel the leather away.

"Come on, come on," the doctor said. "There are people waiting out there."

She kicked away her shoes and stepped on the scales. She stared at the paint on the wall, and then, nerving herself, she glanced down. She couldn't see past herself, to read the figure.

"Oh, dear, oh, dear," the doctor said. "Get the nurse to test your wee. You're probably diabetic. I suppose we ought to get your cholesterol checked, though I don't know why we bother. Be cheaper to send a patrol officer to confiscate your crisps and beer. When did you last have a blood-pressure check?"

She shrugged.

"Sit here," he said. "Never mind your shoes, we haven't time for that, you can get back into your shoes when you get outside. Roll up your sleeve."

Al touched her own warm skin. She was wearing a short-sleeved T-shirt. She hardly liked to draw attention to it. "It is rolled up," she whispered.

The doctor clasped a band around her arm. His other hand began to pump. "Oh, dear, oh, dear. At this level I would always treat." He shot a glance upward, at her face. "Thyroid's probably shot, come to that."

He turned away and tapped his keyboard. He said, "We don't seem to have seen you before."

"That would be right."

"You're not registered with two doctors, are you? Because I should have expected a person in your state to be in here twice a week. You're not moonlighting? Signed up with another practice? Because if you are, I warn you, the system will catch up with you. You can't pull that stunt."

Her head began hurting. The doctor typed. Al fingered her scalp, as if feeling for the lumpy thread of an old scar. I got that somewhere in my past lives, she thought, when I was a labourer in the fields. Years passed like that, back bent, head down. A lifetime, two, three, four. I suppose there's always a call for labourers.

"Now I'm going to try you on these," the doctor said. "These are for your blood pressure. Book in with the nurse for a three-month check. These are for your thyroid. One a day. Just one, mind. No point you doubling the dose, Miss—er—Hart, because all that will do is ensure your total endocrine collapse takes place sooner than scheduled. Here you are."

"Shall I come back?" she asked. "To see you personally? Though not too often?"

"See how it goes," the doctor said, nodding and sucking his lip. But he was not nodding to her in particular. He was already thinking of the next patient, and as he wiped her from the screen, he erased her from his mind, and a well-drilled cheeriness overtook him. "Oh, yes," he said, rubbing his forehead, "Wait, Miss Hart—not depressed at all, are you? We can do a lot for that, you know."

When Colette saw Al shuffling down the passage into the waiting area, trying to keep her unbuckled sandals on her feet, she threw down her magazine, drew her feet from the table, and leaped up, balancing sweetly like a member of a dance troupe. It's nice to be lighter! she thought; Al's diet was working, though not for Al. "Well? So have you got MS?"

"I dunno," Al said.

"What do you mean, Al, you *don't know*? You went in there with a specific question, and I should think you could come out with an answer, yes or bloody no."

"It wasn't that simple," Al said.

"What was the doctor like?"

"He was bald and nasty."

"I see," Colette said. "Fasten your shoes."

Al bent at the waist: where her waist would be. "I can't reach," she said pitifully. By the reception desk, she put one foot on a vacant chair and bent over. A receptionist tapped the glass. *Tap-tap, tap-tap.* Startled, Al wobbled; her body trembled; Colette leaned against her, to prop her upright. "Let's go," Al said, limping faster. When they reached the car she opened the door, plopped her right foot on the doorsill, and fastened her sandal.

"Just get in," Colette said. "In this heat, doing up the other foot will kill you."

Al heaved herself into her seat, scooping up her left shoe with her toe. "I could have made him a prediction," she said, "but I didn't. He says it could be my thyroid."

"Did he give you a diet plan?"

Al slammed the passenger door. She tried to worm her swollen foot into her shoe. "I'm like an Ugly Sister," she said. She took out a cologne tissue and fumbled with the sachet. "Ninety-six degrees is too much, in England."

"Give it here." Colette snatched the sachet and ripped it open.

"And for some reason, the neighbours seem to think I'm responsible."

Colette smirked.

Al mopped her forehead. "That doctor, I could see straight through him. His liver's beyond saving. So I didn't mention it."

"Why not?"

"No point. I wanted to do a good action."

Colette said, "Oh, give over!"

They came to a halt in the drive of number twelve. "You don't understand," Al said. "I wanted to do a good action but I never seem to manage it. It's not enough just to be nice. It's not enough just to ignore it when people put you down. It's not enough to be—forbearing. You have to do a good action."

"Why?"

"To stop Morris coming back."

"And what makes you think he will?"

"The tape. Him and Aitkenside, talking about pickles. My feet and hands tingling."

"You didn't say this was work-related! So we've been through this for nothing?"

"You haven't been through anything. It's only me had to listen to that stinky old soak criticizing my weight."

"It can stand criticism."

"And though I could have made him a prediction, I didn't. A good action means—I know you don't understand, so shut up now, Colette, you might learn something. A good action might mean that you sacrificed yourself. Or that you gave your money away."

"Where did you get this stuff?" Colette said. "Out of RE at school?"

"I never had religious education," Alison said. "Not after I was thirteen. I was always made to stand in the corridor. That lesson, it would tend to lead to Morris and people trying to materialize. So I got sent out. I don't seem to feel the lack of it. I know the difference between right and wrong. I'm sure I always did."

"Will you stop this drivel?" Colette said, wailing. "You never think of me, do you! You don't seem to realize how I'm fixed! Gavin's going out with a supermodel!"

A week passed. Al had filled her prescriptions. Her heart now beat slowly, thump, thump, like a lead weight swinging in space. The change was not disagreeable; she felt slower, though, as if her every action and perception were deliberate now, as if she was nobody's fool. No wonder Colette's been so spiteful, she thought. Supermodel, eh?

She stood at the front window, looking out over Admiral Drive. A solitary vehicle ploughed to and fro across the children's playground, turning up mud. The builders had put down asphalt at one stage, but then the surface had seemed to heave and split, and cracks developed, which the neighbours stood wondering at, leaning on the temporary fence; within a week or two weeds were pushing through the hard core, and the men had moved in again to break up what remained with pneumatic drills, dig out the rubble, and reduce it back to bare earth.

Sometimes the neighbours accosted the workmen, shouting at them over the noise of their machines, but none of them got the same story twice. The local press was strangely silent, and their silence was variously attributed to stupidity and bribes. From time to time the knotweed rumour resurfaced. "You can't keep down knotweed," Evan said. "Especially not if it's mutated." No actual white worms had been spotted, or none that anyone had admitted to. The residents felt trapped and baffled. They didn't want public attention, yet they wanted to sue somebody; they thought it was their entitlement.

Al caught sight of Mart, down at the children's playground. He was wearing his brickie's hat, and he appeared so suddenly in the middle distance that she wondered if he'd come up through one of the secret tunnels the neighbours were speculating about.

"How are you doing?" he yelled.

"Okay." Her feet were moving sideways and every which ways, but by tacking to the left then abruptly changing course she managed to manoeuvre herself down the hill towards him. "Are you working here, then, Mart?"

"I've been put on digging," he said. "We're remediating, that's the nature of it and the job description. Did you ever have a job description?"

"No, not me," she said. "I make it up as I go along. So what's remediating?"

"You see this soil?" He pointed to one heap. "This is what we're taking off. And you see this?" He pointed to another heap of soil, very similar. "This is what we're putting down instead."

"So who are you working for?"

Mart looked wild. "Subcontracting," he said. "Cash in hand."

"Where are you living?"

"Dossing at Pinto's. His floor got put down again."

"So you got rid of the rats?"

"In the end. Some pikey come round with a dog."

"Pikey?"

"You know. Gypsy fella."

"What was his name?"

"He didn't say any name. Pinto met him down the pub."

Al thought, if a man is always no more than three feet from a rat—or is it two?—how does that feel from the rats' point of view? Do they spend the whole of their lives in trembling? Do they tell each other nightmare stories about a gypsy with a terrier on a rope?

"How's the old shed?" Mart said. He spoke as if it were some foolish indulgence of his youth.

"Much as you left it."

"I was thinking I might get the odd night there. If your friend had no big objection."

"She does have a big objection. So do the neighbours. They think you're an asylum seeker."

"Oh, go on, missus," Mart said. "It's just for when Pinto says, Mart, take a walk. Then we could have a chat again. And if you've got the money we could get a takeaway."

"Are you remembering your pills, Mart?"

"On and off. They're after meals. I don't always get a meal. It was better when I was living in your shed and you was bringing a tray and reminding me."

"But you know that couldn't go on."

"Because of your friend."

I will continue to do a good action, she thought. "Wait there, Mart," she said. She went back into the house, took a twenty out of her purse. When she got back, Mart was sitting on the ground.

"They're going to be water-jetting the sewers soon," Mart said. "It's due to complaints and concerns."

"You'd better look busy," she said. "Or you'll get the sack."

"The lads have gone on their lunch," Mart said. "But I don't have a lunch."

"Now you can get one," she said, handing over the bank note.

Mart stared at it. She thought he was going to say, that's not a lunch. She said, "It represents a lunch. You get what you want."

"But I'm barred."

"Your mates will go for you."

"I'd rather you made me a lunch."

"Yes, but that's not going to happen."

She turned her back and plodded away. I want to do a good action. But. It won't help him to hang around here. On the doorstep of the Collingwood she turned and looked back at him. He was sitting on the ground again, in the freshly dug soil, like a gravedigger's assistant. You could spend your life trying to fit Mart together, she thought. There's no cause and effect to him. He feels as if he might be the clue to something or other, made up as he is out of bits and pieces of the past and the fag end of other people's phrases. He's like a picture where you don't know which way up it goes. He's like a walking jigsaw, but you've lost the box lid to him.

She was closing the front door, when he called out to her. She stepped outside again. He loped towards her, his twenty screwed up in his fist.

"Forgot to ask you. If in case of a terrorist outrage, could I come in your shed?"

"Mart," she said warningly, and began to close the door.

"No, but," he said. "It was at the Neighbourhood Watch last week."

She stared at him. "You went to the meeting?"

"I sneaked in the back."

"But why?"

"Keep my eye on Delingbole."

"I see."

"And the message was, in case of terrorist outrage or nuclear explosion, go indoors."

"That seems sensible."

"So if there's one of those, can I come back and live in the shed? You're supposed to stock up with a first-aid kit to include scissors, a wind-up radio—but I dunno what one is—and tins of tuna fish and beans, which I have, plus a tin opener to open them with."

"And then what do you do?" She thought, I wish I'd gone to this meeting.

"Then you sit tight, listen to the radio, and eat your beans."

"Till such time as?"

"What?"

"I mean, when is it safe to come out?"

Mart shrugged. "I suppose when Delingbole comes round and tells you. But he might not ever tell me because he hates me. So I'd just starve to death."

Alison sighed. From under his brickie's hat, Mart rolled a fallow eye at her. "Okay," she said. "How about this? In case of terrorist outrage or nuclear explosion, never mind the shed, you can come and live in our house."

"But she won't let me."

"I'll tell her you're my guest."

"That won't make no difference."

He shows sense, Al thought.

"A bloke was here," he said, "looking for you. Yesterday. In a van."

"Oh, that would be the courier," she said. They were expecting some more party packs from Truro.

"You was out."

"Funny he didn't leave a card. Unless Colette picked it up and didn't say."

"He didn't leave a card, he didn't leave a trace," Mart said. He clapped his belly. "How about tea?"

"Mart, get back over there and start digging. These are testing times. We've all got to put a bit of effort in."

"You wouldn't give me a hand, would you?"

"What, with the digging? Look, Mart, I don't do outdoors, horses for courses, I'm in here earning a twenty so I can give it you. What would your mates say if they came back and found me doing your job for you? They'd laugh at you."

"They laugh at me anyway."

"But that's because you don't get on with the job. You should have self-respect! That's what's important to all of us."

"Is it?"

"Yes. That's what people used to call it, now they call it self-esteem, but same difference. People are always trying to take it away from you. Don't let them. You have to have backbone. Pride. So! You see! Get digging!" She stumped away, then stopped and turned. "This man, Mart, this courier. What did it say on the side of his van?" As an afterthought, she added, "Can you read?"

"I can," Mart said, "but not a plain van with no writing. It didn't say his name or anything. There was mud up the side of it, though."

"So did he speak to you? I mean, did he have a box that he was wanting to leave, did he have a clipboard or one of those computers that you sign on, you know?"

"He had boxes. He opened the back doors and I looked in. He had boxes stacked up. But he didn't leave any."

A terrible uprush of fear swept over her. She thought her new heart pills prohibited such a feeling. But seemingly not.

"What type of bloke was he?" she said.

"He was one of them type of blokes what always hits you. The kind that, you're in a pub, and he says, oi, mate, what you looking at? and you say, nothing, mate, and then he says—"

"Yes, I get the picture," Al said.

"—and then the next thing you know is you're in the hospital," said Mart. "Having yourself stitched together. Your ears all sliced and blood down your jersey, if you have a jersey. And your teef spitting out of your head."

• • •

In her own room, Alison took an extra heart pill. For as long as she could en-
dure, she sat on the edge of the bed, hoping it would take effect. But her
pulse wouldn't slow; it's remarkable, she thought, how you can be both
bored and frightened at the same time. That's a reasonable way, she thought,
to describe my life with the fiends: I lived with them, they lived with me, my
childhood was spent in the half-light, waiting for my talent to develop and my
means of making a living, knowing always, knowing always I owed my existence to them; for didn't a voice say, where d'you fink your mum gets the
money to go down the shop and get instant mash, if it ain't from your uncle
Morris; where d'you fink your mum gets funding for her little bevvy, if it ain't
from your uncle Keef?

She took off her clothes: peeling them wetly from her body, dropping
them on the floor. Colette was right, of course; she should be on a diet, any
diet, all the diets at once. If TV, as people said, put extra weight on you, then
she would look like—she couldn't think what she would look like, something
ridiculous, perhaps faintly menacing. Something from a sci-fi channel. She
felt her aura wobbling around her, as if she were wearing a giant's cape made
of jelly. She pinched herself. The thyroid pills had not made any instant im-
pact on her flesh. She imagined how it would be if she woke up one morning, to find she had shed layers of herself, like someone taking off a winter
coat—then two coats, then three. . . . She took handfuls of flesh from here
and there, repositioned and resettled them. She viewed herself from all an-
gles but she couldn't produce a better effect. I try my best with the diets, she
said to herself; but I have to house so many people. My flesh is so capacious;
I am a settlement, a place of safety, a bombproof shelter. *"Boom,"* she said
softly. She swayed on her feet, rocked back on her heels. Through the long
mirror she watched herself, rocking. When she was accustomed to her re-
flection, inured to it, she turned her back; craning her chin over her shoulder,
she could see the raised, silver lines of her scars. In hot weather like this they
seemed to puff and whiten, whereas in winter they seemed to shrink, red-
den, and pull. But perhaps that was her imagination. In her imagination,
someone said, "The tricky little bitch. We'll show her what a knife can do."

Cold sweat sprang out across her back. Colette was right, Colette is right, she has to take me in hand, she has to hate me, it is important someone hates me. I liked it when Mart came and we got the takeaway, but I should have left it all to him. Though in all conscience I didn't do it for the sake of the spare ribs. I did it because I wanted to do a good action. Colette never does a good action because she is being thin; it is what she does instead. See how she has starved herself, just to teach me, just to shame me, and see how impervious I am to example. In the last week or two, Colette's wheat-coloured clothes had hung on her like bleached sacks. So cheer up, Al thought, we can go shopping. We can go shopping, me for a bigger size and Colette for a smaller. That will put her in a good mood.

The phone rang, making her jump. She sat down, naked, to take the call.

"Alison Hart, how may I help you today?"

"Oh, Miss Hart . . . is that you in person?"

"Yes."

"So you are real? I thought you might be a call centre. Do you offer dowsing?"

"It depends what for. I do missing jewellery, old insurance policies, concealed wills. I don't do lost computer files or any type of electronic recovery. I charge a flat-rate call-out fee, which depends on your area, and then after that I work on a no-find no-fee basis. I do indoor work only."

"Really?"

"I'm not suited to distances, or rough terrain."

"But it's the outside that's worrying us."

"Then you need my colleague Raven, who specializes in earth energies, neolithic burials, mounds, caverns, burrows, and henges."

"But you're in my area," the woman said. "That's why I rang. I'm going by your telephone code in your ad."

"What is it you're actually looking for?"

"Actually, uranium," the woman said.

Al said, "Oh, dear. I do think it's Raven you want." I expect he'll be branching out, she thought, if these poisonings continue: knotweed, the bad drains. He'll be branching out into sludge and toxic seepages, and detecting the walls of underground installations. If there were walls beneath my feet, she thought, if there were occult silos and excavations, cavities blasted in the earth, would I know? If there were secret chambers and bricked-in cul-de-sacs, would I sense them?

"Are you still there?" she asked the client. She imparted Raven's details: his e-mail, and so on. It was hard to get the woman off the phone; she seemed to want some sort of free extra, like, I'll throw you in a tarot reading, pick one card of three. It's a while since I unwrapped the cards, Al thought. She said to the woman, "I really ought to go, because I have, you know, another client coming in—well, fifteen minutes, and—oh, dear, what is that smell? Oh, dear, I think I've left something on the stove. . . ." She held the phone away from her ear, and still the woman talked, and she thought, Colette, where are you, get this woman off the line. . . . She threw the receiver down on the bed and ran out of the room.

She stood on the landing, naked. I never did any science at school, she thought, any chemistry or physics, so I can't advise these people about the likelihood of aliens or rabies or uranium or knotweed or anything at all really. Imagine, she said to herself, Morris let loose in a laboratory, all his friends trapped in a test tube, amalgamating and reacting against each other and causing little puffs and whiffs. Then she said to herself, don't imagine, because it is imagining that gives them the door to get in. If you were thinner they would have less space to live. Yes, Colette was right and right again.

She knelt down, leaned forward, and tucked her head down by her knees. "Boom!" she said softly. "Boom!" She crunched herself down as small as she could go and said to herself a phrase she did not know she knew: Sauve qui peut.

She rocked her body, back and to, back and to. Presently she felt stronger: as if a shell, as if the back of a tortoise, might have grown over her spine. Tortoises live for many years, she thought, they outlive human beings. No one really loves them for they have no lovable qualities, but they are admired just for lasting out. They don't speak, they just don't utter at all. They are okay as long as no one turns them upside down and shows their underside, which is their soft bits. She said to herself, when I was a child I had a tortoise for a pet. The name of my tortoise was Alison, I named it after me because it is like me, and with our slow feet we walk in the garden. With my tortoise at weekends I have many enjoyable times. The food of my tortoise is bollocks grass and blood.

She thought, the fiends are on their way, the question is how fast and who is first. If I cannot enjoy a nice childhood thought about a tortoise I might have had but didn't, then I can expect Morris will shortly be limping in my direction though I believed he had gone on to higher things. Unless I am the higher things. After all, I tried to do a good action. I try to be a higher thing myself, but why does something inside me always say, but? Thinking *but*, she squashed herself down hard. She tried to put her chin onto the carpet, so she could look up, as if she were emerging from her shell. To her surprise— she had not tried this sort of thing before—she found it anatomically impossible. What came naturally was to tuck her head into her shielding spine, her plaited fingers protecting her fontanel.

In this position Colette found her, as she scampered lightly up the stairs, coming back from a meeting with their tax advisor. "Colette," she said to the carpet, "you were right all along."

These were the words that saved her; protected her from the worst of what Colette could have said, when she extended a cool hand to help her up and finally, admitting the task beyond her, brought a chair upon which Alison could place her forearms, and from there, lever herself into a position that seemed like an undignified sexual invitation, and from there, upright. One hand was spread across her heaving diaphragm, another crept down to cover her private parts—"which I've seen, already, once this week," Colette snapped, "and once too much, thank you, so if you don't mind getting dressed—or at least covering yourself up decently, if the idea of getting dressed is too challenging—you might come down when you're ready and I'll tell you what Mr. Colefax has to say about short-term savings rates."

For an hour, Alison lay on her bed to recover. A client called for a tarot reading, and she saw her cards so clearly in her mind that really, she might as well have jumped up and done it and earned the money, but she heard Colette making tactful excuses, taking the client into her confidence and saying that she knew she would understand, the unpredictable demands placed on Alison's talent meant that she couldn't always give of her best, so when she said she needed rest that must be respected . . . she heard Colette book the woman in for a callback, and impress on her the fact that she must be standing to attention when it came, ready for Alison, even if her house were on fire.

When she felt able, she sat upright; she ran a tepid bath, dipped herself in and out of it, and felt no cleaner. She didn't want hot water, which would make her scars flare. She lifted her heavy breasts and soaped beneath them, handling each one as if it were a weight of dead meat that happened to adhere to her chest.

She dried herself, put on the lightest dress she owned. She crept downstairs and, by way of the kitchen, into the garden. The weeds between the paving had withered, and the lawn was rock-hard. She looked down; snaky cracks crossed the ground.

"Ali!" came the cry. It was Evan, out poisoning his own weeds, his spray gun slung like a bandolier across his bare chest.

"Evan!" She moved stiffly, patiently, towards the fence. She was wearing her fluffy winter slippers, because her swollen feet wouldn't go into any other shoes; she hoped Evan wouldn't notice, and it was true he didn't notice much.

"I don't know," he said, "why did we ever pay the extra five K for a garden due south?"

"Why did we?" she said heartily, buying time.

"Personally I did it because I was told it would boost the resale value," Evan said. "And you?"

"Oh, the same," she said.

"But we couldn't have known what climate change had in store, eh? Not the most of us. But you must have known?" Evan giggled. "What's tomorrow, eh? Ninety-eight and rising?"

She stood in the doorway of Colette's room, where she did not usually intrude: she stood and watched Colette, who was gazing into her computer screen, and talked to her, in a good-humoured, light sort of way. She said, the neighbours seem to think I have supernatural knowledge of what the weather's going to be, and some of them are ringing me up to search for uranium and dangerous chemicals. I've had to say I don't do that, I've handed them on to Raven, but today's been quite good and quite busy, I've got lots of repeat telephone business,

I know I always say to you I prefer face-to-face, but you always said, it limits you, it really limits you geographically and basically you can do it fine over the phone if you learn to listen hard, well you're right, Colette, I have learned to listen hard and in a different way, you were right about that as you have been right about everything. And thank you for protecting me today from my client, I will phone her back, I will, you did the right thing, you always do the right thing, if I took notice of you, Colette, I would be thin and rich.

Colette saved her screen, and then, without looking at Al, she said, "Yes, all that is true, but why were you naked and curled into a ball at the top of the stairs?"

Al padded downstairs in her furry slippers. Another red, blazing evening had come; when she went into the kitchen, it was filled with a hellish light. She opened the fridge. To her knowledge, she had not eaten that day. Can I please have an egg? she asked herself. In Colette's voice, she said, yes, just one. There was a sound behind her, a little tapping noise. Painfully—every bit of her was stiff and aching—she moved herself around, to look behind her; around again, to take in the whole room. "Colette?" she said.

Tap-tap. Tap-tap. It was coming from the window. No one was there. She crossed the room. She looked out into the garden. It was empty. Or seemed so.

She unlocked the back door and stepped out. She heard the train rumbling through Brookwood, the distant background roar of Heathrow, Gatwick. A few drops of rain fell, hot swollen drops. Lifting her head, she called out, "Bob Fox?"

The rain plopped onto her face and ran backwards into her hair. She listened. There was no reply.

"Bob Fox, is that you? "She gazed out into the milky darkness; there was a fugitive movement, towards the back fence, but that could be Mart, seeking shelter from some civic catastrophe. I could have imagined it, she thought. I don't want to be premature. But.

eleven

You can understand it, Al thought. Fiends would be attracted to any site where there's diggings, workings, companies of men going about men's business, where there's smoking, betting, and swearing; where there are vans running around, and trenches dug where you could conceal things.

She lay on the sofa; the tarot cards slid from her hands and fanned out on the carpet. She levered herself upright, dabbing at her face, to see how the cards had fallen. The two of pentacles is the card of the self-employed, indicating uncertainty of income, restlessness, fluctuation, an unquiet mind, and an imbalance between the output of energy and the inflow of money. It is one of those cards so doubled and ambivalent in its meanings that if you draw it reversed it hardly matters much; it then suggests mounting debt, and the swing between paralyzed despair and stupid overconfidence. It's not a card you want to draw when you're making next year's business plan.

Colette had got her online these days, e-mailing predictions around the globe and doing readings for people in different time zones. "I'd like to make you a global brand," Colette said. "Like . . ." Her sentence had tailed off. She could only think of fat things, like McDonald's and Coca-Cola. In Al's belief, the four of swords governed the Internet. Its colour was electric blue and its influence bore on people in a crowd, on the meetings of groups, on ideas that had mass appeal. Not all the psychics agreed; some backed the claims of the four, five, and six of cups, which govern secret areas of knowledge, recycled concepts, and work pursued in windowless rooms such as cellars or basements. As read by Mrs. Etchells, the four of swords indicated a short stay in hospital.

The weather broke; it thundered, then rained hard. The water ran down the patio doors in scallops and festoons. Afterwards, the gardens steamed under a whitening sky. Then the sun struggled through and the cycle began again, the buildup of unbearable heat. But if you looked into the crystal ball you could see shifting cloudbanks, as if it were making its own weather.

I don't understand it, Colette said, peering in. I cleaned it yesterday.

She read for Colette and said, oh, look, the two of cups. Colette said, wait, I know that one, that means a partner, that means a man for me. Her optimism was endearing, Al supposed. The spread was short on the major arcana, as if Fate wasn't really bothered about Colette.

Colette yelled. "Silvana on the phone. Are you up for team psychics?" Al picked up the phone by her own computer. "Oh, Silvana," she said. "What's team psychics then?"

Silvana said. "It's a way to keep the excitement going, we thought. Up on the stage, twenty minutes, in and out, no time to get into anything deep and sticky; you're on, you're off, you leave them asking for more. Six times twenty minutes with shortest possible changeover is two hours, add in twenty minutes interval, and you're away by ten-thirty, which means everybody can get home the same night, nice hot chocolate and a cheese toastie, tucked up in your own bed by midnight, which means you're fresh the next day and up with the lark and manning the phones. Which looks to me like a good deal all round."

"Sounds all right," Al said, cautiously.

"We'd have come to you first off, except woss-name—Colette—she's always so offhand and snotty."

Yes, I'm afraid she is, Al thought, which is why I was last pick—

"Which is why you were last pick for the hen parties," Silvana said. "But anyway, no hard feelings, Mandy said I should try you. She said one thing about Al, she's nobody's fool but she is the forgiving type, she says, there's no malice or harm in her anywhere. So our problem is, we've advertised Six Sensational Psychics, but Glenora's dropped out."

"Why?"

"She had a premonition."

"Oh, she's always having those. She should get over herself. Where is it?"

"The Fig and Pheasant. You know. The steak house."

Oh, dear. Not one of Colette's favourite venues. "So it's who?"

"Me, Cara, Gemma, Mrs. Etchells, Mandy, and then you."

"You're a bit light on men. Can't you phone Merlyn?"

"We did. But his book came out, and he's gone to Beverly Hills."

It put Colette in a temper, the whole thing: the news about Merlyn, the insult of being called up last, and the fact that they would be performing at short notice in a so-called banqueting suite, cleared for the occasion, where beyond the wall a mega sports screen in the bar would be roaring with football chants, and in the "family area" a bunch of low-rent diners would be grimly hacking their way though honey-basted chicken kebabs.

She made her feelings known.

Alison drew the Papessa, with her veiled lunar face. She represents the inward world of women who love women, the pull of moods and gut feelings. She represents the mother, especially the widowed mother, the bereft *feme sole*, the one who is uncovered and abject and alone. She represents those things which are hidden and slowly make their way to the surface: she governs the virtue of patience, which leads to the revelation of secrets, the gradual drawing back of the velvet cloth, the pulling of the curtain. She governs temperature fluctuation and the body's deep hormonal tides, besides the tide of fortune which leads to birth, stillbirth, the accidents and freaks of nature.

Next morning, when Colette came downstairs, her temper had not improved. "What's this? A fucking midnight feast?"

There were crumbs all over the worktop, and her precious little omelette pan lay across two rings of the hob, skidded there as if by some disdainful hand which had used and abused it. Its sides were encrusted with brown grease and a heavy smell of frying hung in the air.

Alison didn't bother to make excuses. She didn't say, I believe it was the fiends that were frying. Why protest, only to be disbelieved? Why humiliate yourself? But, she thought, I am humiliated anyway.

She rang up Silvana. "Silvy, love, you know at the Fig and Pheasant, will there be a space to set up beforehand, you know, my easel and my picture?"

Silvana sighed. "If you feel you've got to, Al. But frankly, darling, a few of us have remarked that it's time you retired that photo. I don't know where you got it done."

Oh, you *wish*, Al thought, you wish you did, you'd be round there like a shot, getting yourself flattered. "It will have to do me for this week," she said, good-humoured. "Okay, see you tomorrow night."

Next day when they came to pack the car, they couldn't find her silk, her apricot silk for draping the portrait. But it's always, always, she said, in just the same place, unless it's in the wash, and to prove to herself it wasn't she turned out her laundry basket, and then turned out Colette's.

Her heart wasn't in it, she knew it had vanished or been filched. For a week she had noticed the loss of small objects from her bathroom and dressing table.

Colette came in. "I looked in the washing machine," she said.

"And? It's not there, is it?"

Colette said, "No. But you might like to look for yourself."

In the kitchen, Colette had been running the extractor fan, and spraying room freshener. But the odour of burst fat still hung in the air. Al bent down and looked into the washing machine. Her hand shrank from it, but she picked out the object inside. She held it up, frowning. It was a man's sock, grey, woolly, the heel gone into holes.

So this is what it's led to, she thought; Morris going on a course. It's led to him sucking away my silk and my nail scissors and my migraine pills, and taking eggs out of the fridge and frying them. It's led to him intruding his sock into Colette's sight: and soon, perhaps, his foot. She looked over her shoulder, as if he might have materialized entirely; as if he might be sitting on the hob and taunting her.

Colette said, "You've had that vagrant in."

"Mart?" How wrong can you be?

"I've seen him hanging around," Colette said, "but I draw the line at his actual admission to the premises, I mean his using the cooking facilities and our utilities. I suppose that would account for the lavatory seat left up, which I have found on several occasions over the last few days. You have to decide who's living here, Alison, and if it's him or me, I'm afraid it won't be me. As for the frying, and the bread that was obviously brought in somehow, that will have to rest with your own conscience. There isn't a diet on this earth that allows the wholescale consumption of animal fats and burning another person's pan. As for the sock—I suppose I should be glad I didn't find it before it was washed."

The Fig and Pheasant, under a more dignified name, had once been a coaching inn, and its frontage was still spattered with the exudates of a narrow busy A-road. In the sixties it had stood near-derelict and draughty, with a few down-at-heel regulars huddled into a corner of its cavernous rooms. In the seventies it was bought out by a steak-house chain and Tudorized, fitted with plywood oak-stained panels and those deep-buttoned settles covered in stain-proof plush of which the Tudors were so fond. It offered the novelty of baked potatoes wrapped in foil, with butter or sour cream, and a choice of cod or haddock in bread crumbs, accompanied by salad or greyish and lukewarm peas. With each decade, as its ownership had changed, experiments in theming had suceeded each other, until its original menu had acquired retro-chic, and prawn cocktails had reappeared. Plus there was bruschetta. There was ricotta. There was a Junior Menu of pasta shapes and fish bites, and tiny sausages like the finger that the witch tested for plumpness. There were dusty ruched curtains and vaguely William Morris wallpaper, washable but not proof against kids wiping their hands down it, just as they did at home. In the Sports Bar, where smoking was banned, the ceilings were falsely yellowed, to simulate years of tobacco poisoning; it had been done thirty years ago, and no one saw reason to interfere with it.

To get to the function room you had to push through the bar, past the winking fruit machines. Colette got a round in, counting on her fingers: Gemma, Cara, Silvana, Natasha—four large vodka tonics, include me in and make that five, sweet sherry for Mrs. Etchells, and a fizzy water for Alison.

The internal walls were thin, porous; at the noisy reenactment of early evening goals the rooms seemed to rock, and cooking smells crept into the nostrils of the Sensitives as they gathered in an airless hutch behind the stage. The mood was militant. Mandy read out the order.

"I'll only do twenty minutes because of my arthritis," Mrs. Etchells said, and Mandy said, "Look, love, you were only doing twenty minutes anyway, that's the whole idea, it's like a tag team, or passing the baton."

"Oh, I couldn't do anything like that," Mrs. Etchells said.

Mandy sighed. "Forget I spoke. You just do your usual. You can have a chair on stage if you want. Colette, do you think you could find her a chair?"

"That's not my job."

"Perhaps not, but couldn't you show a bit of team spirit?"

"I've already agreed to do the microphone. That's enough."

"I'll get Mrs. E a chair," Al said.

Mrs. Etchells said, "She never calls me granny, you know."

"We can go into that another time," Al said.

"I could tell you a story," Mrs. Etchells said. "I could tell you a thing or two about Alison that would knock your socks off. Oh, you think you've seen it all, you young 'uns. You've seen nothing, let me tell you."

When the card Papessa is reversed, it hints that problems go deeper than you think. It warns you of the hidden hand of a female enemy, but it doesn't oblige by telling you who she is.

"Let's kick it off, shall we?" said Cara. From beyond the wall came a long roar of *Go-o-o-al!*

It's raw, this kind of work, and near the knuckle: unsupported by music, lighting, video screen, it's just you and them, you and them and the dead, the dead who may oblige or may not, who may confuse and mislead and laugh at you, who may give you bursts of foul language very close up in your ear, who may give you false names and lay false trails just to see you embarrassed. There's no leeway for a prolonged course of error and no time to retrieve a misstep, so you must move on, move on. The punters all think they are talented now, gifted. They've been told so often that everyone has dormant psychic powers that they're only waiting for the opportunity for theirs to wake up, preferably in public. So you have to suppress them. The less they get to say, the better. Besides, the psychics need to avoid any charge of complicity, of soliciting information. Times have changed and the punters are aggressive. Once they shrank from the psychics, but now the psychics shrink from them.

"Don't worry," Gemma said, "I won't stand for any nonsense." Her face grim, she stepped out to begin.

"Go, girl!" Cara said defiantly. "Go, go, go!"

It was a low platform; she was only a step above her audience. Her eyes scoured them as if they were a bunch of criminals. "When I come to you shout up. Do not say your name, I don't want to know your name. I want no information from you but yes or no. I need a minute. I need a minute of hush please; I need to attune; I need to tune in to the vibrations of Spirit World." Time was she would have told them to hold hands, but these days you don't want them to strike up alliances.

"I have it, I have it," Gemma said. Her face was strained, and she tapped the side of her head, which was a mannerism of hers. "You, have I ever seen you before, madam?"

"No," mouthed the woman.

Colette stuck the mike under her nose. "Can you give us that again, loud and clear?"

"No!" the woman roared.

Gemma was satisfied. "I'm going to give you a name. Answer yes or no. I'm going to give you the name Margaret."

"No."

"Think again. I'm going to give you the name Margaret."

"I did know a girl called—"

"Answer yes or no!"

"No."

"I'm going to give you the name Geoff. Can you take that?"

"No."

"Geoff is standing here by my side. Can you take that?"

"No," the woman whimpered.

Gemma looked as if she were going to fly from the stage and slap her. "I am going to give you a place. I am going to give you Altrincham, Cheshire, that is to say Greater Manchester. Can you take Altrincham?"

"I can take Wilmslow."

"I am not interested in Wilmslow. You, can you take Altrincham?" She jumped from the stage, gestured to Colette to hand her the microphone. She paced the aisle between them throwing out names; Jim, Geoff, Margaret. She spun a series of questions that dizzied the punters; she tied them in twisting knots with her yes or no, yes or no?; before they could think or draw breath, her fingers were clicking at them, "no need to think it over, darling, just tell me, yes or no." Yes breeds further yes and no breeds yes too. They haven't come out for the evening to say no. People aren't going to go on and on refusing her offers, or with a contemptuous hitch of her shoulders she will move on to the next prospect. "Yes? No. No? Yes."

A loud humming began inside Al's head; it was the brush of skin as a thousand dead people twiddled their thumbs. God, it's boring, this, they were saying. Her mind wandered. Where's my silk? she wondered. Whatever has Morris done with it? Her photograph on its easel looked bare without it. In the picture her smile looked thinner, almost strained, and her glowing eyes seemed to stare.

Gemma swished past her, coming off to a spatter of applause. "On you go, take your time," Silvana said to Mrs. Etchells.

Mrs. Etchells toddled forward. As she passed Alison, she muttered again, "Never called me granny."

"Get out there, you batty old witch," Gemma breathed. "You next, Cara."

"What a joy to see your faces," Mrs. Etchells began. "My name is Irene Etchells, I have been gifted with second sight from an early age, and let me tell you there has been a great deal of joy in my life. There is no place for gloom when we reach out to Spirit World. So before we can see who's with us tonight, I would like you all to join hands, and join me in a little prayer. . . ."

"She's up and running," Silvana said, satisfied.

A moment or two, and she was eliciting symptoms from a woman in the second row left: palpitations, light-headedness, a feeling of fullness in her abdomen.

Gemma stood in the wings, prompting, "Yes or no, answer yes or no."

Alison sighed. "Let her do it in her own sweet way."

"Oh, I can't do with that yes-no malarkey," Mrs. Etchells said, apparently to no one. The woman with the fullness paused, and looked offended. "There's a gentleman coming through from Spirit who's trying to help me," Mrs. Etchells said. "He begins with a K, can you take a K?"

They began negotiations. Kenneth? No, not Kenneth. Kevin? Not Kevin.

"Think, dear," Mrs. Etchells urged. "Try and think back."

In the house before Al left that evening, there had been further signs of a creeping male presence. There had been a whiff of tobacco and meat. As she was getting changed she had stepped on something with her bare foot, something rolling, round and hard. She had picked it up from the carpet; it was the gnawed stump of a pencil, the kind of pencil someone used to wear behind his ear. Aitkenside? Or Keef?

"It's Keith," Mrs. Etchells said. "K for Keith. Do you know a Keith, dear?"

I used to know one, Al thought, I used to know Keef Capstick, and now I've re-created him, brought him to mind, his pals can't be far behind. She stood up, her breathing tight, wanting to get out. The room had a close smell, damp and medicinal, like mould under a box lid.

Onstage Mrs. Etchells was smiling. "Keith is suggesting an answer to your problem, dear. About your swollen tummy. He says, well madam, are you in the pudding club?"

There was a yelp of laughter from the audience: of indignation, from the woman in the second row left. "At my age? You must be joking."

"Chance would be a fine thing, eh?" said Mrs. Etchells. "Sorry, dear, but I'm only passing on what the spirits tell me. That's all I can do, and what I'm bound to do. Keith says, miracles can 'appen. Those are his exact words. Which I have to agree with, dear. Miracles can happen, unless of course you've had a little op?"

"Dear God," Gemma whispered, "I've never known her like this."

"Been at the cooking sherry," Mandy said. "Before she came out."

"I'd have smelled it on her breath," Silvana snapped.

"Have you placed Keith, yet?" Mrs. Etchells asked. "He's laughing, you know, he's quite a joker. He says, you wouldn't catch him wiv his trousers down in your vicinity, but some geezers don't bother. They say, you don't look at the mantelpiece when you're poking the fire."

There was a puzzled silence in the hall; laughter from some; from others a hostile mutter. "They're turning," Silvana said, a warning in her voice. "Can we get her off?"

"Leave her be," Mandy said. "She's been working with Spirit more years than you've had hot dinners."

"Oops," said Mrs. Etchells. "Somebody's got their wires crossed. Now I look at you, dear, I see you're not of an age for any how's-your-father. Let's clear the vibrations, shall we? Then we'll have another go at it. You have to be able to laugh at yourself, don't you? In Spirit World there's lots of laughter. After the sunshine comes the rain. A chain of love links us to the world beyond. Let's just tune in and have a little chat."

Alison peeped out. She saw that Colette stood at the back of the room, ramrod-straight, the mike in her hand. "There's a gentleman in the back row," Mrs. Etchells said. "I'm coming to you, sir."

Colette looked up, her eyes searching the platform for guidance. Her difficulty was clear. The back row was empty. From the wings Silvana cooed, "Mrs. E, dear, he must be in spirit, that gentleman, the audience can't see him. Pass on, dear."

Mrs. Etchells said, "That gentleman at the back, on the end there, have I seen you before? Yes, I thought I had. You've got a false eye now. I knew something was different. Used to wear a patch, didn't you? I remember now."

Alison shivered. "We must get her off," she said. "Really, Mandy, it's dangerous."

A little louder, Silvana called, "Mrs. Etchells? How about some messages for the people in front?"

The audience were turning around, craning their necks and swivelling in their seats to see the empty back row: to giggle and jeer. "Aren't they ungrateful!" Cara said, "You'd think they'd be glad of a manifestation! There's obviously somebody there. Can you see him, Al?"

"No," Al said shortly.

Mrs. Etchells beamed down at the hecklers. "Sometimes I wonder what I've done to be surrounded with so much love. God gave us a beautiful world to live in. When you've had as many ops as me you learn to live for the moment. As long as the youngsters are willing to listen and learn, there's hope for this world. But now they're only willing to put dog shit through your letter box, so I don't see much hope. God has put a little light inside of us and one day we will rejoin the greater light."

"She's gone on automatic," Cara said.

"Which one of us is going to get her?" Mandy said.

"Mrs. Etchells," Silvana called, "come on now, time's up. Come on for your cup of tea."

Mrs. Etchells flapped a dismissive hand towards the wings. "Ignore that raddled little madam. Silvana? That's not her name. They none of them have their right names. She's light-fingered, that one. She comes into my house to collect me, and the next thing is the milk money's gone, the milk money that I left behind the clock. Why does she give me a lift anyway? It's only because she thinks I'll leave her something when I go over. And will I? Will I buggery. Now let us link hands and pray. Our prayers can put a chain of love around—"

She looked up, dumbfounded; she had forgotten where she was.

The audience shouted up with various silly suggestions: Margate, Cardiff, Istanbul.

"I've never seen such unkindness," Mandy breathed. "Listen to them! When I get out there, I'll make them sorry they were born."

Silvana said, "She has a nerve! That's the last lift she'll get from me."

Al said quietly, "I'll get her."

She stepped out onto the platform. The lucky opals gleamed dully, as if grit were embedded in their surface.

Mrs. Etchells turned her head towards her and said, "There's a little flower inside us that we water with our tears. So think of that, when sorrows come. God is within all of us, except Keith Capstick. I recognize him now, he had me there for a minute, but he can't fool me. He only once did a good action and that was to drag a dog off a little girl. I suppose God was within him, when he did that."

Alison approached, softly, softly, but the stage creaked beneath her.

"Oh, it's you," Mrs. Etchells said. "You remember when you used to get belted for playing with knitting needles?" She turned back to the audience. "Why did her mum have knitting needles? Ask yourself, because she never knitted. She had 'em for sticking up a girl when she's in trouble, you don't have to do that these days, they vacuum it out. She stuck a needle up herself but the baby never come out till it was good and ready, and that was Alison here. You'd see all manner of sharp objects in her house. You'd go in and the floor would be all rolling over with little dead babies, you wouldn't know where to put your feet. They all brought their girlfriends round—Capstick, MacArthur, that crew—when they found themselves with a bun in the oven."

So, Al thought, my brothers and sisters, my half brothers and sisters—every day, when I grew up, I was treading on them.

"There was hardly anybody up that way knew the joy of motherhood," Mrs. Etchells said.

Al took her arm. Mrs. Etchells resisted. Sedately, she and Mrs. Etchells tussled, and the audience laughed, and gradually Al inched the old woman towards the edge of the platform and behind the scenes. Colette stood there, a pale burning figure, like a taper in fog.

"You could have done something," Al complained.

Mrs. Etchells shook off Al's hands. "No need to molest me," she said. "You've pulled my nice new cardigan all out of shape, you've nearly had the button off. No wonder they're laughing! A laugh's all right, I like a laugh but I don't like people pointing fun at me. I'm not going back out there because I don't like what I've seen. I don't like who I seen, would be a better way to put it."

Al put her mouth close to Mrs. Etchells's ear. "MacArthur. Isn't it?"

"Yes, and the other bloody shyster, Bob Fox. All along the back row."

"Was Morris with them?"

Mandy said, "Cara, you're next, go on."

"Not me," Cara said.

Mrs. Etchells sat down and fanned herself. "I've seen something you wouldn't want to see in a month of Sundays. I saw Capstick at the back there. And the rest. All that old gang. I recognized them large as life. But they've got modifications. It was horrible. It turned me up."

Mandy stepped out onstage. Her chin jutted and her voice was crisp. "There will be a short delay. One of our Sensitives has been taken ill."

"How short?" a man shouted.

Mandy gave him a baleful glance. "As short as we can contrive. Have some compassion." She turned her back on them. Her heels clicked, back to the hutch. "Al, it's for you to decide, but I don't like the feel of Mrs. Etchell's blood pressure, and I think Colette should call an ambulance."

"Why me?" Colette said.

"Colette could drive her," Cara said. "Where's the nearest A and E?"

"Wexham Park," Colette said. She couldn't resist supplying the information, but then added, "I'm not taking her anywhere on my own. Look at her. She's gone weird."

Said Mrs. Etchells, "I could tell you a thing or two about Emmeline Cheetham. No wonder the police were always around her place. She was a big drinker and she knew some terrible people. Judge not, that ye may not be judged. But there is a word for women like her and that word is prostitute. Soldiers, we all know soldiers—Tommies, no harm in 'em. Have a drink, have a laugh, we've all done it."

"Really?" Silvana said. "Even you?"

"But no two ways about it. She was on the game. Gypsies and jockeys and sailors, it was all the same to her. She used to go down to Portsmouth. She went off after a circus once, prostituting herself to dwarves and the like, God forgive her, foreigners. Well, you don't know what you'll catch, do you?"

"Quick!" Mandy said. "Loosen her collar. She can't get her breath."

"She can choke for all I care," Silvana said.

Mandy struggled with the buttons of Mrs. Etchells's blouse. "Colette, call nine-nine-nine. Al, get out there, darling, and keep it going for as long as needed. Cara, go through into the bar and find the manager."

Al stepped out onto the stage. She took in the audience, her gaze sweeping them from left to right, front row to the back row, which was empty: except for a faint stirring and churning of the evening light. She was silent for a long moment, letting their scattered wits regroup, their attention come to rest. Then she said, slowly, softly, almost drawling, "Now, where were we?" They laughed. She looked back at them, grave, and slowly let her smile spread, and her eyes kindle. "We'll drop the yes and no," she said, "since tonight has not turned out the way we expected." She thought, but of course I have expected it, I have done nothing but expect it. "I suppose it teaches us," she said, "to expect the unexpected. It doesn't matter how many years' experience you have, Spirit can never be anticipated. When we work with Spirit we are in the presence of something powerful, something we don't completely understand, and we need to remember it. Now I have a message for the lady in row three, the lady with the eyebrow piercing. Let's get the show back on the road."

Behind her, she heard the slamming of doors. Manly cheers burst through, from the sports bar. She heard snatches of voices, a moan from Mrs. Etchells, the low rumbling voices of ambulance men: she heard Cara wailing, "She's left her chakras open. She'll die!"

They drove home. Colette said, "They took her out on a stretcher. She was a bad colour."

Al glanced down at her hands, at the leaden sheen of her rings. "Should I have gone with her? But somebody had to hold the evening together."

She thought, I didn't want that shower in the back row following me, not to a public hospital.

"She was breathing all wrong. Sort of gasping. Like, 'urg—ee, urg—ee. . . .'"

"I get the picture."

"Silvana said, she can snuff it for all I care, she can rot in hell."

"Yes."

"She said, 'I've bloody had enough of it, running around after her like a nanny, have you got your door keys, Mrs. Etchells, have you got your teeth in, have you got your spare pad for the toilet'—did you know Mrs. Etchells had an irritable bladder?"

"It might come to all of us."

"Not to me," Colette said. "If I can't get as far as the lavatory, I'll top myself. Honestly. There's only so far you can sink in self-esteem."

"If you say so."

They drove in silence, to the next traffic light. Then Al lurched forward in her seat; her seat belt dragged her back. "Colette," she said, "let me explain to you how it works. If you have lovely thoughts, you get attuned to a high level of Spirit, right? That's what Mrs. Etchells always said."

"I wouldn't call that a high level of Spirit, the one who said that old biddy was up the duff."

"Yes, but then a spirit—" she gulped; she was frightened to name him— "but then a spirit, you know who he was, had broken in on her, like a burglar—she couldn't help it, she was just transmitting his message. But you see, Colette, some people are nicer than you and me. Some people are much nicer than Mrs. Etchells. They do manage to have lovely thoughts. They have thoughts that are packed inside their head like the chocolates in an Easter egg. They can pick out any one, and it's just as sweet as the next."

The lights changed; they shot forward. "What?" Colette said.

"But other people's heads, on the inside, the content is all mixed up and it's gone putrid. They've gone rotten inside from thinking about things, things that the other sort of people never have to think about. And if you have low, rotten thoughts, not only do you get surrounded by low entities, but they start to be attracted, you see, like flies around a dustbin, and they start laying eggs in you and breeding. And ever since I was a little kid I've been trying to have nice thoughts. But how could I? My head was stuffed with memories. I can't help what's in there. And with Morris and his mates, it's damage that attracts them. They love that, some types of spirits, you can't keep them away when there's a car accident, or when some poor horse breaks its leg. And so when you have certain thoughts—thoughts you can't help—these sort of spirits come rushing round. And you can't dislodge them. Not unless you could get the inside of your head hoovered out. So if you ask why I have an evil spirit guide instead of an angel or something—"

"I don't," Colette said. "I've lost interest. I'm past caring. I just want to get in and open a bottle of wine."

"—if you ask why I have an evil guide, it's to do with the fact that I'm a bad person, because the people who were around me in my childhood were bad. They took out my will and put in their own. I wanted to do a good action by looking after Mart, but you wouldn't let me—"

"So everything's my fault, is that what you're saying?"

"—and they wouldn't let me because they want the shed to themselves. They want me, and it's because of me that they can exist. It's because of me that they can go on the way they do, Aitkenside and Keef Capstick as well as Morris, and Bob Fox and Pikey Pete. What can you do? You're only human, you think they'll play by earthside rules. But the strong thing about airside is that it has no rules. Not any we can understand. So they have the advantage there. And the bottom line is, Colette, there are more of them than us."

Colette pulled into the drive. It was half-past nine, not quite dark.

"I can't believe we're home so early," Al said.

"We cut it short, didn't we?"

"You could hardly expect Cara to go on. She was too upset."

"Cara gets on my tits. She's a wimp."

Al said, "You ask why I have an evil spirit guide, instead of an angel. You might as well ask, why do I have you for my assistant, instead of somebody nice?"

"Manager," Colette said.

As they stepped out of the car, Pikey Paul, Mrs. Etchell's spirit guide, was weeping on the paving by the dwarf conifers that divided them from Evan next door.

"Pikey Paul!" Al said. "It's years since I seen you!"

"Hello, Alison dear," sniffed the spirit guide. "Here I am, alone in this wicked world. Play your tape when you get in. She's left you a few kindly sentiments, if you want to hear them."

"I'm sure I shall!" Alison cried. She sounded, in her own ears, like someone else; someone from an earlier time. "Why, Paul," she cried, "the sequins is all fell off your jacket!"

Colette removed Al's portrait from the boot of the car. "They're right," she said. "You need to get this picture redone. No point in fighting reality, is there?"

"I don't know," Al said to her: temporizing. Said Paul, "You might fetch out a needle and a scarlet thread, darling girl, then I can stitch up my glad rags and be on my way to my next post of duties."

"Oh, Pikey Paul," she said, "do you never rest?" and "Never," he said. "I'm on my way to link up with a psychic in Wolverhampton, would you know anyone who could give me a lift up the M6?"

"Your nephew is around here somewhere," she said.

"Never speak of Pete, he's lost to me," said Paul. "I want no truck with his criminal ways."

She stood by the car, her hand resting on its roof, her face entranced.

"What's the matter with you?" Colette said.

"I was listening," she said. "Mrs. Etchells has passed."

Torches crept over Admiral Drive. It was the Neighbourhood Watch, beginning their evening search among the cow parsley meadows that led to the canal, for any poor wastrels or refugees who had grubbed in for the night.

• • •

Colette played the messages on the answering machine; several clients wanting to set up readings, and Mandy's cool level voice. . . . "on a trolley in the corridor . . . didn't linger . . . mercy really . . . given your name as next of kin." Once she had shot her first draught of sauvignon blanc down her throat, she wandered into the sitting room to see what Al was doing. The tape recorder was in action, emitting chirps and coughs.

"Want a drink?" Colette said.

"Brandy."

"In this heat?"

Al nodded. "Mrs. E," she said, "what's it like there?"

"It's interactive?" Colette asked.

"Of course it is." She repeated, "Mrs. E, what's it like in Spirit?"

"Aldershot."

"It's like Aldershot?"

"It's like home, that's what it's like. I've just looked out of the window and it's all happening, there's the living and there's the dead, there's your mum reeling down the road with a squaddie on her arm, and they're heading for hers to do the unmentionable."

"But they've demolished those houses, Mrs. Etchells. You must have been past, you only live down the road. I went past last year, Colette drove me. Where my mum used to live, it's a big car showroom now."

"Well, pardon me," said Mrs. Etchells, "but it's not demolished on this side. On this side it looks the same as ever."

Alison felt hope drain away. "And the bath still in the garden, is it?"

"And the downstairs bay got a bit of cardboard in the corner where Bob Fox tapped on it too hard."

"So it's all still going on? Just the way it used to?"

"No change that I can see."

"Mrs. Etchells, can you have a look round the back?"

"I suppose I could." There was a pause. Mrs. Etchell's breathing was laboured. Al glanced at Colette. She had flung herself onto the sofa; she wasn't hearing anything. "Rough ground," Mrs. Etchells reported. "There's a van parked."

"And the outbuildings?"

"Still there. Falling down, they'll do somebody a damage."

"And the caravan?"

"Yes, the caravan."

"And the dog runs?"

"Yes, the dog runs. Though I don't see any dogs."

Got rid of the dogs, Al thought: why?

"It all looks much the same as I remember," Mrs. Etchells said, "not that I was in the business of frequenting the back of Emmeline Cheetham's house, it wasn't a safe place for an old woman on her own."

"Mrs. Etchells—listen now—you see the van? The van parked? Could you have a peep inside?"

"Hold on," Mrs. Etchells said. More heavy breathing. Colette picked up the remote and began to flick through the TV channels.

"The windows are filthy," Mrs. Etchells reported.

"What can you see?"

"I can see an old blanket. There's something wrapped up in it." She chuckled. "Blow me if there isn't a hand peeping out."

The dead are like that; cold-blooded. Nothing squeamish left in them, no sensitivities.

"Is it my hand?" Al said.

"Well is it, I wonder?" Mrs. Etchells said. "Is it a little chubby baby hand, I wonder now?"

Colette complained, "It's like this every summer. Nothing but repeats."

"Don't torment me, Mrs. E."

"No, it looks like a grown-up woman's hand to me."

Al said, "Could it be Gloria?"

"It could at that. Now here's a special message for you, Alison dear. Keith Capstick has got his balls armour-plated now, you'll not be able to get at 'em this time. He says you can hack away all bloody day, with your scissors, carving knife or whatever you bloody got, but you'll not get anywhere. Excuse my language, but I feel bound to give you his very words."

Alison clicked off the tape. "I need a breath," she said to Colette. "A breath of air."

"I expect there'll have to be a funeral," Colette remarked.

"I expect so. I don't suppose the council will agree to take her away."

"Oh, I don't know. If we doubled her up and put her in a black bag."

"Don't. It's not funny."

"You started it." Colette made a face behind her back. Alison thought, I have seen, or I have dreamed of, a woman's body parts wrapped in newspaper. I have seen men's hands smeared with something glutinous and brown as they unloaded parcels from the back of the van, wobbling packages of dog meat. I have heard a voice behind me say, fuck, Emmie, got to wash me hands. I have looked up, and where I thought I would see my own face in the mirror, I saw the face of Morris Warren.

She went out into the garden. It was now quite dark. Evan approached the fence, with a flashlight. "Alison? We had the police out earlier."

Her heart lurched. She heard a low chuckle from behind her; it seemed to be at knee height. She didn't turn, but the hair on her arms stiffened.

"Michelle thought she saw somebody snooping about your shed. You had that tramp, didn't you, broke in? She thought it might be him again. Take no chances, so she called them out. Constable Delingbole came in person."

"Yes? And?"

"He checked it over. Couldn't see anything. But you can't be too careful, when you've got kids. That type want locking away."

"Definitely."

"I'd throw away the key."

"Oh, so would I."

She stood waiting, her hands joined at her waist, the picture of patient formality, as if she were Her Majesty waiting for him to bow out of her presence.

"I'll be getting in, then," Evan said. But he shot her a backward glance as he crossed his balding lawn.

Alison turned and stooped over a large terra-cotta pot. Bending her back, she heaved it aside, managing only to roll it a few inches. The gravel beneath appeared undisturbed; that is to say, no one had dug it up. She straightened up, rubbing the small of her back. "Morris," she said, "don't play silly beggars." She heard a scuffling; then the chuckle again, faintly muffled by the soil, coming from the very depths of the pot.

twelve

Next morning, when she was eating her lo-salt cornflakes with skimmed milk, Morris put his head around the door. "Have you seen Keith Capstick?" he asked. "Have you seen MacArthur? He has a false eye and his earlobe chewed off, and he wears a knitted weskit? Have you seen Mr. Donald Aitkenside?"

"I think I'd know them if I saw them." The skin of her entire body crept at the sight of him, as if there were a million ants walking under her clothes; but she wasn't going to let him know she was scared. "Have you forgotten who you're talking to?" she said. "Anyway, why the formality? What's this about *Mister* Aitkenside?"

Morris puffed up his chest, and tried to straighten his buckled legs. "Aitkenside's got made up to management. Aren't you informate with our new terms of employment? We've all got our training under our belt and we've all been issued wiv notebooks and pencils. Mr. Aitkenside's got certificates, too. So we're supposed to be foregathering."

"Foregathering where?"

"Here is as good as any."

"What brings you back, Morris?"

"What brings me back? I have got a mission. I have got a big job on. I have got taken on a project. You've got to retrain these days. You've got to update yourself. You don't want to go getting made redundant. There's no such thing anymore as a job for life."

Colette came in with the post in her hand. "Usual catalogues and junk mail," she said. "Mayan calendar workshop, no thanks. . . . Shamanic requisites by return. . . . What about mixed seeds from Nature's Cauldron? Henbane, wolfsbane, skullcap, hemlock?"

"Some might blow over to next door."

"That's what I was thinking. By the way, do you know you're on the phone from eleven till three?"

Al groaned. Morris, squatting before the empty marble hearth, glanced up at her and began to roll up his sleeves.

"And we've had a call from those people near Gloucester, saying are you going on the Plutonic symbolism weekend? Only they need to know how many to cater for." She laughed nastily. "And of course, they count you double."

"I'm not sure I want to go away by myself."

"Count me out, anyway. They say it's in an idyllic location. That means no shops." She flicked through the letters. "Do you do exorcisms for eating disorders?"

"Pass it on to Cara."

"Will you go over to Twyford? There's a woman got a loose spirit in her loft. It's rattling around and she can't get to sleep."

"I don't feel up to it."

"You're entitled to postpone things if you've had a bereavement. I'll call her and explain, about Mrs. Etchells."

A light blinked at Al from a corner of the room. She turned her eyes and it was gone. Morris was scuttling fast across the carpet, swinging on his knuckles like an ape. As he moved, the light moved with him, a crimson ripple, sinuous, like an exposed vein; it was Morris's snake tattoo, lit and pulsing, slithering along his forearm as if it had a life of its own.

"Tee-hee," Morris chuckled. She remembered what Mrs. Etchells had said: "They've got modifications. It turned me up."

Colette said, "Are you having that yogurt or not?"

"I've lost my appetite." Al put her spoon down.

• • •

She phoned her mum. The phone rang for a long time, and then after it was picked up there was a scuffling, scraping sound. "Just pulling up a chair," Emmie said. "Now then, who is it and what can I do for you?"

"It's me. I thought you'd like to know my grandma's dead."

"Who?"

"My grandma. Mrs. Etchells."

Emmie laughed. "That old witch. You thought she was your grandma?"

"Yes. She told me so."

"She told everybody that! All the kids. She wanted to get 'em in her house, captive bloody audience, innit, while she goes on about how she's had bouquets and whatnot, little op, chain of love, then when the time's right she's offering 'em around the district to all comers. I should know, she bloody offered me. Same with you, only the lads got in early."

"Now just stop there. You're saying my grandmother was a—" She broke off. She couldn't find the right word. "You're saying my grandmother was as bad as you?"

"Grandmother my arse."

"But Derek—listen, Derek *was* my dad, wasn't he?"

"He could of been," her mother said vaguely. "I think I done it with Derek. Ask Aitkenside, he knows who I done it with. But Derek wasn't her son, anyway. He was just some kid she took in to run errands for her."

Al closed her eyes tight. "Errands? But all these years, Mum. You let me think—"

"I didn't tell you what to think. Up to you what you thought. I told you to mind your own business. How do I know if I done it with Derek? I done it with loads of blokes. Well, you had to."

"Why did you have to?" Alison said balefully.

"You wouldn't ask that question if you were in my shoes," Emmie said. "You wouldn't have the cheek."

"I'm going to come over there," Al said. "I want to put a few straight questions to you. About your past. And mine."

Her mother shouted, "You hear that, Gloria? She's coming over. Better bake a cake, eh? Better get the fancy doilies out."

"Oh, you're not on that again, are you?" Al's voice was weary. "I thought we'd got Gloria out of our lives twenty years ago."

"So did I, pardon me, till she turned up on me doorstep the other night. I never had such a thunderclap. I says, Gloria! and she says, hello, and I says, you've not changed a bit, and she says, I can't say the same for you, she says, give us a fag, I says, how'd you track me down in Bracknell? She says—"

"Oh, Mum!" Alison yelled. "She's *dead*!"

I said it, she thought, I uttered the word no Sensitive ever uses: well hardly ever. I didn't say passed, I didn't say gone over, I said dead, and I said it because I believe that when it comes to dead, Gloria is deader than most of us, deader than most of the people who claim to be dead: in my nightmares since I was a child she is cut apart, parcelled out, chewed up.

There was a silence. "Mum? You still there?"

"I know," said Emmie, in a small voice. "I know she's dead. I just forget, is all."

"I want you to remember. I want you to stop talking to her. Because it's driving me round the twist and it always did. It's not as if you made a living out of it. So there's no use fooling yourself. You may as well get it straight and keep it straight."

"I have." Emmie sounded cowed. "I have, Alison. I will."

"So do you want to come to Mrs. Etchells's service?"

"Why?" Emmie was mystified. "Is she getting married?"

"We're burying her, Mum. I told you. Cremating. Whatever. We don't know what her wishes would have been. I was hoping you could shed some light, but obviously not. Then as soon as that's over, I'm coming to see you, and we're going to sit down and have a heart-to-heart. I don't think you're fit to live on your own. Colette says you should be living in a warden-assisted bungalow. She says we ought to make you a care plan."

"You hear that, Gloria?" said Emmie. "We'll have to polish the silver, if Lady Muck is coming to tea."

For a few days the fiends were faintly present, flickering at the corner of her eye: throughout her whole body, they left their mark. It's as if, she thought, they're walking in one by one, and wiping their feet on me. Her temperature dropped; her tongue furred up with a yellow-green coating. Her eyes looked small and bleary. Her limbs tingled and she lost sensation in her feet; they still seemed intent on walking off, leaving the whole mess behind, but though the intention was there, she no longer had the ability.

Morris said, got to get the boys together. We will be wanting a knees-up, seeing as Etchells is fetched away, and we are fully entitled in my opinion, there's one we can tick off—well done, lads—there weren't no messing about with Etchells.

"You arranged it?" she said. She had hoped their appearance in the back row of the dem might be coincidental—or rather, the kind of coincidence with unpleasant events that they liked to arrange for themselves.

" 'Course we did," Morris boasted. "What is our mission? It is to track down useless and ugly people and recycle them, and with Etchells we have made a start. I says to Mr. Aitkenside, do you mind if I kick off the project wiv a bit of personal business, and he says, Morris, old son, if I could give you the nod I would, but you know it is more than my skin's worth, for you know old Nick, his temper when he is roused, and if you don't go right through the proper procedure and your paperwork all straight he will take a pencil and ram it through your ear hole and swivel it about so your brain goes twiddle-de-dee, he says, I seen it done, and Nick has a special pencil he keeps behind his ear that makes it more painful. I says to him, Mr. Aitkenside, sir, upon my mother's life I would not ask you to take any such risk of having your brain twiddled, forget I asked, but he says, Morris, old son, we go back, he says, we go back you and me, I tell you what I'll do for you, when I happen to catch old Nick in a mellow mood—let us say we have had a good session in the back bar at the Bells of Hell, let us say Nick has won the darts, let us say we have had a barbecue on the back lawn and the great man is feeling at ease with himself—I'd say to him, Your 'Ighness, how would it be if my friend and yours Morris Warren were to do a bit of personal business, a bit of tidying up he has left over? For Nick was in the army, you know, and he likes things tidy."

"What army?" Al said.

"I don't know." Morris sounded impatient. "The army, the navy, the forces, innit, bomber command, special boat squadron, there's only one army, and that's ours. Will you stop interrupting?"

"Sorry."

"So it all worked out just like Mr. Aitkenside said it would, and I got leave, and off I go, rounding up a few of the lads *as* I go, and we pop up there and give the old biddy the fright of her life."

"What had she ever done to you?"

"Etchells? She put me out in the street. She kicked me off Spirit Guide, she wanted Pikey Paul with his shiny outfits, Poncey Paul as I call him; if he wasn't the uncle of Pete who is a mate of mine, I could cast aspersions there, I really could. I had to live in a builder's skip, under an old broken fireplace, till I could happen to move in with you."

"It's a long time to hold a grudge."

"It's not a long time, when you're dead and you've bugger-all else to do. You can't treat a guide like that—maltreat him, and it comes back on you. So anyway . . . we got ourselves down the Fig and Pheasant, we tampered with the optics and nipped the little girls' bottoms that was serving behind the bar, we strolled into the function room cool as you like and then we lined up on the back row. Etchells, blimey, you should have seen her face."

"I did."

"But you didn't see our modifications."

"So what are those? Apart from your tattoo?"

"Lifelike, innit?" Morris said. "I got it done when we was on a spot of R and R in the Far East. We got leave halfway through our course. Still, you ain't seen nothing till you seen young Dean. We oldsters, we've got enough to sicken folk as it is, by God have we a collection of scars, there's Mac with his eye socket and his chewed-off ear and Capstick with his private problem that he don't like mentioned. Pikey Pete booked in to have his teeth filed, but Dean said, you could get that earthside nowadays, mate, you could get your teeth filed and your tongue slit. Oh, but Dean did rib him! So Capstick says, I'll show willing, I'll lay my money out, so he's had his hair stood on end and his tongue rasped, but the youngsters don't think nothing of that. They've all got these new tongue extensions. You can have it hung further back so it's re-tractable, or you can have your palate heightened so your tongue rolls up neatly till required. Now Dean has opted for the last one, it costs you but it's more neat and tidy, doesn't slide out when you're walking, and Mr. Aitkenside is teaching him to take a pride in his appearance. He's going for the full scroll-out, so he'll have to wear a guard till he gets used to it, but he claims it's worth it, I dunno. He's gone in for his knees swivelled as well, so he's walking backwards when he's walking forwards; you have to see it to appreciate it, but I can tell you it's comical. Mr. Aitkenside has got six legs, so he has got six boots; that's because he has got made up to management, that's all the better for kicking them with."

Colette came in. "Al? Cara's on the phone—do you think Mrs. Etchells would have liked a woodland burial?"

"I don't think so. She hated nature."

"Right," Colette said. She went out again.

Al said, "Kicking who?"

"Not just kicking, kicking out. We are chasing out all spooks what are asylum seekers, derelicts, vagrants, and refugees, and clearing out all spectres unlawfully residing in attics, lofts, cupboards, cracks in the pavement, and holes in the ground. All spooks with no identification will be removed. It ain't good enough to say you've nowhere to go. It ain't good enough to say that your documents fell through the hole in your breeches. It's no good saying that you've forgot your name. It's no good pretending to go by the name of some other spook. It's no good saying you ain't got no documents because they ain't invented printing yet—you got your thumb print, ain't you, and it's no good saying they cut off your thumb—don't come that, they all say that. Nobody is to take up room they ain't entitled to. Show me your entitlement or I'll show you the boot—in Aitkenside's case, six boots. It's no good trying to bamboozle us because we have got targets, because Nick has set us targets, because we have got a clear-up rate."

Al said, "Is Nick management?"

"You're joking me!" Morris said. "Is Nick management? He is the manager of us all. He is in charge of the whole blooming world. Don't you know nothing, girl?"

She said, "Nick's the devil, isn't he? I remember seeing him, in the kitchen at Aldershot."

"You should have taken more notice. You should have been respectful."

"I didn't recognize him."

"What?" Morris said. "Not recognize a man wiv a leather jacket, asking for a light?"

"Yes, but you see, I didn't believe in him."

"That's where you was under a mistake."

"I was only a girl. I didn't know. They kept throwing me out of the RE class, and whose fault was that? I hadn't read any books. We never got a news-paper, except the ones the blokes brought in, their racing paper. I didn't know the history of the world."

"You should have worked harder," Morris said. "You should have listened up in your history lessons, you should have listened up in your Hitler lessons, you should have learned to say your prayers and you should have learned some manners." He mimicked her: " 'Is Nick the devil?' 'Course he's the de-vil. We have only been under pupillage with the best. Who have you got to put up against him? Only mincey Mandy and the rest, they're not worth MacArthur's fart. Only you and stringbean and that sad bastard used to live in the shed."

As the week passed, her parade of business-as-usual became less convincing, even to Colette, whom she sometimes caught gazing at her dubiously. "Is something troubling you?" she said, and Colette replied, "I don't know that I trust that doctor you saw. How about a private health check?"

Al shrugged. "They'll only talk about my weight again. If I'm going to be insulted, I'm not paying for it. I can get insults on the NHS." She thought, what the doctors fail to realize is that you need some beef, you need some heft, you need some solid substance to put up against fiends. She had been alarmed, climbing out of the bath, to see her left foot dematerialize. She blinked, and it was back again; but she knew it was not her imagination, for she heard muffled laughter from the folds of her bath towel.

That was the day they were getting ready for Mrs. Etchells's funeral. They had opted for a cremation and the minimum of fuss. A few elderly practi-tioners, Mrs. Etchells's generation, had clubbed together for a wreath, and Merlyn sent a telegram of sympathy from Beverly Hills. Al said, "You can come back to my house afterwards, Colette's got some sushi in." She thought, I ought to be able to count on my friends to help me, but they'd be out of their depth here. Cara, Gemma, even Mandy—they've had nothing like this in their lives, they've never been *offered*. They've sold spirit services; they haven't been sold, like me. She felt sad, separate, set apart; she wanted to spare them.

"Do you think in Spirit she'll be at her best age?" Gemma said. "I find it hard to picture what Mrs. Etchells's best age might have been."

"Sometime between the wars," Mandy said. "She was one of the old school, she went back to when they had ectoplasm."

"What's that?" Cara said.

"Hard to say." Mandy frowned. "It was supposed to be an ethereal substance that took on the form of the deceased. But some people say it was cheesecloth they packed in their fannies."

Cara wrinkled her nose.

"I wonder if she left a will?" Colette said.

"No doubt behind the clock, with the milk money," Gemma said.

"I hope you're not looking at me," Silvana said. She had threatened to boycott the ceremony, and only turned up out of fear that the other Sensitives might talk about her behind her back. "I don't want anything from her. If she did leave me anything, I wouldn't take it. Not after those wicked things she said about me."

"Forget it," Mandy said. "She wasn't in her right mind. She said herself, she saw something in the back row she couldn't stomach."

"I wonder what it was," Gemma said. "You wouldn't have a theory, Al, would you?"

"Anyway," Mandy said, "somebody ought to see about her affairs. You've still got a key, Silvy?" Silvana nodded. "We'll all come over. Then if there's no will in the obvious places, we can dowse for it."

"I'd rather not, myself," Al said. "I try to steer clear of Aldershot. Too many sad memories."

"There would be," Mandy said. "God knows, Al, I don't think any of us had what you'd call a regular upbringing, I mean when you're a Sensitive it's not like a normal childhood, is it? But those kind of old people tend to keep cash lying about. And we'd want a responsible witness. A relative ought to be present."

"I'm not," Al said. "A relative. As it turns out."

"Don't listen to her," Colette said. If there were any bundles of fivers to be picked up, she didn't see why Alison should lose out. "It's just what her mum's been putting into her head."

"Didn't your mum want to come today?" Gemma asked.

But Alison said, "No. She's got a house guest."

Guilty—knowing they'd been fed up with Mrs. Etchells, knowing they were glad to have her off their patch—they let the conversation drift back to discounts, to advertising rates, to Web sites, and to supplies. Gemma had found a place on the North Circular that undercut the Cornwall people on crystal-gazing kits. "Nice cauldrons," Gemma said. "Very solid. They're fibreglass, of course, but as long as they look the business. You don't want to be lugging cast iron around in the boot of your car. They go from mini to three gallon. Which is going to set you back a hundred quid, but if that's what you need, you've got to invest, haven't you?"

"I don't do much with Wicca anymore," Cara said. "I got bored of it. I'm more interested in personal development, and ridding myself and others of limiting beliefs."

"And are you still rubbing people's feet?"

"Yes, if they'll sign a disclaimer."

"It can't be very nice, remembering the womb," Gemma said.

There was a feeling among them, in fact, that nothing about the day was very nice. Mandy's nose kept twitching, as if she could smell spirits. Once the sushi and meringues were consumed, they showed no wish to linger. As they parted on the doorstep, Mandy took Al's arm and said. "If you want a bolt-hole, you know. You can soon be down in Hove. Just pick up the car keys and come as you are."

She was grateful for Mandy's tact. She obviously had her suspicions that Morris was back, but she didn't want to say anything in case he was listening in.

Sometimes Morris's voice was in her head; sometimes she found it on the tape. Sometimes he seemed to know everything about their past life together; he would talk, reprising the Aldershot days, running them back on a kind of loop, as if, like Mrs. Etchells at the dem, he'd gone on automatic. She tried every means she knew to tune him out; she played loud music, and distracted herself by long phone calls, going through her contacts book for the numbers of psychics she had known years ago, and calling them up to say, "Hi, guess who?"

"Al!" they would say. "Have you heard about Merlyn? He's gone to Beverly Hills." Then, "Shame about Irene Etchells. Sudden, wasn't it? I never quite got it straight. Was she your gran, or not? Did you ever trace your dad? No? What a shame. Yes, Irene dropped in. I was just cleaning my crystal, and whoops, there she was, swimming about inside. She warned me I might have to have a little op."

But, as she chatted, the past was chatting inside her: how's my darling girl, Mrs. McGibbet, poxy little boxer, Keef are you my dad? If you're going to chuck up go outside and do it. Fuck, Emmie, I've got to wash me hands. Dog-meat, Gloria, Gloria, dogmeat: there's an evil thing you wouldn't want to see. Round and round it went: there's an evil thing you wouldn't want to see at all. Morris was giving her earache, about the old days: the fight game, the scrap-metal game, the entertainment game. All the same, she felt there was some-thing he wasn't saying, something that he was holding back, perhaps some memory he was teasing her with. At other times, he seemed to be hazy about whom he was addressing; he seemed to be talking to the air.

He said, "Have you seen MacArthur? He's the cove that owes me money. If you see him you'll know him, he's missing one eye. Have you seen young Dean? He's got his head shaved and Rule Britannia stamped on it. Have you seen Pikey Pete? I've been down the waste ground and Pete ain't there. Been up the waste tip—civic amenity, they call it now—I expect to see him rum-maging but he's not. Totting you call it, totting's in his blood, together wiv scrap metal, his uncle were the biggest scrap-metal merchant in the Borders in the old days."

"The Borders," she said, "that's a bit out of the way for you, how did you get up there then?"

Morris said, "Circus used to go up that way, didn't it? Then in later years when I got kicked out of the circus I got a ride off Aitkenside. Aitkenside and his truck was always very handy, if you wanted picking up, if you want drop-ping off, post yourself by the side of a major trunk road and Aitkenside will be there. Very handy, a truck like that, when you've got boxes, when you've got a consignment, a van is very nice for a small consignment but nowadays we are trucking spookies by the score, gel. We bring 'em in by the hundreds, they are migrating from the east for a better life. But we charge, mind, and at the same time as we're bringing 'em in we are kicking 'em out, it's all part of the same racket, now you might not understand that but if you'd been on a course with Nick he'd make you understand: Comprenez? he'd say and hang you up by your feet until you answered yes. Now Aitkenside is management we have incentives for good work. We have vouchers to spend on modifications and we have family leisure breaks. We pack off on the weekends to the country, and we make crop circles. We fly over the fields and we make high-pitched whistling sounds, causing alarm to farmers and ramblers. We go on theme parks—that's what they call a fair these days—and we hang off the rides and lie by night unscrewing the screws to cause fatalities. We go out to golf clubs to dig up the greens and they think we're moles. Only you don't want to go on a driving range, a spirit can get tangled up easy in them big nets. That's how we found young Dean, we had to rescue him. Somebody shouted 'old Nick's coming' and Dean being new, he panicked and run off, he run head first into one of them nets—well, where his head would be. It was Aitkenside what extricated him, using his teef." Morris cackled. "Old Nick, if he sees you where he didn't ought, he will spit your bollocks on his toasting fork. He will melt you on a brazier and sip the marrow out your bones."

"Why did you get kicked out of the circus?" she asked. "I never heard that before."

Morris didn't answer. "Got kicked out of the circus," he said. "Got kicked out of the army. Got kicked out of Etchells's place and had to live in a skip. Story of my life. I don't know, I don't feel right in myself till I meet up with Pete. Maybe there's a horse fair. Do you reckon there's a horse fair? Maybe there's a cockfight somewhere, Pete enjoys that."

When she saw MacArthur again, materializing in the kitchen after this gap of many years, he had a false eye, just as Mrs. Etchells had suggested. Its surface was lustrous but hard, and light bounced from as it did from the surface of her lucky opals on the days when they refused to show their depths. Morris said, "Say what you like about MacArthur, but he was an artist wiv a knife. I seen him carve a woman like a turkey."

The tape unspooled in the empty room, and Morris, speaking from the distant past, could be heard puffing and grunting into the microphone, as if he were carrying a heavy and awkward burden. "Up a bit, left a bit, mind the step, Donnie. Right, I've got her. You grab your corner of the blanket there . . . steady as she goes. . . . Fuckit, I'm going in the kitchen, I've got to wash me hands. They are all over sticky stuff."

Colette came in from the garden, indignant. "I've just been in the shed," she said. "Mart's been back. Come and look, if you don't believe me."

Alison went down the garden. It was another of those hot, clammy days. A breeze stirred the saplings, bound to their posts like saints secured for burning, but the breeze itself was fevered, semitropical. Al wiped her hand across her forehead.

On the floor of the shed were a scatter of Mart's belongings: a tin opener, some plastic cutlery nicked from the supermarket café, and a number of rusty, unidentifiable keys. Colette scooped them up.

"I'll pass these on to PC Delingbole. Perhaps he can reunite them with their owners."

"Oh, don't be so spiteful!" Alison said. "What did Mart ever do to you? He's been kicked out of any place he could call home. There's no evil in him. He isn't the sort to cut a woman up and leave her in a dirty van."

Colette stared at her. "I don't think you ought to go to Aldershot," she said. "I think you ought to have a lie-down." She ducked out of the Balmoral, and stood on the lawn. "I have to tell you, Alison, that I am very disturbed at your behaviour lately. I think we may have to reconsider the terms of our arrangement. I'm finding it increasingly untenable."

"And where will you go?" Alison jeered. "Are you going to live in a shed as well?"

"That's my business. Keep your voice down. We don't want Michelle out here."

"I wouldn't mind. She could be a witness. You were down and out when I met you, Colette."

"Hardly that. I had a very good career. I was regarded as a highflyer, let me tell you."

Alison turned and walked into the house. "Yes, but psychically, you were down and out."

• • •

On the way to Mrs. Etchells's house, they did not speak. They drove through Pirbright—by the village green, by the pond fringed with rushes and yellow iris—through the black-shaded woodlands of the A324, where bars of light flashed through the treetops to rap the knuckles of Colette's tiny fists clenched on the wheel: by the ferny verges and towering hedges, by deep-roofed homesteads of mellow timbers and old stock brick, the sprinklers rotating on their velvet lawns, the coo of wood pigeons in their chimney stacks, the sweet smells of lavender and beeswax wafting from linen press, commode, and étagère. If I walked out on her now, Colette thought, then with what I have got saved I could just about put a deposit on a Beatty, though to be frank I'd like somewhere with a bit more nightlife than Admiral Drive. If I can't live here where the rich people live I'd like to live on a tube line, and then I could go out to a club with my friends and we could get wrecked on a Friday like we used to, and go home with men we hardly knew, and sneak off in the mornings when only the milk trucks are out and the birds are singing. But I suppose I'm old now, she thought, if I had any friends they'd all have kids by now, they'd be too old for clubbing, they'd be too grown-up, in fact it would be their kids that would be going out, and they'd be sitting at home with their gardening manuals. And I have grown up without anyone noticing. I went home with Gavin once, or rather I pressed the lift button to his hotel floor, and when I tapped at his door he looked through his spyhole and he liked what he saw—but would anybody like me now? As the first straggle of the settlement of Ash appeared—some rotting sixties in-fill, and the sway-walled cottages by the old church—she felt penetrated by a cold hopelessness, which the prospect before her did nothing to soothe.

Much of the district had been razed; there were vast intersections, grassy roundabouts as large as public parks, signs leading to industrial estates. "Next right," Al said. Only yards from the main road, the townscape dwindled to a more domestic scale. "That's new." She indicated the Kebab Centre, the Tanning Salon. "Slow down. Right again." Between the 1910 villas some new-build terraces were squeezed, bright blue plastic sheeting where their window glass would be. On a wire fence hung a pictorial sign that showed a wider, higher, loftier, and airier version of the building it fronted: LAUREL MEWS, it said. MOVE IN TODAY FOR NINETY-NINE POUNDS.

"How do they do that?" Al said, and Colette said, "They offer to pay your stamp duty, your surveyor's fees, all that, but they just stick it on the asking price and then they tie you into a mortgage deal they've picked out, you think you're getting something for nothing but they've got a hand in your pocket at every turn."

"They want their pound of flesh," Al said. "Pity. Because I thought I could buy one for Mart. You'd think he'd be safe, in a mews. He could keep that sheeting over the windows, so nobody could see in."

Colette hooted. "Mart? Are you serious? Nobody would give Mart a mortgage. They wouldn't let him near the place."

They were almost there: she recognized the dwarf wall, its plaster peeling, the stunted hedge made mostly of bare twigs. Mandy had pulled her smart little soft-top off the road, almost blocking the front door. Gemma had given Cara a lift, and she and Silvana were parked in the road, bumper-to-bumper.

"You want to watch that," Silvana said, indicating Mandy's car. "In a neighbourhood like this."

"I know," Mandy said. "That's why I pulled as close as I could."

"So where do you live, that's so special?" Colette asked Silvana. "Somewhere with security dogs?"

Mandy said, trying to ease relations, "You look nice, Colette. Have you had your hair done? That's a nice amulet, Cara."

"It's real silver, I'm selling them," Cara said promptly. "Shall I send you one? Postage and packing free."

"What does it do?"

"Sod-all," said Silvana. "Silver, my arse. I had one off her. It makes a dirty mark round your neck, like a pencil mark, looks as if somebody's put a dotted line round for snipping your head off."

Colette said, "I'm surprised anyone notices it. Against your natural deep tan."

Silvana put the key in the door. Alison's heart squeezed small inside her chest.

"You nerved yourself, love," said Mandy in a low voice. "Well done." She squeezed Al's hand. Al winced as the lucky opals bit into her flesh.

"Sorry," Mandy whispered.

"Oh, Mand, I wish I could tell you the half of it." I wish I had an amulet, she thought, I wish I had a charm against the stirring air.

They stepped in. The room felt damp. "Christ," Silvana said, "where's her furniture gone?"

Alison looked around. "No milk money. No clock."

In the front parlour, nothing was left but a square of patterned carpet that didn't quite meet the sides of the room, and an armchair hopelessly un-sprung. Silvana wrenched open the cupboard by the fireplace; it was empty, but a powerful smell of mould rushed out of it. In the kitchen—where they had expected to find the crumbs of Mrs. Etchells's last teatime—there was nothing to find but a teapot, unemptied, on the sink. Alison lifted the lid; a single teabag was sunk in brown watery depths.

"I think it's obvious what's happened here," Gemma said. "I believe if we inspect the windows at the back we'll find signs of forced entry." Her voice faded as she walked down the passage to the scullery.

"She used to be married to a policeman," Cara explained.

"Did she?"

"But you know how it is. She got involved in his work. She tried to help out. You do, don't you? But she got strangled once too often. She lived through the Yorkshire Ripper, she had all sorts of hoaxers coming through, she used to report them to his seniors but it didn't stop her having to walk about all day with an axe in her head. She gave him an ultimatum, get out of the CID, or we're history."

"I suppose he wouldn't quit," Colette said.

"So he was history." Al sounded awed.

"She left him, moved down south, never looked back."

"She must be older than she says, if she was married when it was the York-shire Ripper."

"We're all older than we say." Gemma was back. "And some of us, my dears, are older than we know. The windows are intact. They must have got in upstairs. The back door is locked."

"Funny, to come in upstairs, if you're going to make off with the furniture," Colette said.

Alison said, "Colette is nothing if not logical." She called out, "Pikey Pete? You bin in here?" She dropped her voice. "He's part of a gang that used to run about round here, Mrs. Etchells knew them all. He's what you call a totter, collects old furniture, pots and pans, anything of that sort."

"And he's in Spirit, is he?" Gemma said. She laughed. "That explains it, then. Still, I've never seen such a wholesale teleportation of anybody's goods, have you?"

"It's a shame," Al said. "It's just plain greedy, that's what it is. There are people earthside could have used the things she had. Such as nutmeg graters. Toby jugs. Decorative pin cushions with all the pins still in. She had a coffee table with a glass top and a repeat motif of the Beatles underneath, printed on wallpaper—it must have been an heirloom. She had original Pyrex oven dishes with pictures of carrots and onions on the side. She had a Spanish lady with a flouncy skirt that you sat on top of your spare loo roll. I used to run to her house when I wanted to go to the toilet because there was always some bloke wanking in ours. Though God knows why they were wanking because my mum and her friend Gloria was always ready to give them hand relief."

Mandy put an arm around her. "Shh, lovey. Not easy for you. But we all had it rough."

Alison scrubbed the tears out of her eyes. Pikey Paul was crying in the bare corner of the room. "It was me what gave her that Spanish lady," he said. "I won it on a shooting stall in Southport on the pleasure beach. I'd a lift all the way from Ormskirk and down the East Lancs Road, and then I had the malfortune to be picked up by a chap in a truck called Aitkenside, which was the origin of the sad connection between my fambly and yours."

"I'm sorry, Pikey Paul," Alison said. "I do sincerely apologize."

"I carried it all the way down the country wrapped in a cloth, and Aitkenside he would say, what's that you've got between your legs, employing the utmost ambiguity, till finally he made a dive for it. So I held it out of the way, the dolly, above my head while Aitkenside had his way, for I wasn't about to get Dolly spoiled, and I had a good inkling as to his nature, for those men's men they are all the same."

"Oh, I do agree," said Alison.

"For it is all they can think of, those men's men, rifling about in a boy's tight little matador pants till they can find his wherewithal. But still and all it was worth it. You should have seen Irene smile, when I gave her the presentation. Oh, Paul, she said, is that dolly all for me? I never told her of the perils I'd been assaulted with. Well, you don't, do you? She was a lady. I don't say you're not, but Mrs. Etchells wouldn't have understood a thing like that. Whereas now it's more the modern style. They're all at it. They don't like to miss any pleasure. They're having extensions so they can fuck themselves, and whores will be out of business."

"Pikey Paul!" said Alison. "Keep it low! Don't talk so obscene. You never used to have such a filthy tongue in your head!"

"They're queueing up for multiple tongues," Paul said. "I seen 'em. What I say is mild, believe me. You want to hear 'em in the years to come. No sentence will be clean."

"I can believe it," Alison said. She began to cry. "All the same, Paul, I wish I'd had a spirit guide like you. Morris never brought me a present. Not so much as a bunch of flowers."

"You should have kicked him out," Paul said. "You should have kicked him out like Mrs. Etchells kicked him out. Soon as she saw my Spanish dolly, she hoisted him up in her arms—she was sinewy in those days, and you know how squat he is—she carried him down the road and she dumped him in a skip. Then she come back and cooked us some pancakes. I was uncommonly fond of pancakes with syrup, but now I lay off 'em, as I've to watch my waistline, which don't we all. Now I was looking for a place to call my own, and I had a billet where I could come and go, ask me no questions and I'll tell you no lies, she was easygoing, was Mrs. Etchells. We was suited—that's how you could express it. Little op, chain of love, joys of motherhood, she never varied it and why should she? Meanwhile I got on with my own life. She had a stack of testimonials, handwritten, some of them in real fountain pen by titled people, stacked up in that sideboard there."

"What sideboard?" Al said.

"That sideboard that one of my fambly has removed, namely Pikey Pete. To sell it on."

"He should be ashamed," Alison said. The Sensitives, acting on instinct or by training, had formed a semicircle around Al, aware that she was experiencing a manifestation. Only Colette walked away, bored, and stood with drooping head, her fingers flaking yellowed paint from the front windowsill. Silvana rubbed and rubbed at a spot below her jawline: trying, perhaps, to ease her teak-coloured line of tan into the tint of her flesh. The women stood, patient, till Pikey Paul vanished in a dull red flash, his suit of lights depleted, bagged at the knee and sagged at the seat, his aura—trailing on the air—resembling no more than a greasy smear of old-fashioned men's hair cream.

"That was Pikey Paul," Al said. "Mrs. E's guide. Unfortunately he didn't say anything about the will."

"Okay," said Cara. "Dowsing it is. If it's here at all, it can only be under the lino or slid behind the wallpaper." She opened her beaded satchel and took out her pendulum.

"Oh, you use a bobber," Mandy said, interested. "Brass, is it? I swear by a Y-Rod, myself."

Silvana took out of a carrier bag what looked like a length of lavatory chain, with a metal nut on the end. She glanced at Colette, as if daring her to say something. "It was my dad's," she said. "He was a plumber."

"You could be done for carrying that around," Gemma said. "Offensive weapon."

"Tools of her trade," Mandy said. "Did you get your Sight from your dad, then? That's unusual."

"Alison doesn't know who her dad was," Colette said. "She thought she had it worked out, but her mum knocked her theory on the head."

"She's not the only one," Mandy said. "I believe that in your case too, Colette, what's on the birth certificate isn't quite the same as what's in the genes."

Al's been gossiping, Colette thought: and yet she said it was all in confidence! How could she? She stored it up, for a future row.

"I don't even have a birth certificate," Al said. "Not that I know of. To be honest, I'm not really sure how old I am. I mean my mum gave me a date, but it might not be true. I can never remember my age when things were done to me or when things happened. It's because they always said to me, if anybody asks, you're sixteen, right? Which is confusing when you're only about nine."

"Poor love," Mandy breathed.

"You must be recorded somewhere," Colette said. "I'll look into it. If you had no birth certificate, how did you get a passport?"

"That's a point," Al said. "How did I? Maybe we can dowse for my documentation, when we're done here. Okay, look, ladies, you do down here—don't forget to take that armchair apart. I'll go and check upstairs."

"Do you want somebody with you?" Gemma asked.

Mandy said in a low voice, "Let her have some privacy. Doesn't matter whether she was her gran or not, she looked up to Irene Etchells."

Pete had stripped out the stair carpet, so the creak of each tread carried to the women back in the parlour and, as their pendulums twitched, each tiny impulse registered an answering twitch in Alison, just above her diaphragm. The rooms were bare, but when she opened the wardrobe, a row of garments still hung there, close-covered against moths. She parted their calico shrouds; her hand brushed silk and crepe. They were Mrs. Etchells's performance gowns, from her days of triumph on distant platforms. Here was a peacock green faded to grey, here a rose-pink faded to ash. She examined them: crystal beads rolled beneath finger and thumb, and a scatter of pewter-coloured sequins drifted to the floor of the wardrobe. She leaned in, breathing the smell of cedar, and began to scoop them into her cupped hand, thinking of Pikey Paul. But as she straightened up, she thought, no, I'll buy him new. I'm patient for sewing, as long as it's spirit sewing, and he'll appreciate something more shiny than these. I wonder why Pete left her frocks? Probably thought they were worth nothing. Men! He had plundered the saggy polyester skirts and the cardigans that Mrs. Etchells usually wore; these, Al supposed, he would be selling onto some poor Iraqi grandma who'd lost everything but what she stood up in, or somebody who'd been bombed out in the Blitz; for in Spirit World, wars run concurrently.

She let the sequins drift, between her fingers, to the bare boards; then picked two empty wire hangers from the wardrobe. She wrenched them out of shape, formed each into a rod with a hook for a handle, and held them in front of her. She followed their guidance into the back room. They bucked and turned in her hand, and while she waited for them to settle she looked out of the uncurtained window onto the site of urban clearance beyond. Probably going to build a mews, she thought. For now, she had a clear view of the back plots of the neighbouring street, with its lean-tos and lockup

garages, its yellowed nylon curtains billowing from open windows, its flori-
bundas breaking through the earth and swelling into flagrant blood-dark
bloom: a view of basking men throwing sickies, comatose in canvas chairs,
their white bellies peeping from their shirts, their beer cans winking and
weakly dribbling in the sun. From an upper storey hung a flag—ENGLAND—
red on white: as if it could be somewhere else, she thought. Her eye carried
to the street beyond, where on the corner stood municipal receptacles for the
sorting and storage of waste, disposal bins for glass, others for grass, others
for fabrics, for paper, for shoes; and at their feet clustered black sacks, their
mouths tied with yellow tape.

The rods in her hands convulsed, and their hooks cut into her palms. She
followed them to the corner of the room, and at their direction, laying them
down, she tore into a foot of rotting linoleum. Her nails clawed at a seam; she
inched two fingers under it and pulled. I should have a knife, she thought,
why didn't I bring a knife? She stood up, took a deep breath, bent again,
tugged, tugged. There was a crack, a splintering; floorboards showed; she
saw a small piece of paper, folded. She bent painfully to scoop it up. She un-
folded it, and as she did so the fibres of the paper gave way, and it fell apart
along the folds. My birth certificate, she thought: but no, it was barely six
lines. First a blurred rubber stamp—PAID TO—then *Emmeline Cheetham* was
written beneath, in a florid, black hand: THE SUM OF SEVEN SHILLINGS AND SIX-
PENCE. Underneath came another stamp, at an angle to the above, RECEIVED
WITH THANKS: and then in her mother's youthful hand, her signature, *Emmeline Cheetham*: below that, IN WITNESS WHEREOF: *Irene Etchells (Mrs.)*. Beneath
the signature, the paper had a brown indentation, as if it had been ironed
briefly on a high setting. As the nail of her little finger touched the scorch
mark, the paper flaked away, leaving a ragged gap where the mark had been.

She kicked the divining rods away from her feet, and went downstairs;
clattering, tread by tread. They were gathered in the kitchen, turned to the
foot of the stairs and awaiting her arrival. "Anything?" Mandy said.

"Zilch. Nix."

"What's that? That paper?"

"Nothing," Al said. She crumpled the paper and dropped it. "God knows.
What's seven shillings and sixpence? I've forgotten the old money."

"What old money?" Cara said.

Mandy frowned. "Thirty-three pence?"

"What can you get for that?"

"Colette?"

"A bag of crisps. A stamp. An egg."

When they went out, pulling the front door behind them, Mandy stood aghast at the sight of her car. "The sneaky bastards! How did they do that? I kept looking out, checking."

"They must have crawled," Silvana said. "Unless they ran up on very little legs."

"Which, sadly, is possible," Alison said.

Mandy said, "I cancelled a half day of readings to get here for this, thinking I was doing a favour. You try to do a good action, but I don't know. Dammit, where does it get you?"

"Oh well," Cara said, "you know what Mrs. Etchells used to say, as you sow shall you reap, or something like that. If you have done harm you'll get it back threefold. If you've never done any harm in your life, you've nothing to worry about."

"I never knew her well," Mandy said, "but I doubt that, with her long experience, Irene thought it was that simple."

"But there must be a way out of it," Al said. She was angry. "There must be a route out of this shit." She took Mandy's arm, clung to it. "Mandy, you should know, you're a woman of the world, you've knocked about a bit. Even if you have done harm, if you've done really bad harm, does it count if you've done it to evil people? It can't, surely. It would count as self-defence. It would count as a good action."

Colette said, "Well now, Mandy, I hope you're insured."

"I hope I am too," Mandy said. She freed herself from Al. Tenderly, she passed her fingers over her paintwork. The triple lines were scored deep into the scarlet, as if scraped with a claw.

Tea, tea, tea! said Colette. How refreshing to come into the cleanliness and good order of the Collingwood. But Colette stepped short, her hand on the kettle, annoyed with herself. A woman of my age shouldn't be wanting tea, she thought. I should be wanting—I don't know, cocaine?

Alison was rummaging in the fridge. "You're not eating again, are you?" Colette said. "It's coming to the point where I'm getting ashamed to be seen with you."

There was a tap on the window. Alison jumped violently; her head shot back over her shoulder. It was Michelle. She looked hot and cross. "Yes?" Colette said, opening the window.

"I saw that stranger again," Michelle said. "Creeping around. I know you've been feeding him."

"Not lately," Alison said.

"We don't want strangers. We don't want pedophiles and homeless people around here."

"Mart's not a pedophile," Al said. "He's scared to death of you and your kids. As anybody would be."

"You tell him that the next time he's seen the police will be called. And if you don't know any better than aiding and abetting him, we're going to get up a petition against you. I told Evan, I'm not too happy anyway, I never have been, two single women living together, what does that say to you? Not as if you're two girls starting out in life."

Colette lifted the steaming kettle. "Back off, Michelle, or I'm going to pour this over your head. And you'll shrivel up like a slug."

"I'll report you for threatening behaviour," Michelle said. "I'll call PC Delingbole." But she backed away. "I'm going round right now to see the chairman of the Neighbourhood Watch."

"Oh yes?" Colette said. "Bring it on!" But when Michelle had ducked out of sight, she slapped the kettle down and swore. She unlocked the back door, and said, "I've had enough of this. If he's in there again I'm going to call the police myself."

Alison stood by the kitchen sink, swabbing up the hot water that Colette had spilled from the kettle. Out in the garden there was seething activity, at ankle height. She couldn't see Morris, but she could see movement behind a shrub. The other spirits were crawling about, prone on the lawn, as if they were on some sort of military exercise. They were hissing to each other, and Aitkenside was gesticulating, as if urging the others forward. As Colette crossed the grass they rolled over and kicked their legs; then they rolled back and followed her, slithering along, pretending to nip her calves and slash at them with spirit sticks.

She saw Colette push at the door of the Balmoral, and step back. Step forward and push again. Her face turned back towards the house. "Al? It's stuck."

Al hurried down the garden. The spirits edged away and lay in the verges. Dean was whistling. "Cut that out," Morris said, speaking from within his bush. "Watch and observe. Watch how she goes now. Now she says to stringbean, well, what's sticking it? Is it swollen up wiv damp? Stringbean says, what damp, it ain't rained for weeks. Watch 'em now. Now she pushes. Watch how she breaks out in a sweat."

"There's something heavy behind the door," Al said.

Dean giggled. "If she was any good at predictionating, she'd know, wouldn't she? What we've done?"

Al crouched down and looked in at the window. It was dusty and smeared, almost opaque. Behind the door was an area of darkness, a shadow, which thickened, took on form, took on features. "It's Mart," she said. "Stopping the door."

"Tell him to get away," Colette said. She banged on the door with her fist, and kicked it. "Open up!"

"He can't hear you."

"Why not?"

"He's hanged himself."

"What, in our shed?"

There was a spatter of applause from the margins of the lawn.

"I'll call nine-nine-nine," Colette said.

"Don't bother. It's not an emergency. He's passed."

"You don't know. He might still be breathing. They could revive him."

Al put her fingertips against the door, feeling for a thread of life through the grain of the wood. "He's gone," she said. "Goddammit, Colette, I should know. Besides, look behind you."

Colette turned. I still forget, Al thought, that—psychically speaking—Colette can't see her hand in front of her face. Mart was perched on the top of the neighbours' fence, swinging his feet in their big sneakers. The fiends now roused themselves, and began to giggle. By Al's feet, a head popped up out of the soil, "Coo-ee!"

"I see you turned up, Pikey Pete," Al said. "Fresh from that little job of yours at Aldershot."

"Would I have missed this?" the fiend replied. "Rely on me for a nice noose, don't they? I had a great-uncle that was an hangman, though that's going back."

Dean lay on top of the shed on his belly, his tongue flapping like a roller blind down over the door. Morris was urinating into the water feature, and Donald Aitkenside was squatting on the grass, eating a sausage roll from a paper bag.

"Ring the local station and ask for PC Delingbole," Al said. "Yes, and an ambulance. We don't want anybody to say we didn't do it right. But tell them there's no need for sirens. We don't want to attract a crowd."

But it was school-out time, and there was no avoiding the attention of the mums bowling home in their minivans and SUVs. A small crowd soon collected before the Collingwood, buzzing with shocked rumour. Colette double-locked the front door and put the bolts on. She drew the curtains at the front of the house. A colleague of Delingbole's stood at the side gate, to deter any sightseers from making their way into the garden. From her post on the landing, Colette saw Evan approaching with a ladder and his camcorder; so she drew the upstairs curtains too, after jerking two fingers at him as his face appeared over the sill.

"We'll have the media here before we know it," Constable Delingbole said. "Dear, oh, dear. Not very nice for you two girls. Forensics will be in. We'll have to seal off your garden. We'll have to conduct a search of the premises. You got anybody you could go to, for the night? Neighbours?"

"No," Al said. "They think we're lesbians. If we must move out, we'll make our own arrangements. But we'd rather not. You see, I run my business from home."

Already the road was filling with vehicles. A radio car from the local station was parked on the verge, and Delingbole's boy was attempting to move back the mothers and tots. The kebab van was setting up by the children's playground, and some of the tots, whining, were trying to lead their mothers towards it. "This is your fault," Michelle shouted up at the house. She turned to her neighbours. "If they hadn't encouraged him, he'd have gone and hanged himself somewhere else."

"Now," said a woman from a Frobisher, "we'll be in the local paper as that place where the tramp topped himself, and that won't be very nice for our re-sale values."

Inside, in the half-dark, Delingbole said. "Do I take it you knew him, poor bugger? Somebody will have to identify him."

"You can do it," Al said. "You knew him, didn't you? You made his life a misery. You stamped on his watch."

When the forensic team came, they stood thigh-deep in the low, salivating spirits that cluster at the scene of a sudden or violent death. They stood thigh-deep in them and never noticed a thing. They puzzled over the multiple footprints they found by the shed, prints from feet that were jointed to no ordinary leg. They cut Mart down, and the length of apricot polyester from which they found him suspended was labelled and placed carefully in a sealed bag.

"He must have taken a long time to die," Alison said, later that night. "He had nothing, you see, Mart, nothing at all. He wouldn't have a rope. He wouldn't have a high place to hang himself from."

They sat with the lamps unlit, so as not to attract the attention of the neighbours; they moved cautiously, sliding around the edges of the room.

"You'd have thought he could have jumped on the railway track," Colette said. "Or thrown himself off the roof of Toys 'R' Us; that's what they mostly do round Woking, I've seen it in the local paper. But oh no, he would have to go and do it here, where he would cause maximum trouble and inconvenience. We were the only people who were ever kind to him, and look how he repays us. You bought him those shoes, didn't you?"

"And a new watch," Al said. "I tried to do a good action. Look how it ended up."

"It's the thought that counts," Colette said. But her tone was sarcastic, and—as far as Alison could discern her expression in the gloom—she looked both angry and bitter.

In spirit, Mart had looked quite chipper, Al thought, when she saw him

perched on the fence. When she sneaked into the kitchen, in search of sup-
per, she wondered if she should leave him out a plate of sandwiches. But I
suppose I'd sleepwalk in the night, she thought, and eat them myself. She believed she caught a glimpse of him, behind the door of the utility room; livid
bruising was still fresh on his neck.

Later, as she was coming out of the bathroom, Morris stopped her. "I suppose you think we was out of order?" he said.

"You're an evil bastard, Morris," she said. "You were evil when you were
earthside, and now you're worse."

"Oh, come on!" Morris said. "Don't take on! You're worse than your
bloody mother. We wanted a laugh, that's all. Not as if the cove was doing
much good this side, was he? Anyway, I've had a word with Mr. Aitkenside,
and we're going to take him on to clean our boots. Which is currently young
Dean's job, but with Mr. Aitkenside getting fitted with the sets of false feet,
Dean could do with some assistance. He has to start at the bottom, you
know, that's the rule. I reckon he'll shape up. He's no more gormless than
Dean was when we picked him out of the golf net. If he shapes up, in about
fifty years he might get to go on Spirit Guide."

"Don't expect me to thank you," said Al.

"That's just like you, innit?" Morris said. His features convulsed with spite,
he bounced up and down on the landing. "No bloody gratitude. You talk
about when I was earthside, you give me the character of an evil bastard, but
where would you be if it weren't for me? If it hadn't been for me, the boys
would have cut you up a bloody sight worse. You'd be disfigured. Aitkenside
said, she has to learn respect for what a knife can do, and they all said, all the
boys, quite right, she has to learn, and your mum said, fine, you carve her, but
don't go carving her face, the punters won't like it. She said, it's all very well
your squabbles, but when you gentlemen have all got bored of her, I've still
got to sell her on, ain't I? And I supported her, didn't I? I backed her up. I said
to Aitkenside, quite right, show her what's what by all means, but don't make
her into a bloody liability."

"But Morris, why did they do it?" Al cried. "What did I ever do to you? I
was a child, for pity's sake, who would want to take a knife and slice up a
child's legs and leave her scarred?" I must have screamed, she thought, I

must have screamed but I don't remember. I must have screamed but no one heard me.

"There was nobody to hear," Morris said. "That's why you have to have an outbuilding, innit? You have to have an outbuilding or a shed, or a caravan if you can't manage that, or at least a trailer. You never know when you need to show some little shaver what's what or hang some bugger what's getting on your nerves."

"You haven't answered me," Al said. She stood in his path, fingering the lucky opals as if they were weapons. He tried to swerve past her, but her aura, welling out and smothering him, forced him back. Gibbering with frustration, he condensed himself, and slid under the carpet, and she stamped on him hard saying, "Morris, if you want to keep your job, I want some answers. If you don't give me answers I'm going to give up this game. I'll go back and work in a cake shop. I'll work in the chemist like I used to. I'll scrub floors if I have to. I'm going to give it up, and then where will you be?"

"Ho," said Morris, "you don't frighten me, gel, if you go and work in the chemist I shall make myself into a pill. If you get a job in a cake shop I shall roll myself into a Swiss roll and spill out jam at inopportune moments. If you try scrubbing floors, I will rise up splosh! out of your bucket in a burst of black water, causing you to get the sack. Then you will be wheedling me around like you used to, oh, Uncle Morris, I've no spending money, oh Uncle Morris I've no money for me school dinners, I've no money for me school trip. And all the time going behind my back with the same sob story to MacArthur, and whining for sweeties to Keith. Too generous by half, that's Morris Warren. The day I was taken over, there wasn't five bob in my pocket. I was taken over and I don't know how, taken over wiv money owing to me." Morris began to whimper. "MacArthur owes me. Bill Wagstaffe owes me. I've got in my black book who owes me. Bloody spirits is devious, innit? Always some reason they can't pay. 'My pocket vapourized. Holy Bloody Ghost got my wallet.' So there I was turning up airside, they says, turn out your pockets, and when they saw that was all the money I had to my name they bloody laughed. They said, you don't work you don't drink, me old mate. That's the rule here. Then I got put on Spirit Guide. First I got Irene Etchells, and then you, God help me. I say God help me but the bugger never does. That's why

I bother wiv Nick, wiv Nick you get a career opportunity. You get sent on courses."

"If you get promoted," Al said, "nobody will be happier than I will. The only bit of peace and quiet I had was when you were on your course."

"Peace and quiet?" Morris yelped. "How could you have peace and quiet? Wiv a past like yours? Not ten years old, and a man's testicles on your conscience."

"What testicles?" Alison yelled.

Across the landing, Colette's door opened. She stood in her bedtime T-shirt, very white and severe. "That's it," she said. "I don't intend to spend another night under this roof. How can I live with a woman who has rows with people I can't see, and who stands outside my bedroom door shouting 'What testicles?' It's more than flesh and blood can stand."

Alison rubbed her forehead. She felt dazed. "You're right," she said. "But don't be hasty."

"It's simply not acceptable conduct. Not even by your standards."

Alison moved her foot, so Morris could slide from under it. "At least wait until the morning."

"I don't believe it's safe to wait until morning. I shall pack a small bag and I shall send someone for the rest of my things in due course."

"Who?" Al said, in simple wonderment. "Who will you send?" She said, "You can't just rush off into the night. That's silly. You owe it to me to talk it over."

"I owe you nothing. I built your business up from scratch. It was a blundering amateur mess when I came on board."

"That's what I mean. Come on, Colette! We've been through such a lot."

"Well, from now on you're on your own. You've got plenty of company, I would have thought. Your special sort of company."

"I've got my memories." Al said. "Yes. That's fine."

She turned away. I won't entreat you anymore, she thought. She heard low voices from downstairs. It sounded as if Aitkenside and the rest had come in and were making themselves a snack. Colette closed her door. Al heard her talking. For a moment she stood still, in astonishment. Who has she got in there with her? Then she realized that Colette was using her cell phone, and was making arrangements to depart.

• • •

"Wha?" Gavin said. "Who's this?" He spluttered, coughed, blew his nose twice; he sounded like a bear that has been hibernating at the bottom of a pit.

"It's not that late," she snapped. "Wake up, Gavin. Are you awake? Are you listening to me? This is an emergency. I want you to get me out of here."

"Oh," said Gavin, "it's you, Colette. How've you been?"

"I've been better. I wouldn't ask, except I need to get out right now, and I need somewhere to stay, just for tonight. I'm packing a bag as we speak."

There was a silence. "So let me get this straight. You want me to come over there?"

"Yes. At once."

"You want me to drive over there and get you?"

"We used to be married. Is it too much to ask?"

"Yes—no—it's not that—" He broke off. To consult Zoë, perhaps? Now he was back on the line. "The problem's my car, you see, it's—well, it's in the garage."

"What a time to pick!" she snapped. "You should have a little Japanese one like ours, never lets us down."

"So why don't you, you know, get in it?"

"Because it's hers! Because she's the owner and I don't want a dispute. Because I don't want her near me, or anything that belonged to her."

"You mean Fat Girl? Are you running away from her?"

"Look, I'll call a cab. Only be ready to let me in when I get there. It may take a while."

"Oh, I've got wheels," Gavin said. "I can come. No problem. As long as you don't mind it. I mean, it's not my usual standard."

"Gavin, come now, in whatever you happen to be driving."

She clicked the phone off. She put her hand on her solar plexus, and tried to breathe deeply, calmly. She sat on the side of the bed. Vignettes from her life with Al ran through her mind. Alison at the Harte and Garter, the day they got together, arranging the sugar straws and pouring the milk. Alison in a hotel in Hemel Hempstead, trying on earrings at the dressing table, between each pair dabbing at her earlobes with cotton wool balls soaked in vodka from the minibar. Alison wrapped in a duvet, on the night the princess died, her teeth chattering on the sofa of the flat in Wexham. As she hauled down a bag from the top of the wardrobe and pushed into it a wash bag and some underwear, she began to rehearse her explanation to Gavin, to the world. A vagrant hanged himself in the shed. The air grew thick and my head ached. She stamped outside my room and shouted, "What testicles!" She snapped her bag shut, and lugged it downstairs. At once she thought, I can't turn up like this, what about Zoë, she'll probably be wearing designer lingerie, maybe a one-off a friend has made for her, something chiffon, something silk, I wouldn't like her to see these sweatpants, she'll laugh in my face. She ran upstairs, took off her clothes, and stood before her open wardrobe, wondering what she could find to impress a model. She glanced at her watch: how long would it take Gavin to get over from Whitton? The roads will be empty, she thought. She dressed; she was not pleased by the result; maybe if I do my makeup, she thought. She went into the bathroom; painstakingly she drew two eyes and a mouth. She went downstairs again. She found she was shivering, and thought she would like a hot drink. Her hand reached for the kitchen light switch, and drew back. We're not supposed to be here; the neighbours think we left. She crossed the room and began to inch up the kitchen blind.

It was three-thirty, and already the short midsummer darkness was becoming a smoggy haze. Aluminium barriers had been erected around the Balmoral, and on them a line of magpies was bouncing, as if they were sharing a joke. Behind her, she heard a footstep on the vinyl floor. She almost screamed. Al crossed the kitchen, bulky in her voluminous cotton nightgown. She moved slowly, as if drugged, hypnotized. She slid open the cutlery drawer, and stood looking down into it, fingering the knives and forks.

This is the last of it, Colette thought. A phase of my life ends here; the hidden *clink, clink* of the metal from inside the drawer, the conversational sound of the birds, Alison's absorbed face. Colette crossed the room and passed her without speaking. She had to push past; she felt as if Al's white gown had swelled out to fill the room, and the substance of Al's flesh had swollen with it. In the distance she heard the sound of a car. My chariot, she thought. Gavin may not be much of a man, but he's there for me in a crisis. At least he's alive. And there's only one of him.

•   •   •

From the kitchen, Al heard the front door close behind Colette. The letter box opened, keys dropped to the carpet, the letter box flipped shut. That was a bit dramatic, Al thought, there was no need for her to do that.

She limped to a kitchen chair, and sat down. With some difficulty, she raised one calf and crossed her ankle over the opposite knee. She felt the drag and pull on the muscle beneath her thigh, and she had to hang on to her shin bone to stop her foot from sliding off and back to the floor. She bent her back, hunched forward. It was uncomfortable; her abdomen was compressed, her breath was squeezed. It's a pity Cara's not here, she thought, to do it for me, or at least to instruct me in the proper technique; she must have got her diploma by now. I'll just have to rub away and hope for the best; I'll have to go back by myself, back to Aldershot, back to the dog runs and the scrubby ground, back to the swampish waters of the womb, and maybe back before that: back to where there is no Alison, only a space where Alison will be.

She felt for the underside of her toes, and delicately, tentatively, began to massage the sole of her foot.

thirteen

At some point on your road you have to turn and start walking back towards yourself. Or the past will pursue you, and bite the nape of your neck, leave you bleeding in the ditch. Better to turn and face it with such weapons as you possess.

Her feet feel more swollen than usual. Perhaps she's kneaded them too hard. Or perhaps she's just reluctant to walk down this road, back through her teenage years, fireside chats with Emmie, happy schooldays, kindergarten fun. She hears Colette drop her keys through the door. Back, back. She hears the engine of a small car, struggling uphill on Admiral Drive; it's Gavin.

Back, back, back to yesterday. The police are searching the house. Colette says, what are you looking for, Constable Delingbole, surely you don't think we've got another corpse? Delingbole says, rather self-conscious, would you not call me that anymore? I'm Sergeant Delingbole now.

Lovely house, the policewoman says, looking around. Alison says, can I make you a cup of tea? and the policewoman says, oh no, you've had a fright, I'll do the tea.

Al says, there's lemon and ginger, camomile, Earl Grey, or proper tea, there's a lemon in the fridge and semi-skimmed, there's sugar on the top shelf there if you want it. Sergeant Delingbole plunges a long stick down the waste disposal, fetches it up again and sniffs it. Just routine, he says to Al. By the way, that's quite a set of knives you've got there. I love those Japanese ones, don't you? So chic.

The policewoman says, what do these houses come in at, then?

Back, back. Her fingers are pressed to the door of the shed, feeling for Mart's pulse. She is coming down the garden towards the Balmoral. Colette is gesturing that the door is stuck. She is standing at the sink swabbing the spilled water. The kettle is boiling. Michelle's face appears. Back, back. They are closing the door on Mrs. Etchells's house. As you sow so shall you reap. She is holding a piece of paper with a scorch mark. Her head is in the wardrobe and she is breathing in camphor, violets, a faint body smell persisting down the years. They always said to me, if anyone asks you're sixteen, right? I can never remember my age when things were done to me or when things happened. I'm not sure how old I am.

With each step backwards she is pushing at something light, tensile, clinging. It is a curtain of skin. With each step the body speaks its mind. Her ears pick up the trickle and swish of blood and lymph. Her eyes turn back and stare into the black jelly of her own thoughts. Inside her throat a door opens and closes; no one steps in. She does not look into the triangle of shadow behind the door. She knows a dead person might be there.

She hears a *tap-tap*, a knuckle on glass. "Are you there, Mr. Fox?" she says. She always says *mister*: when she remembers. The men say, here, you bloody tell her, Emmie; tell her politeness costs nothing.

There is a noise that might be crockery smashing, and a chair being knocked over. A door in her mind opens, and at first, once again, no one enters. She waits, holding her breath. It might be Keef, or it might be Morris Warren, or it might be their mate MacArthur, who always winks at her when he sees her.

But it's her mum who staggers in, rights herself with some difficulty. "Whoops!" she says. "Must be my new pills. Blue, they is. That's unusual, ain't it. Blue? I says to him at the chemist, are you sure these are right? He says, lovely shade, he says, not blue, you'd not call that blue. It's more heliotrope."

She says, "Mum, did Donnie Aitkenside leave you any wages when he went off this morning? Because you know that magic shilling, that we have to put in the gas meter? He took it with him."

Her mum says, "Donnie? Gone?"

"Yes," she says, "he was creeping downstairs with his shoes in his hand, and he took our shilling for the gas. I thought maybe it was his change."

"What in the Lord's name is the girl talking about now, Gloria?"

"If we don't have that shilling we need real money for the meter. It's cold out and I haven't had my breakfast."

Her mother repeats, "Donnie? Gone?"

"And if he's not paid you, we've no money for my school dinner."

"And who gave you permission to call him Donnie, you stuck-up little madam? If a child such as you talked back in my day there'd be bloody blue murder."

She says, there is anyway, innit? It's bloody blue murder every day here. Her mum says, there you go again, if he takes his belt off to you I'll not be surprised, I'll not be the one holding him back, I'll tell you: and there, thumping her fist on the wooden draining board, her mum is saying what they'll do, what they'll do and what they won't, how they're going to thrash her till she's the texture of a jellyfish and she has to crawl to school on her belly, till she begins to wail and cry and say, but what can I eat for my breakfast? and her mum says, cornflakes if there's no gas, and she says, but there's no milk, and her mum says, so am I black and white, am I stood in the fucking meadow, and if not, what leads you to believe I am a fuck-ing cow?

And that concludes it. It has to. Emmie falls over, knocked out by the force of her own sentence. Alison goes to school on an empty stomach. The lesson is scripture and she is thrown out to stand in the corridor. She is just standing there, doing no wrong. The headmaster sees her. "You again!" he bellows. She draws down the secret flaps, the membranes that cover her ears, and watches him gesticulating at her, his forehead creasing with fury. At playtime Tehera buys her a bag of crisps. She hopes they will give her a school dinner on credit but she doesn't have a token so she is turned away. She says, the dogs have eaten my token, but they laugh. She gets half of a quarter of a marmite sandwich from Lee. On her way home she keeps her eyes down, searching the pavement for a magic shilling: or any money really, or a pin to pick up. She just thinks she sees a pin when wham! she walks straight into MacArthur. Hello, Mr. MacArthur, she says. All the day you'll have good luck. He stares at her, suspicious. He says to her, your mam says you need a lesson. He puts out his hand, grabs her right nipple and twists it. She cries out. There's one, he says, do you want me to do the other side? He winks at her.

Daylight has come to Admiral Drive. Dare she pull back a curtain? She is stiff and cold, except for her feet, which are burning. She limps into the kitchen. For a moment she stands paralyzed before the gas rings, thinking, how will I light them, when Aitkenside has taken our shilling? Then she depresses the ignition switch and the blue flame leaps up. She pours milk into a pan and sets it on the flame.

The telephone rings. It will be Colette, she thinks, wanting to come back. The cooker's digital clock glows green, lighting the kitchen tiles with their frieze of fishes, lighting their slippery scales. Don't be silly, she says to herself, she'll barely be arrived in Whitton yet. She had thought a much longer time had elapsed: years. She stands with her cold hands stretched over the pan, and lets the machine take the call. Her message plays: there is a click. She thinks, it is the neighbours, trying to trick me into picking up; they want to know if I'm here.

Tentatively, she pulls up the kitchen blind. The clouds are charcoal and thick and grey, like the smoke from burning buildings. The full moon burrows into them and is immersed, swallowed. There is a tension headache at the back of her neck and, at the auditory rim, a faint high-pitched singing, like nocturnal wildlife in an equatorial forest, or God's fingernail scraped against glass. The sound is continuous, but not steady; it pulses. There is a feeling that something—a string, a wire—is being stretched to its limit. She lowers the blind again, inch by inch, and with each inch the years fall away, she is in the kitchen at Aldershot, she is twelve, thirteen, but if anyone asks, she is sixteen of course.

"Mum," she says, "did you run away with a circus?"

"Oh, circus, that was a laugh!" Her mum is merry from three strong lagers. "Your Uncle Morris was in that circus, he did sawing the lady in half. He wanted me to be sawed but I said, Morris, on your bike."

"What about Gloria?"

"Oh yes, they sawed Gloria. Anybody could saw her. She was that sort of girl."

"I don't know what that sort would be. The sort of girl who lets herself be sawed in half."

"Yes, you do," her mum says, as if she is prompting her to remember. "They was always practicing on you. Morris, he liked to keep his hand in. Used to say, you never know when the old tricks will come in useful, you might have to turn your hand to it again. Many's the time I seen your top half in the scullery and your bottom half in the front room. I seen your left half out the back in the shed and your right half God knows where. I says to Morris, I hope you know what you're doing, I want her stuck together before you leave here tonight."

Mum takes a pull on her can. She sits back. "You got any ciggies?" she says, and Al says, "Yes, I got some here somewhere, I nicked 'em for you." Her mum says, "That's nice: it's thoughtful. I mean, some kids, they only go nicking sweeties, just thinking about themselves. You're a good kid, Ali, we have our ups and downs, but that's in the nature of mother and daughter. We're alike, you see. That's why we don't always see eye to eye. When I say alike, I mean, not to look at obviously, plus we're not in the same class when it comes to brains, you see I was always quick when I was at school, and as for weight I was about half the weight of a whippet, whereas you, I mean, you're not the sharpest knife out of the drawer, you can't help that, love, and as for your size it's no secret some men like that type, MacArthur, for instance. When I took his deposit on you, he says, Emmie, it's a good thing you're not selling her by the pound."

She asks, "Did MacArthur say that?"

Her mum sighs; her eyelids flutter. "Al," she says, "get me one of my new blue pills. The helicopter ones. Would you?"

What year is this? Al runs a hand over her body. Has she breasts now, or just the promise of them? There is no point, when it comes to your own flesh, trying to knead it into precision; flesh doesn't yield that kind of answer. She pours the hot milk onto a spoonful of instant coffee. Then she is too weak to do any more, and she sits down.

• • •

"They used to disappear you," Emmie says. "For a laugh. Sometimes you'd be gone half an hour. I'd say, here, Morris, where's Alison? That's my only daughter you've disappeared. If she don't come back I'll sue you."

"And did I?" she says. "Come back?"

"Oh yes. Else I really would. I'd have seen him in court. And Morris knew it. There was all sorts of money tied up in you. Trouble is with me I couldn't keep me books straight."

"You didn't have books. You had a vase."

"I couldn't keep me vase straight. Bob Fox was always dipping in it. And then the boys fell to quarrelling about who was to go first at you. MacArthur put down his deposit, but oops! You see, I had borrowed money off Morris Warren. Morris said money owed counts for more than money down. And he wouldn't leave it alone, I'm owed this, I'm owed that."

Al says, "He's still the same."

"But then Keith Capstick got in anyway, before either of them could do the business, on account of your turning to him after the dog bite. The ones that weren't there when the dog broke in, the ones that didn't witness it, they couldn't understand the way you was wiv Keith, making up to him and kissing him and all. So there was bound to be disputes. So then they was mired in a three-way fight. And MacArthur come first versus Keith, and Keith got a pasting.

"But Morris, he just maintained the same, Keith Capstick owes me money, Mac owes me, he said Bill Wagstaffe owed him, I could never see how that was, but I suppose it was a bet on the horses and boys will be boys. Morris said, I will go to my grave buried with my little black book saying who owes me what, I will never rest till I get my money's worth, dead or alive."

"I wish I'd known," Alison says. "If I'd known all he wanted was a refund, I could have written him a cheque myself."

"And Aitkenside," her mum says, "was overseeing it all. Thank the Lord for Donnie Aitkenside. He was advising me, like. But then how was I supposed to make a living, after you was offering all-in for a shilling? I even lent you my nightdress, and that's all the thanks I get."

"You said I was a good kid."

"When?"

"A while back."

"I changed my mind," said Em, sulking.

Her coffee is cold, and she raises her head to the *tap-tap-tap*. Mr. Fox, are you there? Are your friends with you? Click by click, she lifts the kitchen blind. Dawn: there is a dazing light, a bar of thunderous black across the sky: hailstones are falling. These summers since the millennium have been all the same: days of clammy unnatural heat, sapping to the will. She puts her fingers against her forehead and finds her skin damp, but she couldn't say whether she's hot or cold. She needs a hot drink, to banish that deep internal quaking; I could try again, she thinks, with the kettle and a teabag. Will the police come back? She hears the neighbours chanting *Out out out*: a swell of distant voices, like a choir.

"Jesus," Colette said. "Where did you get this clapped-out dodgem car?"

"My garage lent it. It's only temporary. A courtesy car." Gavin looked at her out of the tail of his eye. "You look done in," he said.

"Done in," she said. "Tired out."

"Washed up," Gavin offered.

"Look, I realize this isn't convenient for you. I promise I won't be in your way. I just need a few hours to catch up on my sleep, then I can think straight. I'll soon put my life to rights. I'm by no means penniless, I just need to work out how to extricate myself from my ties with Alison. I may need to see a solicitor."

"Oh. She in trouble?"

"Yes."

"Small businesses going under all over the show," Gavin said. "Easy to run up a tax bill. They claim there's not a recession, but I dunno."

"What about you, did you get fixed up?"

"Bit of contract work. Take it as it comes. Here and there. As and when."

"Hand to mouth," she said.

For a while they drove in silence. The suburbs were beginning to wake up.

"What about Zoë?" Colette said. "What will she think about me turning up like this?"

"She'll understand. She knows we used to be related."

"Related? If that's what you call it."

"Married is a relation, isn't it? I mean, you're related to your wife?"

"She's got no cause for jealousy. I shall make that perfectly clear. So don't worry. It's just for the emergency. It's strictly temporary. I'll make sure she knows that. I'll soon be out of her way."

"Anyway," her mum says, "Gloria got sawed once too often. And then they had to get rid of her, didn't they? It wasn't even on the premises, that was the big nuisance of it. They had to fetch her back as consignments. But then the dogs came in handy, didn't they? But Pete said, you got to watch them dogs now, Keith. You got to watch dogs, once they get a taste for human flesh. Which was proved, of course. With the dog flying out at you. And then the way he cleaned his dish, when you served him up a slice of Keith."

She leaves the house now, young Alison, she leaves the house at Aldershot, kicking open the back door that is swollen with damp. MacArthur sees her go. He winks at her. It has rained that day and the ground is soft underfoot as she makes her way towards the lockup garages.

Emmie says, "Where there is waste ground, there is outbuildings. It stands to reason. That's where the boys used to keep their knocked-off ciggies and their bottles of spirits, they was always bringing in spirits by the case—oops, I think I've spoken out of turn now, it's a good thing MacArthur's not around, he'd have walloped me one, do me a favour and don't mention to the boys it was me what told you."

"I'm not the police," Al says.

"Police? That's a laugh. They was all in on it, only you don't want to mention it to MacArthur. I'll only get my eye blacked and my teef knocked out—not that I have any teef, but I wouldn't like a smack in the gums. Police used to come round, saying I'm after the whereabouts of MacArthur, I'm attempting to locate a gypsy fella name of Pete, they was having a laugh, they weren't locating, all they was wanting was a rolled-up fiver in their top pocket and a glass of whisky and lemonade, and if I couldn't oblige them, on account of I'd spent me last fiver and you'd drunk the lemonade, they'd say, well now, Mrs. Cheetham, well now, I'll just get my leg over before I depart your premises."

She walks past the van, young Alison, the van where Gloria rests in pieces: past the dog run, where Harry, Blighto and Serene lie dreaming; past the empty chicken runs, where the chickens are all dead because Pikey Pete has wrung their necks. Past the caravan with its blacked-out windows: back to the hut where she lies and howls. She peeps in, she sees herself, lying bleeding onto newspapers they've put down: it will be hygienic, Aitkenside says, because we can burn them once she's clotted.

Aitkenside says, you'd better stay off school, till it scabs over. We don't want questions asked, into our private business. If they say anything to you, say you was trying to jump barbed wire, right? Say you did it scrambling over broken glass.

She lies, moaning and thrashing. They have turned her over on her back now. She screams out: if anybody asks I'm sixteen, right? No, officer sir, my mummy is not at home. No officer sir, I have never seen this man before. No, officer, sir, I don't know that man either. No sir, for certain I never saw a head in a bath, but if I do I will be faithfully sure to come to the station and tell you.

She hears the men saying, we said she'd get a lesson, she's had one now.

The telephone again. She won't answer. She has lowered the kitchen blind, in case despite the new locks the police have installed the neighbours are so furious as to swarm over the side gate. Colette was right, she thinks; those gates are no good, really, but I don't think she was serious when she mentioned getting barbed wire.

She goes upstairs. The door of Colette's room stands open. The room is tidy, as you would expect; and Colette, before leaving, has stripped the bed. She lifts the lid of the laundry basket. Colette has left her soiled sheets behind; she stirs them, but finds nothing else, not a single item of hers. She opens the wardrobe doors. Colette's clothes hang like a rack of phantoms.

They are in Windsor, at the Harte and Garter. It is summer, they are younger; it is seven years ago; an era has passed. They are drinking coffee. She plays with the paper straws with the sugar in. She tells Colette, a man called M will enter your life.

At Whitton, Colette's hand reached out in the darkness of the communal hall; accurately, she found the light switch at the foot of the stairs. As if I'd never been away, she thought. In seven years they say every cell of your body is renewed; she looked around her and remarked, the same is not true of gloss paintwork.

She walked upstairs ahead of Gavin, to her ex-front door. He reached around her to put the key in the lock; his body touched hers, his forearm brushed her upper arm.

"Sorry," she said. She inched aside, shrinking herself, folding her arms across her chest.

"No, my fault," he said.

She held her breath as she stepped in. Would Zoë, like Alison, be one of those people who fills up the rooms with her scent, a person who is present even when she's absent, who sprays the sheets with rose or lavender water and who burns expensive oils in every room? She stood, inhaling. But the air was lifeless, a little stale. If it hadn't been such a wet morning, she would have hurried to open all the windows.

She put her bag down and turned to Gavin, questioning.

"Didn't I say? She's away."

"Oh. On a shoot?"

"Shoot?" Gavin said, "What do you mean?"

"I thought she was a model?"

"Oh, yes. That. I thought you meant like on safari."

"So is she?"

"Could be," Gavin said, nodding judiciously.

She noticed that he had placed his car magazines on a low table in a very tidy pile. Other than that, there was very little change from the room she remembered. I'd have thought he'd have redecorated, in all these years, she said to herself. I'd have thought she'd have wanted to put her stamp on it. I'd have thought she'd throw all my stuff out—everything I chose—and do a make-over. Tears pricked her eyes. It would have made her feel lonely, rejected, if she'd come back and found it all changed, but that fact that it was all the same made her feel somehow . . . futile.

"I suppose you'll want the bathroom, Gav," she said. "You'll have to get off to work."

"Oh no. I can work from home today. Make sure you're all right. We can go out for a bite of lunch if you feel up to it later. We could go for a walk in the park."

Her face was astonished. "A what, Gavin? Did you say a walk in the park?"

"I've forgotten what you like," he said, shuffling his feet.

In the corner of Colette's room, where the air is turbulent and thickening, there arises a little pink felt lady whom Al has not seen since she was a child.

"Ah, who called me back?" says Mrs. McGibbet.

And she says, "I did, Alison. I need your help."

Mrs. McGibbet shifts on the floor, as if uncomfortable.

"Are you still looking for your boy Brendan? If you help me, I'll swear I'll find him for you."

A tear creeps out of Mrs. McGibbet's eye, and makes its way slowly down her parchment cheek. And immediately a little toy car materializes by her left foot. Alison doesn't trust herself to pick it up, to handle it. She doesn't like ap-ports. Start on that business, and you'll find some joker trying to force a grand piano through from the other side, pulling and tugging at the curve of space–time, wiping his boots on your carpet and crying, "Whew! Blimey! Left hand down a bit, steady how she goes!" As a child, of course, she had played with Brendan's toys. But in those days she didn't know how one thing led to another.

"I don't know how many doors I've knocked on," says Mrs. McGibbet. "I've tramped the streets. I've visited the door of every psychic and Sensitive from here to Aberdeen, and attended their churches though my priest told me I must not. And never a sighting of Brendan since the circus fellas put him in a box. He says, 'Mam, it is the dream of every boy to join the circus, for hasn't my sister Gloria a costume with spangles? And such a thing was never seen in these parts.' And that was true. And I didn't care to spell out to him the true nature of her employment. So he was taken on as box boy."

"They put him in a box?"

"And fastened round the chain. And box boy will burst out, they said. A roll on the drums. The audience agog. The breath bated. The box rocking. And then nothing. It ceases to rock. The man MacArthur comes with his boot, oi, box boy!"

"Was MacArthur in the circus?"

"There wasn't a thing that MacArthur wasn't in. He was in the army. He was in the jail. He was in the horse game, and the fight game, and the box game. And he comes with his boot and kicks the side of the box. But poor Brendan, he makes not a murmur; and the box, not an inch does it shift. And a deadly silence falls. So then they look at each other, at a loss. Says Aitkenside, Morris, have you ever had this happen before? Says Keith Capstick, we'd better open it up, me old china. Morris Warren protests at the likely damage to his special box, but they come with a lever and a bar. They pull out the nails with pliers and they prize off the lid. But when they open it up, my poor son Brendan is gone."

"That's a terrible story, Mrs. McGibbet. Didn't they get the police?"

"The police? Them? They'd be laughed out of the place. The police are the king of boxes. It is well known in every nation that people who trouble them disappear."

"That's true," Alison said. "You've only to watch the news."

"I would help you out," the little lady said, "with your memorizing and all, but I'm sure the topic of MacArthur's eye is not a topic for decent people. I'm sure I wasn't looking, though I do recall the man MacArthur lying drunk as a lord on your mammy's couch, for though I might have shifted his head to see if Brendan was under the cushion, if he then fell back into his stupor I barely recall. And if the man they call Capstick was incapable too, lying with his head under the table, I'm sure I was too busy to notice. I can't recall at all you stooping over them vermin and patting their pockets, hoping for a shilling to roll out, for I wouldn't know where the minimart was or what sort of sweeties you were fond of spending on. Now one or the other might have roared 'bleeding thief,' but then it could have been 'bleeding Keith' for I can't claim I was paying attention—and you wouldn't mention to them, would you, that it was me, McGibbet, that told you nothing at all about it, for I'm in mortal fear of those fiends? I'm sure I wasn't seeing a little girl with a pair of scissors in her hand, snipping about a man's private parts. I'm sure I was too busy about my own business to notice whether that was a fork you were carrying, or that was a knife, and whether you had a spoon in your pocket, or whether your mouth was bristling with pins. I'm sure I wouldn't have known if you were carrying a knitting needle, for there were several on the premises, but I'm sure I was too busy seeking my boy Brendan to know whether you had opened the drawer and took one out. And I wouldn't say I saw you go down the garden to feed the dogs, neither. If I hadn't been peeping under the furniture as was my habit, I might have seen a smile on your face and a bowl in your hand, and a trickle of blood running down each arm. But your age I couldn't swear to, it was no more than eight years, nine or ten. And I never saw the fella called Capstick run out and collapse on the ground at the side of the house, shouting *Ambulance, ambulance!* Nor did I see Morris God-curse-him Warren and the other bloody bleeder come up at the trot, his name I don't suppose would be Aitkenside. I didn't notice them haul up Capstick by his oxters and dump him in the bath that was kept out on the road in front of your mother's premises. There was a deal of shouting then, but it was that sort of neighbourhood, so I couldn't say he was crying out to the whole street, where's my bollocks, find the fuckers for they can stitch them back on, beg your pardon but that's the exact truth of what he might have said at the time, if I had been able to hear above the racket. And Morris Warren said something back to him, I dare say, but I wouldn't like to quote you his words, which were too late I regret my son, for your bollocks are all eaten by the dogs, they cannot sew them back when they are swallered, not to my way of thinking, and to my way of thinking they are swallered good and proper and the dogs have cleaned their bowls. And he, Morris Warren, it's possible he could not forbear to laugh, for he had told Capstick he should not interfere with your good self without paying money for it, and now you get paid out, he said, and now you get what's coming to you, the little girl herself pays you out for being a dirty bugger."

I paid him, Alison thought. At least one of the bastards is paid out. Or did I pay out two? "Mrs. McGibbet," she urged, "go on."

"I'm sure," said Mrs. McGibbet, "I never heard the moment Morris Warren ceased to laugh. I never looked in the dogs' bowls, curious to see what they were eating, for if you came near them they'd bite your leg off. And therefore I couldn't have noticed MacArthur's eye plop off a spoon and fall into a dish—surely I must have dreamed it, for such a thing could never be. And if your little self, no more than eight, nine, ten years old, were to have cried out, 'Now wink at me, can you, you bloody bastard?' I wouldn't have known it because I was searching down the back of a cupboard for Brendan. And if Mr. Donald Aitkenside ran down the road in a panic, I wouldn't have seen him. Still less the fella they call Pikey Pete jump in his van and drive screaming in all directions at once."

Al walks down the road. She is eight, nine, ten. Once again she hasn't got her swimming kit or her gym shoes or anything else she should have for school. Lee and Tehera are just behind her, then comes Catherine Tattersall; she looks back for Catherine, who is lagging, and there on the pavement she sees MacArthur's eye, rolling along. "Look," she says, and they say, "What?" She points, "Look at that," she says, "at that." Catherine steps right on MacArthur's eye, and squashes it into the ground. "Yeachh!" Al says, and turns aside. "What's up wiv you, Al?" Catherine says. When Al looks back, the jelly has bounced back again, to a perfect orb, and MacArthur's eye continues to roll along.

It followed her to school one day, it was against the rule:
It made the children laugh and play, to see an eye at school.

It is evening. She is coming home from school. At the street corner, the half-crippled little bloke called Morris Warren leans against the wall. Eff off, she says under her breath. As she approaches, she expects him to reach out and make a grab at her breasts, as this is his usual habit. She prepares to swerve; that is her usual habit, too.

But today he doesn't grab. He just looks at her, and as he looks, he almost falls over. It seems as if his crooked legs won't support him; he grabs the wall for support, and when he speaks, his tone is amazed. He says, "Take off his bollocks, yes! But take out a cove's eye? I've never heard of it before."

She bangs into the house, casting a glance down into the stained bathtub, thinking, I better get something and scour that out, it looks bad. Emmie comes at her as soon as she gets in the door: "I saw MacArthur's eye on a spoon, I saw MacArthur's eye on a fork."

"Which?"

"I saw you standing there with a knitting needle in your hand, young lady. He didn't deserve that. He was only doing what men do. You was all over Cap-stick when he pulled the dog off you, but then you was all over MacArthur when he bought you sweeties. So what was he to think? He used to say, Emmie, what have you bred there? She'll do anything for a bag of chocolate raisins."

Al sits in her kitchen, her kitchen at Admiral Drive. Older now, suddenly wiser, she asks the empty air, "Mum, who's my dad?"

Emmie says, "Leave off, will you!"

She says, "I cannot rest, till I know. And when I know, then possibly I still cannot rest."

"Then you have to ask yourself what's the use," Emmie says. "I dunno, girl. I would help you, if I could. It could be any one of 'em, or it could be six other fellas. You don't see who it is, because they always put a blanket over your head."

Back, back, go back. She is at Aldershot. Darkness is falling, darkness is falling fast. The men are moving a bundle of something. They are passing it between them. It is limp, doll-sized, swaddled. She pulls the blanket aside with her own hand, and in its folds, dead-white, waxy, eyes closed tightly, she sees her own face. And now back she goes, back and back, till she is smaller and smaller, before she can walk, before she can talk: to the first wail, the first gasp: to the knitting needle pricking her skull and letting in the light.

At Whitton, Colette opened the wardrobe. "Where are Zoë's things? Surely she doesn't take everything with her when she travels?"

A pity. She had been looking forward to trying her clothes on, when Gavin went to work. She wished he would clear off, really, and let her go through all the drawers and cupboards, instead of hanging about in a sheepish way at the back of her and sighing like that.

Back and back. There is an interval of darkness, dwindling, suspension of the senses. She neither hears nor sees. The world has no scent or savour. She is a cell, a dot. She diminishes, to vanishing point. She is back beyond a dot. She is back where the dots come from. And still she goes back.

It is close of day, and Al is plodding home. The light is low and greyish. She must make it before dark. Clay is encrusted on her feet, and beneath them the track is worn into deep ruts. Her garments, which appear to be made of sacking—which may, indeed, be sacks—are stiffening with the day's sweat, and chafing the knotty scars on her body. Her breath is coming hard. There is a stitch in her side. She stops and drinks from the ditch, scooping up the water with her fingers. She squats there, until the moon rises.

In the kitchen Colette was opening cupboards, staring critically at the scanty stocks. Zoë, she thought, is one of those people who lives on air, and has no intention of putting herself out to cook for Gavin; which is a mistake, because left to himself he reverts to fried chicken, and before you know where you are he's bursting out of his shirts.

She opened the fridge, she pushed the contents about. What she found was unappealing: a half-used carton of full-fat long-life milk, some Scotch eggs, a lump of orange cheese which had gone hard, and three small blackened bananas.

"Didn't anyone ever tell Zoë," she said, "not to keep bananas in the fridge?"

"Feel free," Gavin said.

"What?"

"Look in all the cupboards, why don't you? Look in the dishwasher. Don't mind me. Look in the washing machine."

"Well, if it's empty," she said, "I'll just pop in one or two things of mine that I brought with me. I didn't like to leave my dirty laundry behind."

He followed her into the sitting room as she went to pick up her bag. "You're not going back then?"

"No chance. Gavin, excuse me, don't stand in my way."

"Sorry." He sidestepped. "So won't you miss her? Your friend?"

"I'll miss my income. But don't worry. I'll get it sorted. I'll ring up some agencies later."

"It's quiet," Gavin warned.

"Anything at your place?"

"My place? Dunno."

She stared at him, her pale eyes bulging slightly. "Gavin—correct me if I'm wrong." She squatted and opened her bag. "Would I be near the truth if I said you're still out of a job?"

He nodded.

She plucked out her dirty washing. "And would I be near the truth if I said you made Zoë up?"

He turned away.

"And that rustbucket out there, it really is your own car?" Damn, she thought, isn't that just typical, he's more embarrassed about the car than everything else put together. Gavin stood rubbing his head. She passed him, went into the kitchen with her bundle.

"It's temporary," he said. "I traded down. But now you're back—"

"Back?" she said coldly. She bent down and retrieved a grey sock from the washing machine. It was a woolly sock, the kind you darn; the heel had gone into holes. "How long were you intending to leave it before you told me Zoë didn't exist?"

"I thought you'd work it out for yourself. Which you did, didn't you? I had to say something! You went on about this Dean guy, and the rest. Dean this and Donnie that. I had to say something."

"To make me jealous?"

"Yes. I suppose."

"I only mentioned Dean once, as far as I remember."

"He going to come after you, is he?"

"No," she said. "He's dead."

"Christ! Really? You're not winding me up?"

She shook her head.

"Accident, was it?"

"I believe so."

"You'd lost touch? I'm glad he's dead. Suppose I shouldn't say it, but I am." She sniffed. "He was nothing to me."

"I mean, I hope he didn't suffer. Kind of thing."

"Gavin, is this sock yours?"

"What?" he said. "That? No. Never seen it before. So what about this psychic stuff, have you given it up?"

"Oh, yes. That's all finished now." She held up the sock to examine it. "It's not like you usually wear. Horrible grey thing. Looks like roadkill." She frowned at it; she thought she'd seen the other half of the pair, but couldn't think where.

"Colette . . . listen . . . I shouldn't have told you lies."

"That's all right." She thought, I told you some. Then, in case she seemed to be excusing him too readily, she said, "It's what I expect."

"Doesn't seem like seven years. Since we split."

"Must be. Must be about that. It was the summer that Diana died." She walked around the kitchen, her finger dabbing at sticky surfaces. "Looks like six years and three hundred and sixty-four days since you gave these tiles a wipe-down."

"I'm glad now we didn't sell up."

"Are you? Why?"

"It makes it like before."

"Time doesn't go backwards."

"No, but I can't remember why we split." She frowned. Neither could she, really. Gavin looked down at his feet. "Colette, we've been a couple of plonkers, haven't we?"

She picked up the woolly sock, and threw it in the kitchen bin. "I don't think women can be," she said. "Plonkers. Not really."

Gavin said humbly, "I think you could do anything, Colette."

She looked at him; his head hanging like some dog that's been out in the rain. She looked at him and her heart was touched: where her heart would be.

• • •

Admiral Drive: Al hears the neighbours, muttering outside. They are carrying placards, she expects. Sergeant Delingbole is speaking to them through a megaphone. You can't scare Al. When you've been strangled as often as she has, when you've been drowned, when you've died so many times and found yourself still earthside, what are the neighbours going to do to you that's so bloody novel?

There are several ways forward, she thinks, several ways I can go from here. She accepts that Colette won't be back. Repentance is not out of the question; she imagines Colette saying, I was hasty, can we start again, and herself saying, I don't think so, Colette: that was then and now it's now.

Time for a shake-up. I'll never settle here after all the name-calling and disruption. Even if, when all this dies down, the neighbours start to cosy up to me and bake me cakes. They may forget but I won't. Besides, by now they know what I do for a living. That it's not weather forecasting; and anyway, the Met Office has moved to Exeter.

I could ring an estate agent, she thinks, and ask for a valuation. (Colette's voice in her ear says, you ought to ring three.) "Miss Hart, what about your shed, which is of local historic interest? And what about the black cloud of evil that hovers over your premises. Will you be leaving that?" Memories are short, she thinks, in house sales. She will be forgotten, just like the worms and voles who used to live here, and the foetus dug in under the hedge.

She calls Mandy.

"Natasha, Psychic to the Stars?"

"Mandy, Colette's walked out."

"Oh, it's you, Alison. Oh dear. I foresaw as much, frankly. When we were at Irene's, looking for the will, I said to Silvana, trouble there, mark my words."

"And I'm on my own."

"Don't cry, lovie. I'll come and get you."

"Please. For a night or two. Till it dies down. You see, the press are here. Cameras."

Mandy was puzzled. "Is that good? For business, I mean?"

"No, I've got vigilantes. Demonstrators."

Mandy clicked her tongue. "Witch-burning, isn't it? Some people are so narrow-minded. Are the police there?"

"Yes."

"But they're not trying to arrest you or anything? Sorry, silly question; of course not. Look, I'll bring Gemma for a bit of muscle."

"No. Just come yourself."

"Take a nice hot bath, Al. Unplug the phone. Spray some lavender around. I'll be there before you know it. I'll have you out of there. A bit of sea air will do you good. We'll go shopping for you, give you a makeover. I always thought Colette gave you bad advice. Shall I book you a hair appointment? I'll line up Cara to give you a massage."

Three hours later, she is ready to leave the house. The police have not had much success in dispersing the crowd; they don't, they explain, want to get heavy-handed. Sergeant Delingbole says, what you could do, probably it would be for the best, would be to come out with a blanket over your head. She says, do you have an official blanket you use for that, or can I choose my own? They say, feel free: the policewoman helpfully runs upstairs and looks out at her direction her mohair throw, the raspberry-coloured throw that Colette bought her once, in better times than these.

She places it over her head; the world looks pink and fuzzy. Like a fish, or something newborn, she opens her mouth to breathe; her breath, moist, sucks in the mohair. The policewoman takes her elbow, and Delingbole opens the door; she is hurried to a police vehicle with darkened windows, which whisks her smartly away from Admiral Drive. Later, on the regional TV news, she will glimpse herself from the knee down. I always wanted to be on TV, she will say, and now I have; Mandy will say, well, bits of you, anyway.

As they swing onto the A322, she pulls aside the woollen folds and looks around her. Her lips itch from their contact with the throw; she presses them together, hoping not to smudge her lipstick. Sergeant Delingbole is sitting with her: for reassurance, he says. "I've always been fascinated," he says. "The paranormal. UFOs. All that. I mean there must be something in it, mustn't there?"

"I think you tried to come through," she says, "at one of my dems. Couple of years back. Just after the Queen Mother passed."

"God bless her," says Delingbole automatically, and Alison answers, "God bless her."

The day has brightened. At Worplesden, trees drip onto the fairways of the golf club. The policewoman says, "The cloud's lifting. Might see some action at Wimbledon this afternoon."

Al smiles. "I'm sure I couldn't say."

Before they reach Guildford, they pull into an out-of-town shopping centre. The exchange takes place in front of PC World. Mandy clip-clips towards the white van: high-heeled pastel pumps in pistachio green, tight pale jeans, fake Chanel jacket in baby pink. She is smiling, her big jaw jutting. She looks quite lined, Al thinks; it is the first time in years she has seen Mandy in full daylight. It must be Hove that's aged her: the sea breezes, the squinting into the sun. "Got the consignment?" says Mandy, breezy herself, and Delingbole opens the back door and gives Al his arm to help her out of the van. She tumbles to the ground, her sore feet impacting hard.

The soft-top stands by, lacquered once again to a perfect hard scarlet. "There's a new nail bar at the end of our road," Mandy says. "I thought after we've had some lunch we could pop in and treat ourselves."

For a moment Al sees her fist, dripping with gore; she sees herself, bloody to the elbows. She sees, back at Admiral Drive, the tape unspooling in the empty house; her past unspooling, back beyond this life, beyond the lives to come. "That will be nice," she says.

MORRIS: And another thing you can't get, you can't get a saveloy.
CAPSTICK: You can't get tripe like you used to get.
DEAN: When I get my tongue guard off, I'm going for a curry.
MORRIS: You can't get a decent cuppa tea.
DEAN: And then I'm going to get a swastika studded into it. I can hang it over walls and be a mobile graffiti.
MART: Tee-hee. When Delingbole comes you can wag it at him and then bugger off.
AITKENSIDE: Etchells could make a good cuppa.
CAPSTICK: She could. I'll give her that.

MORRIS: By the way, Mr. Aitkenside.

AITKENSIDE: Yes? Speak up.

MORRIS: I only mention it.

AITKENSIDE: Spit it out, lad.

MORRIS: It's a question of fundage.

AITKENSIDE: Warren, you have already tapped me for a sub. When I look in my wages book I find it ain't the first time either. You are spending in advance of your entire income, as far as I can see. It can't go on, me old mate.

MORRIS: I don't want a sub. I only want what's due.

MACARTHUR: He's right, Mr. Aitkenside. It ain't fair that Pete should keep all the money he got from Etchells's personal effects, seeing as we all helped to frighten her to death, and especially me rising up with my false eye rolling.

AITKENSIDE: Pete! What you got to say about this? (*pause*) Pete? . . . Where is he?

CAPSTICK: Bugger me. Taken to the road. His wodge of cash wiv him.

MORRIS: Ain't that his sort all over?

BOB FOX: What can you expect, Mr. Aitkenside, taking on pikeys?

AITKENSIDE: Don't you tell me how to do my job, lad! I've got a diploma in Human Resources from Nick himself. We are working towards equal opportunities for all. Don't tell me how to recruit, or you'll be knocking on windows for all eternity.

CAPSTICK: We'll have to contact the missus, then. If we want our cut. She'll nail down Pikey for us. He likes her. He can't keep away.

AITKENSIDE: Pardon me, but I don't know if you'll see your missus again.

DEAN: You've pissed her off good and proper.

CAPSTICK: What, not see her? Who we going to mediumize, then?

BOB FOX: Morris? Morris, speak up. It's you in charge of this fiasco.

MORRIS: You can't get decent vinegar, neither. You go in for vinegar, there's bloody shelves and shelves of the stuff. There's only one sort of proper vinegar, and that's brown.

CAPSTICK: Morris? We're talking to you.

AITKENSIDE: It was you, Warren, according to my ledger, what requested to have that crustie hanged, that lived in her shed.

MORRIS: He was on my manor! Only just got a proper outbuilding, where I can put me feet up evenings, and some geezer with an 'at moves in.

AITKENSIDE: But what did you fail to see, my son? You failed to see he was her good deed.

WAGSTAFFE: A good deed in a naughty world.

AITKENSIDE: That you, Wagstaffe? Bugger off, we're talking.

MORRIS: Besides, you was all agreeable. Oooh, Morris, you said, let's have an 'anging, haven't had a good 'anging in years, it'll be a right laugh when the little bugger kicks his feet!

AITKENSIDE: You failed to see that little bugger was her good deed. And what's the result? She's looking to commit a few others. They get the habit . . . see? They get the habit. It's sad. But they get the taste for it.

MORRIS: So she don't want to know us no more?

AITKENSIDE: I very much doubt it, old son.

MORRIS: But we go back, me and the missus. (pause) I'll miss her. Be on my own. Won't be the same.

CAPSTICK: Oh, leave off, do! Bring on the bloody violins! You wouldn't think so well of her if she'd had away your balls.

MACARTHUR: You wouldn't think so well of her if you'd seen your eye on her spoon.

DEAN: You can get another place, Uncle Morris.

MORRIS: (sniffs) Won't be the same, Dean lad.

AITKENSIDE: Not the bloody waterworks! Pull yourself together, Warren, or I'll demote you. (Morris sobs.) Look . . . Morris, old son, don't take on. Oh, blast it, ain't nobody round here got a bleeding hankerchief?

WAGSTAFFE: Any handkerchief in particular?

AITKENSIDE: Wagstaffe? Put a sock in it. Listen, lads, I've an idea. Maybe she'll come back if her dad asks for her.

(pause)

MACARTHUR: Who *is* her dad, then?

CAPSTICK: I always thought it was you, MacArthur. I thought that's why she took your eye out.

MACARTHUR: I thought it were you, Keef. I thought that's why she took your bollocks off.

AITKENSIDE: Don't look at me! She's not my daughter, I was in the forces.

MORRIS: She can't be mine because I was still in the circus.

PIKEY PETE: She can't be mine—

MORRIS: Oh, there you are, Pete! We thought you'd scarpered. Give a dog a bad name and hang him! We thought you had made off with the emoluments.

PIKEY PETE: I say, she can't be mine, because I was in jail for painting horses.

CAPSTICK: Painting horses?

PIKEY PETE: You paint one racehorse to look like another, innit?

MORRIS: Don't the paint run off, Pikey, when there's a downpour?

PIKEY PETE: It's an old Romany skill. Anyway, she ain't mine.

CAPSTICK: She ain't mine, because I was in the nick too.

MACARTHUR: And me. Serving five.

AITKENSIDE: So who's left? Bob Fox?

BOB FOX: I never did nothing but tap on the window.

(*pause*)

MACARTHUR: Got to be that Derek bloke. Innit.

AITKENSIDE: Couldn't have been. Bloody errand boy? He never had no money. Emmeline Cheetham, she didn't do it for free.

MACARTHUR: True. You made sure of that.

CAPSTICK: Not like these girls you get these days, eh Dean?

MORRIS: So who's left?

(*pause*)

MACARTHUR: Oh, blimey.

MORRIS: Are you thinking what I'm thinking? Only the great man himself!

CAPSTICK: Well, knock me down with a feather.

MORRIS: I never had such a thunderclap.

PIKEY PETE: You don't want to mess with the fambly of Nick. Because Nick he is a fambly man.

(*pause*)

CAPSTICK: What would he do?

AITKENSIDE: Dear oh dear.

MORRIS: The worst thing that can befall a spirit is to be eaten by old Nick. You can be eaten and digested by him and then you've had your chips.

BOB FOX: You can't get chips like you used to. Not fried in proper lard.

AITKENSIDE: Shut it, Bob, there's a good lad.

CAPSTICK: What, you get et? You get et by Nick? And you don't get another go round?

MORRIS: If he pukes you up you can reform and have another go, but otherwise you're et and that's all.

MACARTHUR: And that's all?

MORRIS: El finito, Benito.

PIKEY PETE: Here, shall we do the share-out of these notes? It's the proceeds from Etchells's furniture. Lads? Where you going? Lads? Wait for me. . . .

October: Al is travelling, in the autumn's first foul weather. There are mud slips and landslides, there are storm drains burst, a glugging and gurgling in sumps, conduits, and wells. There are fissures in the riverbeds, there are marshes, swamps, and bogs, there are cracked pipes and breached seawalls, and outswells of gas on the bubbling floodplain. There is coastal erosion, crumbling defences, spillage and seepages; where the saline and swift-rushing tide meets the viscid slime of swollen sewers, there the oceans are rising, half a metre, half a metre, half a metre onwards. On the orbital road the hazard lights of collided cars flash from the hard shoulder. Cameras flash on the bridges, there is the swish of the wipers against drenching rain, the mad blinking eyes of the breakdown trucks. "On we go!" Alison calls. "Sevenoaks, here we come."

They are singing, Alison and the two little women: a few music hall favorites, but hymns, mostly, for it's what the little women like. She didn't know any of the words, but they have taught her.

Show pity, Lord! For we are frail and faint:
We fade away, O list to our complaint.
We fade away, like flowers in the sun;
We just begin, and then our work is done.

Maureen Harrison says, "Have we been to Sevenoaks?" and Alison says, "Not with me, you haven't."

Maureen says, anxious, "Will we get our tea there?" Alison says, "Oh yes, I hear in Sevenoaks you get a very good tea."

"Just as well," says Maureen's friend from the back, "because I could have brought my own Eccles cakes."

"Cakes," says Maureen, "we've had some lovely cakes. Do you remember that one you bought me once, with a walnut on top? You can't get cakes like that these days. Here, lovie, I'll make you one. On your birthday. I always made you a cake on your birthday."

"That would be nice," says Maureen's friend. "And *she* can have some too."

"Oh, yes, we'll give *her* some. She's a lovely girl."

Alison sighs. She likes to be appreciated; and before these last weeks, she never felt she was. They can't do enough for her, the two old ladies, so happy they are to be together again, and when they are talking in the evening, from under a rug and behind the sofa they praise her, saying that they never had a daughter, but if they had, they would have wanted a bonny big girl just like Al. Whenever they set off in the car, they are so excited she has to make them wear incontinence pads. She cries, "Are your seat belts fastened, girls? Are your buttons all sewn on tight?" And they shout, "Yes, miss!" They say, "Look at us, riding in a motor vehicle, a private car!" They will never get tired of the orbital road, no matter how many times they go around it. Even if some image from her former life washes up—the fiends escaping Admiral Drive, vestigial heads trapped under the fences, multiple limbs thrashing, feet entangled in their tongues—even if some moment of dismay fades her smile, chills her, tightens her grip on the wheel or brings a shiny tear to her eye—even if she misses a junction, and has to cross the carriageway—the little women never complain.

They say, "Look at her hair, and look at her lovely rings, look at her frock and look at how she pedals the car—you'd think it would tire her out, but you can't tire her out. Oh, I tell you, Maureen Harrison, we've landed on our feet here." And Maureen adds, "Where our feet would be."

Her cell phone rings. It's Gemma. "How's tricks? . . . Staines on the twenty-seventh? I doubt it, but I'll check my diary when we pull in. . . . *We?* Did I say we? . . . No, not Colette. God forbid. I meant me and my new guides. Colette's gone back to her husband. Near Twickenham. He used to be a, you know, what do they call it, one of those men who sets traps. Sort of gamekeeper."

"Near Twickenham?" Gemma says, surprised, and Al says, "No, in a former life." He was a man, she thought, who kept dogs, but not for pets. A terrier man. Digs out the earths, lays down poisons for hapless small creatures trying to earn a living. "I didn't care for him," she says, "when I ran into him in Farnham." You shouldn't leave bait about for it attracts entities, the slow grub and creep of legless things, feral crawlers looking for wounds to suck or open minds to creep inside. You shouldn't leave traps, for you don't know what will spring them: severed legs, unclaimed and nameless feet, ghouls and spectres looking to stitch themselves together, haunting the roads looking for a hand, an ear, for severed fingers and dislocated thumbs.

She has been, herself, of course, a snapper-up of unconsidered trifles. She doesn't remember, really, if she saw MacArthur's eye in a dish, though she's been trying to remember, just to keep the record straight. It might not have been in a dish; it might have been on a plate, a saucer, a dog bowl. She remembers she had her spoon in her hand, her fork. "Business?" she says. "Business is booming, thanks for asking, Gemma. Give or take the odd quiet midweek, I'm booked out till next Feb."

There are terrorists in the ditches, knives clenched between their teeth. There are fundis hoarding fertilizer, there are fanatics brewing bombs on brown-field sites, and holy martyrs digging storage pits where fiends have melted into the soil. There are citadels underground, there are potholes and sunken shafts; there are secret chambers in the hearts of men, sometimes of women too. There are unlicensed workings and laboratories underground, mutants breeding in the tunnels; there are cannibal moo-cows and toxic bunnikins, and behind the drawn curtains of hospital wards there are bugs that eat the flesh.

But today we are going to Sevenoaks, by way of Junction 5: to see whom fortune favours today. Will it be the brave, or is it the turn of the bloody? Will they be queuing to have their palm prints taken, the legion of the unbowed? Softly the cards are shuffled, whispering to the crimson cloth. A knight in armour is galloping from the battle—or to it. A dog climbs the wheel of fortune, while a monkey descends. A naked girl pours water into a pool, and seven stars shine in the evening sky.

"When is it teatime, miss?" the little woman enquires; and then, "Pedal faster, miss, see if you can beat that one!"

Alison checks her rearview mirror. She pulls out to overtake a truck; she puts her foot down. She moves into the fast lane, half hidden by the spray. Unmolested, unobserved, they flee before the storm. If the universe is a great mind, it may sometimes have its absences. Maureen Harrison pipes up from the back: "This cake we're having: could we have it iced?"

About the Author

Among HILARY MANTEL's novels are *A Change of Climate, A Place of Greater Safety,* and *Eight Months on Ghazzah Street.* She has also written a memoir, *Giving Up the Ghost.* A winner of the Hawthornden Prize, she reviews for *The New York Times* and *The New York Review of Books* and lives in England.